The Atlantean Constellation

By Cassidy Greenberg

ISBN 978-1-64663-260-2

REVIEW COPY: This is an advanced printing subject to corrections and revisions.

Published by

◤ köehlerbooks ™

3705 Shore Drive
Virginia Beach, VA 23455
800–435–4811
www.koehlerbooks.com

The Atlantean Constellation

Cassidy Greenberg

VIRGINIA BEACH
CAPE CHARLES

Dedicated to my grandmother, Dianne Marcum. She inspired and encouraged me to start writing my ideas for stories, which grew into my passion for writing books. This story was inspired by my love for mythology, ancient stories and religions. I truly hope that you enjoy reading these books just as much as I enjoyed writing them.

Thank you and enjoy!

Table of Contents

Prologue

In ancient times there were gods and goddesses. The Egyptian, Greek, Persian, Atlantean, and many other pantheons coexisted on the Earth, each taking care of the lands and people within their realms. Although most gods and goddesses stayed within their family borders, some would stray from their groups, having relations with other deities, mortals, and creatures, mixing bloodlines and creating new beings. They fought beside their allies against common enemies but would turn against one another in an instant.

One of these goddesses, an Atlantean, possessed a strength and power never seen before and coveted by those around her. A power of such importance that even gods could not understand it; that the universe had put her in place for a greater purpose.

She would be the one to change the world forever.

Her name was Cassiopeia.

And now, in the morning light of her mother's bedchamber, she knew the truth and saw the terror in her mother's eyes when she heard the prophecy.

"You must go, Mother," Cassiopeia pleaded with her. "You are in danger! He will come for you, but he won't kill you. He will make me do it."

Chapter 1

The Past

9041 BCE

Love is giving someone the power to destroy you . . .
but trusting them not to.
—E. Lockhart

Cassiopeia walked quickly down the temple palace corridor, Sierra in tow. Dark blonde hair flowed down her back in a waterfall of curls and braids. Her black dress, trimmed in deep cerulean, billowed with every step as tendrils of fabric waved in the wind. She had heard rumors and she needed to know the truth, her blue eyes sparkling with excitement. Sierra, her demon companion, bounced cheerfully as she flew behind Cassiopeia, her wings flapping excitedly. She too possessed beauty, but in her own demonic way. Her wings, such a deep purple that they were almost black, were shaped like a bat's. They seemed too small to hold her above the ground, yet she had impressive grace as she flew through the air. Her dark violet hair was pulled in cornrows of braids down the back of her head with pieces of ribbon tied in throughout, her tiny horns poking through the braids. Her alabaster skin seemed to glow in the light, contrasting her sleeveless, black leather catsuit cinched tight in a corset. She looked beautiful and harmless, especially with no weapons on her, but she was a lethal demon feared by the other pantheons.

Entering through the large golden doors into the chambers of Cassiopeia's mother, they saw one of the handmaidens.

"Where is she?" asked Cassiopeia.

"Through there, goddess." The handmaiden gestured toward the bedroom.

Cassiopeia hurried over, reaching out her hands to push the doors open without touching them. Lilith was a vision of beauty. She was standing at the end of her bed, adjusting her dress. Her long, silver-blonde hair fell down to her waist. Her black dress reached to the floor and trailed behind her when she walked. She looked regal in every sense of the word, queen of the Atlantean gods. Looking up with her grey eyes as the chamber doors opened, her face brightened when she laid eyes on her daughter. At the end of the bed Raffaela, goddess of health and medicine, was packing up her small bag.

"My little star. Why do you enter so urgently?" Lilith asked, as she sat on the bed.

"Mother! Is it true?" Cassiopeia hurried over excitedly to sit next to her mother.

Lilith laughed.

"How did you hear so quickly?"

Cassiopeia tried not to look at the two guilty demons, her mother's companions, standing on the other side of the bed behind Lilith. Normally Lilith would be angry by her companions not keeping this a secret, but she knew why they wanted to tell her daughter. Cassiopeia had been waiting a long time for this.

"Yes." Lilith said reaching down to put both her hands on her belly. "You are going to be a sister."

Cassiopeia smiled in excitement.

"I think it's a boy!" Raffaela said as she headed toward the door to leave. "Just think, a little prince!"

"We must go tell Magnus the good news." Lilith said with a smile.

As they walked down the hall toward the main hall of the Atlantean Parthenon, Cassiopeia looked out the windows at the beach and ocean below. They lived in Vēlatusa, a series of small islands in a separate realm from Earth and home of the Atlantean gods. The main temple—which was more like an immense palace—where her immediate family lived, was on the largest of the islands. On the highest point of all the islands, it overlooked all the other temples that trailed down the cliffside. As she looked out the window, she could see the main path that lead down to the smaller temples for the other gods and goddesses whose importance diminished the farther they were from the main temple.

Cassiopeia loved her home. She had always enjoyed the ocean and she had a perfect view from most places around the temple. When she was quiet, she could almost always hear the ocean waves crashing against the sand, rocks, and cliffsides. She could smell the fresh ocean breeze wafting through the open windows and archways.

When Cassiopeia and Lilith entered the main hall, Magnus was sitting on his throne talking with some of the other gods in their pantheon. He also looked like a godly ruler. His blonde hair fell to his cheeks just below his bright blue eyes in neat waves. He was wearing a traditional Atlantean robe that matched his daughter's in color. Magnus was speaking with Lorcán, god of strength and power, when he saw them enter, smiling at their presence.

"My dears! To what do I owe the pleasure?"

Lilith looked to Cassiopeia.

"You can tell him."

Cassiopeia jumped at the opportunity.

"Mother is pregnant!"

Magnus walked over and pulled Lilith into a warm embrace, surprised and overjoyed.

"That's excellent news! We shall have a party to celebrate! A new god or goddess to enter the pantheon is always reason for celebration."

A new brother. Someone to be a friend and confidant, Cassiopeia thought.

She found it hard to make friends with other gods and goddesses. They tended to be very vain and narcissistic. Everything was about them and nothing else mattered. Very few were more grounded, which made her value her friend, Set, all the more. As a primordial Egyptian god of violence, chaos, and strength, he was powerful in his own right and was also the head of his pantheon. Most gods of his stature were conceited and fueled by power, but he was different, having learned his lesson when his struggle for power caused him to murder his own brother. Since then he had run his pantheon in a more peaceful manner but was not to be underestimated.

Cassiopeia remembered the first time they met. She was walking through the Egyptian market, learning about their culture, when she felt him appear behind her. Instead of trying to philander with her, like most gods did, he just handed her a beautiful white and pink lotus and offered to show her around. They walked through the market for the rest of the day, talking, and had been friends ever since.

"This lotus will never wilt, as long as our friendship exists."

Set had spoken those words before she returned home and the lotus was still in a vase in her room, having never wilted over all of the years. She had no friends in her own pantheon, only acquaintances. Her mother was a shoulder she could lean on, but even she held herself to a higher standard above the gods and mortals below her.

My brother will be different because I will be there for him. He will have me to keep him level-headed and I will have him to protect me, Cassiopeia vowed to herself.

Telling Set the happy news would have to wait, as she must now help her parents plan the next party of the millennia.

Cassiopeia didn't hate trying on all dresses—just the ones that Zaina, goddess of beauty and sexual desires, and her mother picked out. They were too edgy and seductive for her tastes, as she preferred to be more modest. Her father also had to voice his opinion on anything she wore, and he was almost as bad as they were, wanting to show her off like a doll. He wanted her to look like his powerful little star.

This wasn't just a party to announce Lilith's pregnancy; it was meant to also be a party of peace. Magnus was inviting the leviathans. Since the leviathans destroyed the Sumerian pantheon, they had warred between themselves and had become eerily quiet. But a new leviathan had recently been created, only a few decades before, so they had slowly become more active. Leviathans were created by the universe to provide the balance against gods and were the only creatures that were created specifically to kill gods, when necessary. If a god were to kill another god, their power would explode out of them, destroying everything around them, including themselves. Leviathans absorbed the power from the gods they killed, and it made them stronger.

Cassiopeia was the only exception to that rule, though no one knew how or why. She was the only goddess ever known to be able to directly kill a god and absorb their powers with no destruction or adverse consequences.

Cassiopeia tried on the next dress—tight and black, with spaghetti straps, that dipped low in the front, with two long trails of translucent fabric that flowed to the floor from the straps. The fabric was translucent from her thighs down and had a slit down the middle.

"I absolutely love it! It's sexy and fun! *I* want to wear it!" Zaina said that about almost every dress where half of her body was exposed. Cassiopeia looked to her mother with distaste. She hated showing this much skin.

"Mitéra?"

Mother

"It will do but maybe something a little classier? Why don't you go ask Magnus, he has the final say, anyway."

Her mother had seemed a little off the past few days and Cassiopeia couldn't figure out why. Zaina spoke again.

"Let me do your hair and makeup so he can see the whole look!"

Cassiopeia nodded reluctantly. When Zaina was done, Cassiopeia barely recognized herself in the mirror before she flashed to the entrance of the great hall, appearing suddenly just outside its doors. Flashing was the god's form of teleportation. It could transport them to different realms, such as back and forth from their realm to the mortal realm. She rarely used it around the palace, but she was in no mood to struggle to walk in the heels that Zaina had put her in. She heard voices inside the great hall as she walked in. When she saw that her father was meeting with a small group of people, she turned to leave.

"Ah, my little star! Cassiopeia won't you come here. I want you to meet some people." Magnus beckoned to her.

She was not in the mood to meet strangers. She just wanted to show him how inappropriate this dress was, but it did not faze him because he wanted to show her off.

She walked across the hall, her heels clicking on the white marble. As the strangers turned to her, she saw they all wore masks over their eyes. The one at the front, their leader, had an unusual attraction about him. Although she couldn't see his face or his eyes through his mask, she somehow knew that he was handsome. She knew they were all staring at her, but she held her head high as she walked over to her father. She could sense her father's tension and was uncomfortable because of her dress, but for some reason she wasn't nervous or fearful.

"I would like you to meet my daughter and my trophy, Cassiopeia, the killer of gods and teller of fates. She can kill a god with just one touch." Magnus turned to her. "Cassiopeia, these are the leviathans and their leader, Alexander. They will be attending the party for peace."

Leviathans.

They were the true killer of gods. She knew she should be scared, but she found herself looking at their leader and was unafraid.

"Let us give you a demonstration of my daughter's powers," Magnus offered.

"That won't be necessary." Alexander's voice rumbled through the hall.

"I absolutely insist."

Before another word could be spoken, a cage appeared to the right of the leviathans. Cassiopeia reached out her with her powers, like rays of light reaching out to where she directed them. She could feel that the god inside was from the Greek pantheon and wasn't very powerful. He had been caught snooping around the Atlantean palace grounds on Vēlatusa. Cassiopeia hated doing this, but she had to, for her father. Pulling the power of the gods she killed into herself was painful and uncomfortable. Magnus pushed her lightly toward the cage, being careful not to touch her skin. As the cage vanished around him, the god tried to escape, but Cassiopeia was faster.

She flashed herself next to him before he could get away. She could see the fear in his eyes. He tried to back away, but her hand made contact with his skin and he couldn't move, paralyzed by her power and made to only watch as his life flashed before him. Her eyes changed from blue to red, as she pushed her powers out. She saw that he was a god of war and had committed many terrible atrocities in his life, causing unnecessary death, fear, and chaos.

"Enyalius, god of war, I . . ." Before she could finish her sentence and absorb his powers, she felt his lifeforce flow away from her reach. She pulled herself from the trance to see a sword sticking out of the god's back, held by the leviathan leader. She watched as the god's powers streamed out of the god, a black sand-like smoke that spiraled up and went under the leviathan's mask, flowing into him. She was grateful she didn't have to absorb the powers, but she couldn't show it, as she kept her face surprised yet stoic. The leviathan spoke.

"I said it wasn't necessary."

The god's body hit the floor with a sickening thud. Cassiopeia turned to see her father's stone face. He hid his anger, but she knew that inside he was boiling.

"Of course, I assumed you would enjoy watching a god die."

"If I wanted to see a god die, I would kill a god myself," Alexander said. She could have sworn she heard one of the others chuckle lightly.

"We will return tomorrow for the signing of the peace agreement between our people."

"I can't wait." Magnus nodded his head.

Before Magnus could say more, the leviathans left. Magnus's face changed from peaceful and kind to cold and angry. He looked at the body on the floor.

"Someone, get rid of this!" He looked at her, anger still in his eyes. "You should have done it faster," he looked her up and down. "You cannot wear that dress now. They have already seen you in it and I can't have them see you in the same thing twice—that would be ludicrous. Be gone."

Cassiopeia left quickly, walking out of the throne room as her father didn't tolerate flashing in his presence when avoidable. She couldn't stand to be around him when he was in such an angry mood. The only reason he hadn't hit her was because he didn't want to accidentally mar her face before the party tomorrow. She hurried back to her room to tell the others that they had to find a new dress. As she walked quickly back to her bedroom, she thought back to the leviathan leader. Why had he been so alluring to her? He seemed so familiar, like she had met him in another life. She shook her head, trying to stop daydreaming about ridiculous and impossible things.

Lilith and Magnus had decided to make the ball a masquerade because the leviathans didn't want to show their faces. Lilith had given Cassiopeia a dress similar to hers, so that they matched. Floor-length and a dark indigo ombre, the gown was adorned with sparkles, scattered like stars upon it. It had an open back that wrapped around to the front, with mesh down the center of the chest to accentuate her curves while still covering her. The material was an Atlantean silk that looked shiny but felt like soft velvet. The bottom flowed as she walked, with a slit to just above her knees that could only be seen as she moved. It had more material than the other one, while still being alluring and tempting—more fitting for her desire to be somewhat modest. Her mask was simple, made of black lace and covering just around her eyes.

At the entrance to the main hall they announced the arrival of her parents and they regally entered the ball. Then they announced her arrival. Cassiopeia walked in, hating to be the center of attention. As she looked around, she immediately spotted the leviathan leader. She didn't know how she spotted him out of the crowd, he looked just like everyone else with a mask, but somehow, she knew it was him. She walked up the steps to her throne, next to her mother. Everyone bowed and the royals sat as the party continued. While she sat next to her parents, she caught herself continuing to look for the leviathan. Every time she spotted him, he was looking in her direction. After most of the gods and goddess had said their courtesies she was allowed to get up and walk around to socialize, not that any of the gods wanted to speak with her. They either feared her or didn't respect her.

Her mask was driving her crazy, as the lace itched her face. She walked outside and went around the corner to remove it for some relief. Everyone knew who she was anyway, but her father would be angry if she *ruined the illusion* by removing her mask. She heard someone behind her and turned. There was a man standing only a few feet away, tall, his brown hair slicked back neatly. She could see his blue eyes through the holes in his mask.

"May I help you?" She asked warily.

"I guess everyone already knows who you are, so why would you have to wear a mask the whole time."

Cassiopeia was very confused by his behavior and could sense indecision radiating off of him. He was making her nervous and uncomfortable.

"My father told me to wear it. That's why I came here to take it off for a minute. I really should be getting back . . ."

"You can destroy entire pantheons. You can kill anything."

His words were said with respect, but also anger.

"I should go back. People will be wondering where I am." Cassiopeia stepped forward to leave, but he blocked her exit. She reached her powers out lightly, quickly discovering that he wasn't a god. A leviathan.

"Move." She said sternly, in an attempt to be aggressive.

"I just wanted to talk. Are you scared of me?"

A smirk formed on his lips as he spoke, enjoying his power over her. She could feel herself panicking, but she kept her level head.

"You are here on a diplomatic mission. I would hate for you to ruin that with this charade of yours."

"Exactly, we are here as diplomats. Allies." There was a hint of sarcasm and spite in his voice. "So, what's the rush?"

Before she could retort or attempt to grab him, she heard a deep voice behind her.

"Leave. Her. Be."

She knew it was Alexander, the leviathan leader. His stern, masculine voice reverberated through her body, easing her worry. The man in front of her stepped back.

"I was just . . ." the leviathan stammered.

"I don't care. Go inside. Now."

It wasn't a request. It was a listen-or-die kind of demand. The leviathan glared at her for a moment longer before he turned and walked back inside. Cassiopeia took a slight sigh of relief and turned around to thank Alexander, only to realize he stood merely inches behind her. His nearness took her breath away. She could smell jasmine and sandalwood oil on his skin. His mask was black and covered most of his face, there was even mesh over the eye holes so she couldn't see them. She had to fight the urge to reach out and touch him.

"Thank you."

"It's no problem, he needed a lesson in self-control anyway. He never should have cornered you like that."

"Not that I needed your help. I could have dealt with him on my own," Cassiopeia reminded him.

Even though she couldn't see his face she could sense that he was smirking at her.

"I am sure you are fully capable of handling yourself, my goddess."

His endearment surprised her slightly. She had always been told that leviathans were cold and heartless. She expected him to use more aggressive language.

"My goddess? Do I rule over you, leviathan?"

She heard a chuckle rise from his chest. The sound rumbled around her lightly, filling her with comfort and ease. The presence of the other leviathan had caused her to be tense and her skin to crawl, but with him she felt differently.

"And if you did, little goddess, how would you use that power? What would you do to me?"

She felt her cheeks blush lightly. She wanted to answer but she also wanted to change the subject away from the twist that it had taken.

"I don't know. What kind of question is that to ask?"

"It's quite a simple question, I thought. If you had a leviathan at your feet how would you use that power? Would you bend me to your will to use against your enemies or would you show kindness and respect?"

She thought for a moment as he walked over to the ledge that looked over the edge of the gardens. Reaching the stone railing, he turned back to face her as he leaned casually against it.

"All powerful things should be treated with kindness and respect. It isn't just or right to punish something just because it is more powerful than you. That is called cruelty and control. So, to answer your original question, I suppose nothing would change except that I would feel safer knowing that my kindness would be rewarded with loyalty."

He quietly watched her. Cassiopeia wished that she could see his face, or at least his eyes, but he made no moves to remove his mask.

"A wise answer." He said quietly.

They stood there, looking at each other in silence. She couldn't take it any longer.

"Can you remove your mask? I would like to see who I am talking to."

He laughed again.

"The mask stays put."

"Why do you wear it if most of the gods know what you look like anyway?"

He turned his head away to look at the gardens.

"It's to protect my men's identities more so than mine. But I enjoy being able to hide my expressions. Especially from your father. He uses the reactions of others to control conversations. But, with a mask, he can't read my face."

"What would you need to hide from him. If you are here for an alliance, then why hide behind masks?"

"That's my prerogative, not yours, little goddess."

She rolled her eyes, not thinking that he was looking at her. He saw it.

"Is that not an acceptable reason?"

Her cheeks reddened again. She was never good at diplomacy. She was too blunt and timid to play games with words.

"It sounds like an excuse to appease your own needs. You do seem very relaxed right now, for being at a party full of people who hate you."

"Do you hate me?" he asked quietly.

"I don't know you."

"They don't know me either, yet they hate me."

She walked over to lean against the ledge, only a few feet away from him, and looked toward the gardens.

"I don't jump to conclusions about anyone until they prove me otherwise. You don't seem like the heartless, brutal god killer that everyone says you are, but you could always have a proverbial mask on to lower my guard."

"I do have a mask on but not for reasons that you think. I have done a lot of violent things in my life, but I do have my reasons. Some I regret less than others."

"Heartless people don't have regrets. If you are so powerful, why are you trying to build alliances?"

"Alliances aren't just for power. Sometimes they can be used to keep the peace. Even being *all powerful* I would still prefer to have allies rather than enemies. But, on a simpler note, why are you outside all alone?"

"Do I need protection right now? Are you a danger to me, leviathan?"

Even though she asked him that, she felt no danger. If he had wanted to hurt her, he had already had multiple opportunities tonight.

"No, right now you are safe—from me at least."

"Sometimes I just like to get away from everything. Gods and goddesses are too self-consumed for my tastes. Most of them are just using me for their own gains, attempting to befriend me so they have the *god killer* on their side. They act like my friends, but I know that if I tried to touch them, they would just shun away from me."

He stood next to her silently. She realized she had said more than she should have or than he wanted to hear. She suddenly felt uncomfortable.

"Are you worried I will do the same? Befriend you just to use you?" he asked.

"How could you use me? You have the same powers I do, if not more. I have no pull over the decisions of my pantheon, I am just a pawn in their war games. And we have already proven that you are not heartless, therefore you would be too compassionate to use me."

He chuckled again.

"Such a simple view of the world." He could see that his words upset her. "But honest. I like honesty. It's refreshing and pleasant. I am happy to see that your father's cruelty hasn't darkened your heart."

"How would you know how my father treats me?"

His voice lowered. He took a step closer to her, as if someone may be listening.

"My father was cruel too. He also tried to hide it behind a fake facade, but if you looked long enough you could see it bleeding through the cracks. A caring father would never pull you into a room full of leviathans for a display of power and risk something happening to you."

Cassiopeia didn't know why his words angered her. He spoke the truth, yet she felt as though she should defend her father. She stepped away from the ledge to face him. As she did her mask fell to the ground. Before she could bend down to pick it up, he flashed it into his hand and held it out to her. She hadn't noticed that he had gloves on before. They were black and blended in with the black himation he wore over his golden chiton. Now that she was looking at his body, she could tell that he was muscular. He towered over her a good six or so inches. His black hair was pulled back away from his mask and fell to just below his shoulders. She could see a sleeve of tattoos that ran down his exposed right arm. He naturally exuded a deadly and dangerous aura, but she could sense that he was calm and relaxed. Only a foot away from her, she watched as he tensed slightly under her gaze.

She reached up slowly, but her hand went past her mask and up to his shoulder. He tensed more, unsure of what she was about to do as he felt her touch a piece of his hair lightly. When she pulled her hand away, he saw a fallen leaf in her fingers. He exhaled, realizing that he was holding his breath.

"There was a leaf," she said quietly. She placed the leaf onto the ledge and took the mask from his hands. "Thank you."

She could tell that he was staring at her, but finally he responded.

"You are welcome, my goddess."

There was a strange tension in the air around them. As if they were both waiting for the other to make the next move. She had never felt this kind of tension between herself and someone else before.

"I don't know if anyone has told you yet, but you look absolutely stunning. Beautiful as always." His voice was soft and sincere.

She could feel her cheeks reddening at his words as she looked away from his face. She didn't know why his words affected her so much, why she cared about his opinion.

"I . . . umm . . . thank you." She said, flustered. "I should be getting back inside before someone comes looking for me."

"Yes, of course."

It was as if her words snapped him from his trance and he took a large step away from her. She stepped back as well and turned to leave but stopped and turned back to look at him. Her face was stern as she looked at him intensely.

"Can we trust you? Can I trust you?"

He paused.

"Yes. You can trust me."

"Prove it."

Cassiopeia held her hand out, palm up. He didn't move. They both knew that if he touched her, she could see his entire life and, if she wanted to, kill him. So, did he trust her with his life? Was he willing to risk everything for an alliance or was he just hiding behind his mask and charming words? He still hadn't taken her hand.

Just what I thought. Just like the others. Cassiopeia thought.

She turned to walk away when she felt a hand grab hers. Looking down he had taken his glove off and had his bare hand wrapped around hers. He was holding her hand gently but firmly. She was taken aback. He didn't know her as anything other than a killer, a weapon, yet he was risking his life to prove his trust.

"You can trust me." He said again, more intensely.

Cassiopeia looked at his masked face, confused by what to do and what she was feeling. She didn't want to, but she pulled her hand away and started to leave. She got a few feet away and stopped. What her father was planning wasn't justice; it was cruel. Magnus wanted to single out the leviathans and kill them. That was the true purpose of this party. As a goddess of justice, it hurt her to the core to go along with her father's injustice. This man, this leviathan, had honor. He wasn't just some cruel killer and she was going to prove that she had honor too. She turned back and walked over to him quickly and, grabbing his bare hand, she pulled out four decorative pins. Every guest had been given a pin except for the leviathans, as a way to identify them. They were simple golden stick pins with three stones on them that were black, red, and blue. She had gotten them when they were preparing for the party. She placed them inside of his palm before closing his fingers around them.

"You and your men must wear these when you leave, or you will be singled out and killed. You showed me a sign of good faith and trust, so here's mine. Please don't betray me. Please don't make me regret this."

Alexander looked down at her, surprised at what she had just done.

"They can't kill us. If they do the universe will just replace us with new leviathans. There must always be a balance."

"That's the mindset that will get you killed. New, untrained leviathans are easier targets than ones with age and experience."

As she went to move away, he grabbed her arm and stopped her.

"If you disagree with your father's choices then why don't you stand up to him. We both know you have the power to stop him."

"What do you know of my powers?"

"More than you could ever guess, little goddess. Thank you. You will not regret this."

He let go of her arm and watched her place her mask back on to return to the party. She had just risked her life for men she didn't even know, and it shook him to his core. He turned to go back inside and give the pins to his men.

Magnus was furious. His rage shook all of Vēlatusa. All of the guests had gone, including the leviathans, each wearing a pin. Cassiopeia knew Magnus was going to be angry, but she hadn't anticipated this level of furor and wrath. She could hear him ranting about sending her to everyone's quarters to find the *traitor* who had betrayed him. Lilith was finally able to calm him slightly and the ground stopped shaking.

Cassiopeia awoke the next morning to silence. She walked out of her quarters with Sierra, only to be stopped by two Vantha demons.

"We were told that we must escort you, goddess. The leviathans are here, again."

She felt a wave of fear and regret wash over here. If Alexander wanted to, all he had to do was tell her father that it was she who had given them the pins and allowed them to escape. Nothing would be able to stop Magnus's wrath against her. Cassiopeia realized the predicament she had placed herself in for a man she didn't know. She walked quickly toward one of the entrances of the main hall, stopping just out of sight. She could hear angry voices. Alexander's stood out the most.

"We come as a display of peace and you try to trap and kill us? Is that what peace means to you?"

Magnus tried to backpedal.

"I don't know who told you this, but it was a display of peace for us too. I think that . . ."

Before he could finish, she heard small metal tings on the marble floor. The pins. Alexander had thrown the pins onto the ground in front of the Atlantean god.

"Explain this, *god of peace*." His voice was full of venom.

Magnus was at a loss for words. This further confirmed that someone had betrayed him. But before he could try to wiggle his way out of the current predicament, one of the other leviathans stepped forward.

"A prophecy for you, king of the gods of Atlantis. As punishment for trying to destroy peace you will be destroyed. One of your children is not of your blood. When they reach their peak powers, they will destroy Atlantis and the entire Atlantean pantheon. Your actions will cause your own demise. Your choices will be your unraveling."

With those words, the leviathans vanished. Cassiopeia couldn't breathe. She knew her father would send her to kill Lilith. Adulterous behavior was a death sentence in Atlantis, especially against Magnus. Panicking, Cassiopeia flashed to Lilith's room. Her mother was surprised and irritated at her uninvited arrival.

"I have my doors shut for a reason, you know," she said, exasperated.

"Stop!" Cassiopeia didn't have time to say everything that had happened, so she touched her mother and showed her what she had just overheard. Lilith's eyes widened at the impending threat from the prophecy the leviathans issued.

"You must go, Mother," Cassiopeia pleaded with her. "You are in danger! He will come for you, but he won't kill you. He will make me do it."

"You must go as well, my little star! If he discovers that you have warned me, he will hurt you, too. Sierra will protect you with her life. Go!"

Sierra grabbed Cassiopeia and quickly flashed them to her quarters.

"What do I need to do, my goddess?" Sierra asked Cassiopeia, as she sat down on the bed beside her.

"Nothing. We just wait."

Chapter 2

Cassiopeia
9022 BCE

He who controls others may be powerful,
but he who has mastered himself is mightier still.
—Lao Tzu

Cassiopeia took a breath to compose herself before she walked through the portal she had created and into a large throne room. There was a large table in the middle with Vantha demons sitting around it chatting loudly. They looked at her, quieting slightly at her arrival. She looked to the other end of the room toward the empty throne.

Mother must be in the gardens.

She turned out of the room leaving the demons to continue their discussions. It was not unusual for Cassiopeia to appear at random to visit Lilith. She was the only god who visited her on a regular basis. After the prophecy was decreed her mother fled to Khaos, the Atlantean hell realm, where she had ruled before she married Magnus and became queen of the gods. It was here that she had given birth to her son. From there she sent Cassiopeia's baby brother with a demon to be hidden in the mortal realm. Magnus couldn't reach her here, so as her punishment he trapped her in this realm until one of her children died. Here her mother sat in her prison waiting for her child to grow up and destroy the Atlanteans, as the leviathans had prophesied.

Cassiopeia walked down the dark corridor toward the garden. The walls were black marble with gold streaks, like crackling lightning. As she got closer, she could hear the fluttering of moths and smelled the sweet apricot-like smell of oleander mixed with the floral smell of belladonna. She turned the corner and walked into a courtyard in the center of the palace, through the gate, and into the garden. In it grew more than one hundred different types of flowers and plants and, as expected for a garden in the hell realm, all of them were deadly. On the far wall water sprang from a large fountain, which cascaded into a small pool. Her mother liked to sit and look into the water, which showed her what was happening in the other realms.

Today, Lilith was sitting on her favorite bench near the center of the garden. One of her Vantha demon companions was standing over her shoulder as she slowly brushed the goddess' long blonde hair. The demon looked up at Cassiopeia as she entered and whispered to Lilith.

"My little star. So wonderful for you to visit me. I am saddened that I had to send for you to come." Lilith said.

"I'm sorry, Mitéra, but Magnus has been more paranoid than ever as the eighteen-year mark approaches. Every day that passes his anger and frustrations grow. It's been nearly impossible for me to come any sooner."

She felt badly about not visiting her mother more often, but she knew she had to be cautious. Even though Magnus was her father, if he found out she was visiting Lilith he would unleash his wrath on her.

"Well, funny you should mention it, that is why I wanted to speak to you. When your brother, Caelum, gets his powers he is going to need help. Someone to be there for him. To guide him. I want that someone to be you."

Cassiopeia was taken aback by what her mother was asking and slightly angered. Just the fact that she knew where her brother was put her life in danger but now her mother wanted her to go visit him and teach him how to use his powers. If Magnus found out that she not only knew where her brother was but that she helped him become stronger, no amount of family bond could stop his wrath against her, not that their paternal bond overly protected her anyways. Not even his fear of Set or Lilith would stop him from punishing her. Why did Lilith care so much? Her brother had caused all of their current problems. If not for him, Lilith would be free from this domain and living where she belonged, in the pantheon with her daughter and the other Atlantean gods. Cassiopeia would have her mother and not have to sneak around to see her. Caelum, in her mind, had already destroyed the Atlantean pantheon by tearing her family apart. But now her mother asked her to go protect him, to help him become strong and powerful. It hurt her that her mother would put her in danger for the safety of her other child.

"Why me? Why not send a Vantha demon? Why not bring him here and train him yourself?"

"You can teach him more than a Vantha demon could about control. I can't risk bringing him here and Magnus sensing him in my domain." She could hear the aggravation in her mother's voice growing. "Why are you so bothered by this request? He is your brother."

"I'll think about it."

Her mother looked disappointed. Cassiopeia didn't know what else to say without upsetting her. They had fought over this before, many times, and it had never ended well for either of them.

"I should be getting back. I have plans to visit with Set tonight. He found a new amulet, and he wants to see if it can help with my power spikes."

Ever since the Atlantean pantheon had been split by Lilith's banishment Cassiopeia had been having trouble controlling her powers.

She had a nightmare a few weeks ago that nearly destroyed half of her temple on Vēlatusa. Set had a theory that her difficulty controlling her powers was linked to her emotions. That had given him a new life mission to fix her. Normally she would be peeved by his overbearingness but lately she appreciated it. She liked having someone care about her with no gain to themselves. Her mother, on the other hand, despised Set's interest in her daughter.

"Why do you like him?" she said with disgust. "He's so . . . annoying."

"At least he's there for me and doesn't put me in danger."

She regretted it as soon as she said it. Sadness and hurt filled Lilith's eyes. Lilith turned away to face the fountain.

"Mitéra . . ."

"Just go my little star. But promise me you will think over my request."

"I promise."

Cassiopeia left the Atlantean hell realm feeling worse than when she arrived. She could feel her powers pulling at her to use them to solve her problems. To just destroy. Everything. Set was right. Her powers were tied to her emotions and, if she didn't control her emotions, she would lose control of her powers. Her head and body hurt from keeping it all inside. She straightened up in her chambers before she flashed herself to Set's temple in Egypt.

It was out in the middle of the dessert, secluded from the reach of men. Its huge throne room occupied most of the temple's space but just outside in the back was an oasis with a large open arena for sparring and fighting. This was where Set would go to get away from the other gods and goddesses in his pantheon and clear his head.

In the temple the large red pillars rose up from the sandy colored floors. The walls inside of the temple had blood red curtains edged in gold that hung from the fifty-foot ceiling all the way to the floor. Its beauty was infused with an undercurrent of darkness, but she had been raised around gods of destruction, so to her this felt like home. If anything, it was too bright for her tastes, with all of the sand around it reflecting the sun inside through the large entryway and high windows.

"You're early."

She turned around to see the tall, muscular Egyptian god walking toward her. He wore a gold braided headpiece that fell to his shoulders and had bangs that stopped just above his eyes, hiding his short onyx hair. His green eyes were lined in kohl, which caused them to stand out from his golden almond skin.

"Yes. I couldn't just sit in my chambers slowly dying inside."

"That's a little dramatic don't you think?" he said with a smirk, raising his eyebrows and giving her a look. She just rolled her eyes.

"You didn't just get asked by your mother to risk your life for your perfect, golden-child brother. She wants me to defy Magnus and go train Caelum how to use his powers when he receives them."

"You've already defied him by hiding Caelum's location. Why would visiting him and helping him be different?" He paused. "Or, is it possible that you are reflecting your anger with your mother for leaving you toward your brother?"

Cassiopeia felt her anger rising. Why was he toying with her? Why was he upsetting her? She felt her powers surging, screaming to be released on Set.

"It's all his fault. Everything would be fine if he had never come along. We were happy. I was happy."

"Were you happy? Truly? And how could a baby choose to do all these things? Did he do it because he was being malicious? Maybe he's been suffering too. Maybe he's live a tortured life too. He was also abandoned."

"He's been the son of a powerful nobleman."

"That means nothing. You are a like a princess to the gods. Has your life been perfect, with no hardships? No. You'll never know the truth if you don't go see it for yourself. The truth is a powerful thing, as you well know being a goddess of justice. How is it justice to abandon someone in need because of your own petty feelings?"

Damn.

She hated it when he was right, which happened often. Set had gained a lot of wisdom in his tens of thousands of years of walking the Earth. He had made some of his own mistakes that he would have to live with for the rest of eternity. He just didn't want her to make the same errors. Cassiopeia decided that she would go to her brother. She would see the truth and, if he needed it, she would help. She looked over at the wise god.

"I'm not petty."

He laughed.

"No, my sweet flower. You're just hurt." He pulled her into a hug. "I won't abandon you. These wounds will stay with you forever, but the pain will heal."

They stood there for a moment embracing each other. She could sense that Set needed her just as much as she needed him. She had never known why he had taken her under his wing, but she was forever grateful. He was the caring brother that she never had but always needed. She knew he wouldn't leave, like others in her life. Cassiopeia pulled away from their embrace.

"You said you found something that could help with my powers?"

"Ah yes! Well maybe . . . don't get too excited. As you know it's been an interesting quest trying to find something to help."

They walked outside toward the arena.

"Where are we going?" Cassiopeia asked.

"I don't want you destroying my temple if this fails. I don't want to have to build another one—again!"

She laughed. A small box sat on a table at the edge of the arena.

"Amun and Ptah created it and Amunet added her womanly touch. They said it was the hardest thing they have ever created. They couldn't touch it or stay around it for long before it started to drain them. So, hopefully it will be strong enough for you."

He smiled, but she could still see the worry in his eyes.

"Will it drain my powers permanently?"

"No. They will come back shortly after you take it off and put it back in the box."

Cassiopeia walked over to the table. She saw Set back away a few steps. She opened the box to see a black stone in a gold setting. The stone was swirling inside, like a ball of liquid constantly in motion. She could feel her powers waning as she reached for it. The edge that she had been holding back dissipated. When she touched it, she realized she no longer had to hold back her powers. They weren't fighting to be free. They had settled inside of her. She lifted the amulet out of the box, noticing that it was a necklace. The chain was long enough for her to hide under her Atlantean robes. She grabbed the chain and pulled the necklace over her head, letting the gem rest on her chest. She was finally able to relax. It felt wonderful to not be holding all of her energy back. She closed her eyes at the feeling of peace that flowed over her.

"So..." Set asked nervously.

She opened her eyes and looked at Set. He was still standing away from her. She smiled at him.

"It's working."

"Good! Good! They will be very pleased!" Set smiled at her.

"As wonderful as it is, how can I wear this around other gods without them feeling it drain them too?" She asked. He moved closer to her, standing next to her.

"Once it's on they won't feel anything. If you take it off, you must return it to the box immediately, or it will drain anything nearby. Even other magical objects."

"Okay, I understand." She looked down at it. It was a truly beautiful piece of work.

"Why don't you walk over there and try to use your powers. Let's see how much power this amulet can take," Set suggested.

Cassiopeia walked toward the center of the arena. As horribly as her day had started, it was so much better now. She stopped in the middle of the sand and dirt field and turned around to face Set. He had summoned a dummy with her father's likeness onto the field. She smiled, laughing at the joke as she closed her eyes and pulled forth her powers. She focused on the dummy, pulling at all of her restrained emotions. She opened her eyes. Nothing had happened. She looked at Set with a smile.

"That was weak!" he shouted.

She shook her head closing her eyes again. She focused on all her pent-up anger. Focused on all of the pain that she had been suppressing for years. She felt a tug inside but nothing more. She pulled harder and forced up memories that she had long ago repressed. Painful memories and emotions of the past. She felt a ripple through her body. She didn't hold back. She focused only on herself. Every pain she had ever seen, every feeling that had made her lose control. She let the rage take over. The beast, the demon, that had always wanted to be freed inside of her came forward, ready to take control. It clawed its way out of her chest boiling to the top.

Cassiopeia felt something change. Her hair turned pure white and her eyes shifted to a swirling red with gold and black streaks running through them. Her skin changed, becoming so white it was almost grey. She heard a noise and when she opened her eyes everything was tinged red.

Cassiopeia wanted to destroy everything, and she knew she had the power to do it. She could feel every creature touching the earth like their lives were connected with a string. Feeling them breathe, feeling their connection. She knew she could pull at any of the strings and they would be gone. Dead. She was the ultimate destroyer. As she focused her eyes, she saw Set. Someone else was with him. She felt their anger at each other. But she realized something. The stranger had no string. He wasn't connected to the Earth like everything else. Him she couldn't touch. Why? The beast inside of her ebbed back at the realization that something may be stronger. Cassiopeia thought clearly for a moment. Her powers were free. She touched the amulet which was glowing trying to hold her back. It hadn't worked. But she had another problem. She couldn't reign in the power she had released.

Help.

As if he had heard her silent plea, the stranger flashed to her. His black hair whipped in the wind. He had unique eyes. They were glowing a deep purple. He reached out with his right hand and grabbed her arm. She felt the beast inside relax at his touch. It ebbed back, retreating to its cage inside her chest. He stared at her intently, which normally would have bothered her. But she found his eyes to be so mesmerizing and relaxing, like the sound of waves crashing onto the shore. Her powers were still out of control, but she was back in control of her body.

"Close your eyes!" He shouted over the wind and she obliged. "Push your powers into the earth. Let the ground absorb your powers instead of taking from it!"

She had never thought to do that. Every god and goddess had a unique way to charge their powers. She pulled from the earth and charged off of the energy of all of the living things in this realm. So instead of charging from the earth she pushed her powers back into it. She tried for a few moments, but nothing happened. She looked back up at him, worried. Her stress was causing her powers to flare more. He took his hand off her arm and cupped her face in his strong grasp.

"Focus. You can do it."

He was so sure of her. She closed her eyes and tried again. Cassiopeia pushed down with her mind and she felt her powers melt down into the ground. She felt the chaos around her begin to die down slowly.

Cassiopeia continued to push until the wind had stopped completely. When she looked down at her hair it had returned to its normal blonde color. She stopped letting her powers flow and looked up at the stranger who was still staring intently into her eyes. His eyes were no longer glowing deep purple. They were now a soft lavender. His handsome face relaxed and softened, almost lovingly. As he removed his hands from her face, she felt cold at the absence of his touch. Looking down at her chest he lifted up the amulet.

"I think you're going to need a new necklace," he said.

His voice was deep and calming. She could have sworn she had heard it before, but she couldn't place where. She looked down at the amulet and the black swirling stone was now white and still. She looked at the dummy and knocked it over with her mind from across the arena. Cassiopeia could feel her hope dissipating as anger flowed forward and she felt her powers again.

"How do I still have more power! Why can't it go away!"

"You need to learn how to accept it not control it. An aggressive animal is going to become more and more aggressive if you stuff it in a cage, but, if you let it out in a controlled manner you can train and use it. Your powers are the same. If you keep holding them in, they will consume you."

"Teach me. Please."

She saw indecision on his face.

"I can teach you something that helps me. Someone taught me this long ago. When you feel your powers surging, make a fist. Breathe out." She did as he suggested. "Now open your hand, feeling the power grow in the center of your palm. Breathe in." She did. She could see her hands glowing. "Now make another fist but pull the power back into yourself and feel it disintegrate into you. Breathe out." She felt his hand on the back of hers as he gently pushed her hands shut. She curled her fingers shut, feeling the power return to her and ebb down inside of her. She felt a calmness overcome her. When she opened her eyes, he gave her a small smile releasing her hands.

"Better?"

Cassiopeia nodded yes and caught herself just looking at him. His black hair fell in waves to just above his shoulders and he had a clean-shaven face with a strong, chiseled jaw. His lavender eyes stood out from his tawny skin. He wore a simple black peplos with a belt and bronze clasps. His aura felt familiar. As if she knew him. Mesmerized, she reached out to touch his cheek. Her hand was only a few inches away from his face when he quickly grabbed her wrist firmly. Their eyes locked and she saw a profound amount of emotion swirling behind their lavender surface. His hand relaxed and slid from her wrist to her hand, her fingers curling around his thumb. She didn't know why he felt so safe and comforting.

"I . . . I feel like I know you."

His eyes softened and he was about to speak when they heard yelling.

"Is it safe!?" They both turned to look at Set, who was still standing on the other side of the arena. She pulled her hand away from his gentle grip before the Egyptian saw. Set was very protective of her, in a way that a brother is toward his little sister.

"Yes!" She shouted back.

I hope so.

She was still shaken by what had happened. Set appeared next to them. He reached out and lifted the amulet off of her chest.

"Damn. Amun, Ptah, and Amunet are going to be pissed when I tell them I lost their amulet."

"It's not lost. You can give this to them and tell them what happened."

Cassiopeia took off the destroyed amulet and handed it to him. Set looked up at the stranger as if they knew something she didn't. She realized she still had no clue who he was. He had risked his life to help her and she didn't even know his name.

"Wait, I'm confused. Who are you?"

He looked at her almost as if her question hurt him. She could see sadness hidden in his eyes. As if he had already told her and she had forgotten. Did she know him? Set answered for him.

"Cassiopeia, this is Alexander."

The infamous leviathan leader. A god-killer, like her. One of the few of his kind. He had destroyed pantheons and murdered his own. The gods had endless stories of the horrors he had caused. She knew she should fear him, but she didn't. She remembered when they had met at the masquerade party eighteen years earlier. Their conversation was still in her mind even after all this time. This was the masked leviathan who had trusted her all those years ago and hadn't betrayed her. She was drawn to him then too.

"Alexander," She said, as if testing his name on her lips. "The leviathan leader."

He nodded.

"I remember you . . ."

"You should go," Set said, looking at Cassiopeia, pulling her from her thoughts. "The other pantheons are going to be coming to find out what happened, and I don't want you to be here. They don't need to know about your powers. If they ask, you were never here. Gods are jealous. If they learned about your primordial powers, they will try to use you as a weapon . . . even more so than they do now."

"I won't tell anyone."

She looked one last time at Alexander. She would never forget the pain and sadness in his unique eyes, or his simple, gentle touch. She flashed home.

Set looked at Alexander. Neither had ever seen power like that before in their thousands of years of life. Set spoke first.

"We knew she was powerful, but I didn't expect that. We must keep her safe. She will need our help to fight the demon inside of her."

"I agree."

Alexander looked out across the destruction that had occurred. He had never understood how much power she truly had locked up inside until today. She could end the world single-handedly. Set manifested the box and placed the amulet inside, handing it over to Alexander.

"Here's our story. You heard about the amulet and that we made it to control you. You came to take it, and we fought. Unbelievably, you won—I know, shocker. It was close," Set smirked. "You stole the amulet and we almost destroyed the planet."

Alexander shook his head at the prideful god.

"Sounds good to me," he said, "except for one thing."

Alexander turned toward Set, the box disappearing from his hands as he pulled back his arm and punched Set squarely in the jaw. Set fell to the ground.

"What the hell!" Set's eyes began to glow a deep gold.

"For believability. And for being dumb enough to let her unleash her powers and the demon. What were you thinking?" Alexander's eyes matched the intensity of Set's, firing to a deep purple.

"I was trying to help, you ungrateful ass!" Set looked up at him and lunged, tackling Alexander to the ground. As they both got to their feet and circled each other, their powers surged and the wind began to pick up again. They were about to go at each other again when Zeus, Magnus, and Isis appeared at the other end of the destroyed arena, each dressed in full armor. Alexander looked at them and back at Set. He vanished with a wink, returning to his hidden island. Set walked to the other gods, rubbing his jaw.

"Just a difference of opinions."

The other gods looked at each other and then back at him, unamused.

"The whole earth shook," Zeus said.

"You are not the only pantheon with subjects on this planet. Don't destroy it with your petty games," Magnus spat out. Set felt his rage rising toward the Atlantean, but for other reasons.

"It won't happen again. I will assure it. Correct, Set?" Isis looked at him with her sharp angry eyes.

"No, never again. Unfortunately, he got what he came for and won't be back." He looked to the Greek and Atlantean gods. "You can leave my domain now that all is well."

The gods didn't look pleased about being told what to do, but they weren't going to fight with a primordial god who had just survived a fight against a leviathan. They left, leaving Set and Isis alone. She looked at him with anger.

"What are you hiding? I know that if Alexander came here to kill you, he wouldn't have stopped, and as powerful as you are you would be way more busted up. So, what game are you two playing?"

"He stole the amulet that Amun, Ptah, and Amunet made. That's all he came for, and that's all he wanted."

She still looked displeased but more convinced.

"Stop being a child. You are one of the oldest creatures on this planet, but you aren't acting like it. Fix yourself—before I do it for you." She turned to leave, then looked back at him. "Next time you want to lie to me, make a better story."

And with that she left him alone to think about the power he had witnessed Cassiopeia use. If that happened again and Alexander wasn't there, she would be unstoppable. She would be the end of the world.

Cassiopeia appeared back on Vēlatusa. As she looked at her bed, she felt a sudden tiredness fall over her. Walking across the room, she collapsed onto the bed. She pulled one of her pillows to her chest and curled into it. She wished Sierra was here to comfort her. Her demon companion was also her best friend. Her father had banned her from the palace with all of the other Vantha demons after he exiled Lilith. As goddess of the Atlantean realm of death, they fell under her rule and her direct command. Yes, they would listen to their king, but Lilith still had an unspoken pull over them. Cassiopeia felt a heavy weight closing her eyes.

When she opened them again, it was dark outside. She sat up, realizing that she had fallen asleep. Getting up quickly, she knew that if she didn't hurry, she would miss dinner and Magnus would be upset with her.

She hurried down the long corridor toward the dining hall. As Cassiopeia got closer, she heard voices. She was treated with the amazing smells of fennel-roasted lamb over thyme-seasoned lentils and freshly made rabbit stew as she entered the large dining room. There were two huge tables that ran down the length of the hall and at the end there was one golden table that ran perpendicular to the others. Her father was already at the head table. She hurried down the side of the room and took her place in the chair at his side. Maybe he wouldn't notice her tardiness.

"You're late."

Damn.

"I'm sorry, Father. I fell asleep. I haven't been sleeping well."

"It will not happen again."

"Of course."

She placed some of the food on her plate and began to eat, not discovering how famished she was until she took the first bite. She tried to eat in a civilized manner, but all she wanted to do was stuff her face. She saw Serephina lean back in her chair to look at Magnus.

"Do you know what happened in Egypt today?"

As the Atlantean goddess of mischief and trouble, she was curious about the chaos that had ensued. Cassiopeia stopped chewing and turned to look at Magnus.

"Apparently Set and the leviathan, Alexander, got into a fight over an amulet."

"And they shook the earth?" Nikolaus, god of war, shouted.

"So I was told. They were still fighting when I arrived with Zeus and Isis. If it happens again, we may have to band together with the other pantheons to go after and destroy the leviathan."

Cassiopeia didn't know why, but just the thought of that made her stomach turn. Her ravenous appetite left her.

"Maybe it was just a misunderstanding," Cassiopeia said.

All the other Gods got quiet and looked at her. Magnus spoke first.

"Leviathans just destroy. That's all they know how to do and that's all they were created to do. They even destroyed each other. The only reason the pantheons haven't banned together earlier is that they keep to themselves and no one ever sees them. But if one of them, especially their leader, Alexander, is attacking gods and stealing amulets, then maybe we should talk about banding together to remove the common threat."

A few of the other gods and goddesses responded with sounds of agreement. Cassiopeia didn't know why she wanted to argue her point. She had seen goodness in him. He wasn't just a monster to be stopped. Alexander could have killed her today to stop her, but he didn't. He saved her and, in doing so, saved the entire planet. Cassiopeia was tired of dealing with the politics and the power struggles of the gods. Why couldn't they just be happy with the lives they were dealt? They could be worse off. They had never felt hunger or poverty or weakness. Yet they still complained. It made her understand why the universe created leviathans from mortals who lived hard lives and were abused by the gods. They appreciated the gifts they were granted. They didn't abuse others and take advantage of them because they remembered how it felt to have that done to them. The others continued to jibe at the leviathan, and she couldn't listen to them anymore.

"May I be excused? I still don't feel well. I'm going to go lie back down."

Magnus's eyes filled with concern. He went to feel her forehead with his hand then stopped before he made skin contact.

"Should I send in Raffaela?"

"No. I think I just need to rest."

"Okay."

He stood and she rose after him. He embraced her and then let her leave for the night. His embraces were always so cold, so emotionless. He showed concern for her health only because she was an asset to him and not because she was his daughter. She could still remember when his embraces were warm and full of concern, but that was a long time ago. He had been kinder and more caring when she was a girl, but as she grew, she saw his joy and warmth recede, leaving a cold, hard man. She knew he would never be as he was. Her mother and his position in their pantheon had changed him over the years. Power and strength were more important to him now than having kindness and showing love.

When Cassiopeia entered her chambers, she quickly closed the door behind her. She needed to go to Earth and recharge, feeling weak from the events of the day. She also remembered her conversation with Set before everything happened. As she walked out to her balcony, looking out at the ocean and the other islands below her, she took a deep breath, allowing the smell of the salty air to calm her. She closed her eyes, listening to the sounds of the sea. The crashing waves against the rocks below and the smell of the ocean spray always settled her soul. Opening her eyes, she knew what she should do. Even if she didn't want to, she needed to go visit her brother. Tomorrow she was going to meet Caelum.

Chapter 3

Caelum
9022 BCE

Day by day, what you choose,
what you think and what you do is who you become.
—Heraclitus

I awake in my chambers to the blood-curling sound of screams. Sitting up quickly, I look around to see a red fog surrounding me. The fog is too thick to see through as I stumble out of my bed chambers. I run my hand along the wall as I stagger toward the chaos that is occurring before me. As I enter the main hall, the floor is coated in blood. It drips down the steps that lead to the thrones. Even the thrones themselves are dripping with blood. In the air above my head I hear what sounds like the shifting of sands, and I look up to see black god-dust floating in the air and swirling around aggressively, looking for its host. The sounds of the

Atlantean people praying for help fills the air, almost deafening. I cower away, covering my ears to ease the pain from the volume of their noise. As I am crouched there, I see someone walk up to me. I look up to see Lilith standing over me.

"Finish the job," She hisses.

I look past her to see Magnus on his knees. In front of him is a baby, my baby brother. Dead. Lilith touches my shoulder and rage fills me. I lunge forward and rip out Magnus' heart as easy as butter. All the screams stop. The whole world comes to a standstill.

"It is done," Lilith whispers.

I turn to look at her, but suddenly the floor beneath me is gone. I am falling into a dark abyss. When I hit the rocky bottom, I watch as a cage closes around me, trapping me inside. I shout through the bars, but all I can see is the shadow of a figure with demonic eyes, red swirling with gold and black.

Cassiopeia sat up gasping for air. She didn't remember where she was for a moment from the intensity of the dream. This was the worst it had ever been. This time she could even smell the blood and feel his heart. She didn't fully know what it meant, but she knew that it was not a good omen of things to come. As she sat up, she took a deep breath.

I have been having these dreams for years and nothing has come of them. They are just dreams, she thought.

Once she settled her nerves, she looked over to see the sunlight streaming in through the open pillars of her balcony. She felt her aunt's gentle brush on her cheek. As the invisible goddess of the north wind, she only made her presence known occasionally. She couldn't speak but she was always there to help steer the ships of their people and comfort those in need with her gentle caress.

Cassiopeia rolled over, groaning. Caelum. Yesterday had been his birthday. He was now an adult and soon he would discover his powers.

Godly powers usually manifested themselves shortly after adulthood, but it wasn't an exact date. He would get his initial powers—the ability to flash, manifest, use a god bolt, and sense other gods and beings around him—but he would have to harness the world around him to discover what his individual power was, the one that made him different from the gods around him. For Cassiopeia, her powers came from being a goddess of fate and justice. For him it could be anything. She would have to help him if he was to have any chance at being able to control them. She had forgotten her current dilemma. It seemed like even her aunt wanted her to go to him. Cassiopeia didn't want to, but she knew Set was right. If she didn't go and something happened, or she was wrong, she would feel guilty.

"Fine, I will go." She said to the air around her.

She sat up and stretched. Her body felt sore. Yesterday's power excursion had taken its toll on her mentally and physically. She knew she would heal quickly and fought through the soreness, rising out of bed. She changed her clothes into a long Greek peplos. It was cream with a thick border of gold and red edging. The fibulae that held up her peplos had her symbol on it: a perfectly balanced scale whose stand was a sword. Behind it was the black crescent moon of Lilith. She had always wondered why her father wasn't represented in her image but had never questioned. She looked into her mirror.

Everything is going to be fine. Just control your emotions, she thought.

Cassiopeia felt her power rise in her. She did what Alexander had taught her. Fist. Breathe out. Relax. Breathe in. Fist. Breathe out. The edge dissipated. She gave herself a small smile for being able to do it on her own. She was ready. She flashed herself to an island in Greece. The island where her brother lived as a mortal nobleman whose life was about to change forever.

Cassiopeia appeared on a balcony. She could sense that Caelum was close. As she looked through the curtains that billowed gently in the wind at the entry way into the room, she saw a man sleeping in the bed. She quietly crept into the room. It was still early morning in Greece, the sun just beginning to peak over the horizon. As she walked closer, she could see that he was covered in a layer of sweat. He had light blonde hair, just like Lilith, and his skin was tanned from the sun. His face was very handsome and alluring. But the expression on it was twisted in pain and fear. She pushed out with her powers, feeling his mind push back violently. Something was different about him, but maybe he was just destined to be powerful like her.

He started mumbling in his sleep and tossing around. She reached out to him to give him comfort but, as her hand neared him, he awakened. When his eyes opened, they were a light grey, matching her mother's perfectly. He looked like a male version of Lilith, as she could see her mother's features in his face. He focused on her and his eyes widened as he flung himself up and grabbed her, pushing her roughly into the wall. By doing so he grabbed her arm in skin-to-skin contact. Cassiopeia felt her eyes shift from blue to red. His face twisted as he realized he couldn't pull away. She saw his past. She saw everything he had gone through in his life. His mortal family had never truly accepted him as one of their own. They hadn't treated him like a prince. They had treated him worse than a slave. He was tortured and abused. She felt a tear slide down her face. Cassiopeia couldn't watch his horrors anymore and she pushed him away. She looked into his eyes, unable to talk to him after what she had seen. She just couldn't process the brutality of it.

With three words she left him to wonder who she was: "I'm so sorry."

Cassiopeia appeared back in her chambers. She couldn't breathe, feeling horrible. All this time she had left him to his own devices, assuming that he was being taken care of when, in reality, she had abandoned him to be abused, just as she had been at the hands of Magnus. She couldn't go face her mother. She couldn't face Set. Tears streamed down her face as her powers began to surge, the monster inside pounding at her heart, fighting to be freed again. Cassiopeia felt herself panicking over how she had abandoned him, over the guilt she felt. The tightness in her chest was growing. She tried to calm down, but she couldn't regulate her breathing. Vaguely, she heard her chamber doors open but didn't look up as she heard a gasp.

"Are you alright, my little star?"

She heard her father's voice, but she couldn't handle talking to anyone. She grabbed her stomach as she felt it twisting tighter, her stress growing. She backed away and walked out onto the balcony. As she leaned forward, her hair fell into her face. It was white, just like when she used her powers at Set's temple. She needed to get control and quickly.

Think. Relax. Breathe.

She closed her eyes and pictured two deep purple eyes looking back at her. How relaxing they were. She imagined his voice in her ear and his face as his eyes shifted back to their calming lavender.

Focus. You can do it.

Cassiopeia clenched her fists, breathing like he showed her. She felt herself slowly regaining control. She breathed in sync with the tightening and relaxing of her hands. Over and over until she felt herself fill with calmness. When she opened her eyes, she looked for the lavender eyes that she wanted to see, but instead looked into her father's deep blue eyes. She saw worry and took a step back.

"I'm fine. I just . . . it's okay. I'm in control."

He looked at her warily.

"What happened?"

She didn't know what to say. She couldn't tell him about meeting her brother.

"I had a vision." She elaborated, saying, "I've been having nightmares about death and destruction. People screaming. Fire. Flooding. Death. It's been happening for the past week. Last night was worse than usual."

It wasn't a complete lie. Her panic hadn't been caused by her dreams, but she had been plagued by nightmares for the past few days. The only part she left out was that in her dreams she saw Lilith walking the Earth.

"Let's have Raffaela give you something to help you sleep. We can't have you losing control of your powers."

He looked worried. But she could tell it was more worry of her hurting him than of her having bad dreams.

"Okay thank you, Patéras."

Father.

Magnus smiled back, his eyes still filled with false concern. He left her room, closing the doors behind him. It was then that she realized she had to go back to her brother. She was going to be more prepared next time because now she had the truth. She wasn't going to leave and hurt him like others in his life had done. She was going to show him that not everyone leaves. She was going to be as steady and supportive to him as Set had been to her.

Cassiopeia had decided to wait until nightfall to go back, so fewer people would be moving around in his home. They wouldn't have to be as careful. She appeared on his balcony again, this time under the night stars. Cassiopeia walked in and found him already asleep on the bed. She walked toward the bed, then felt someone flash behind her. Two gloved hands grabbed her and pinned her to the pillar by the entrance of the room. She opened her eyes in shock and surprise only to look into two angry, familiar blue eyes that glowed with rage. Magnus. He had waited and followed her to find her brother. She didn't know what to say or do.

"You have some explaining to do, my *loyal* daughter."

His quiet voice was full of venom and malice. Her stomach dropped as she realized he had followed her here. He had easily seen through her lie to him earlier that morning. He knew Cassiopeia would only lie to him about this, nothing else was important enough to risk facing his wrath. She had unintentionally led her father directly to the one thing she was trying to protect.

"I . . . I heard he was here, and I was investigating. This place appeared in my dreams."

She didn't want to lie but she was so scared of his wrath. His face relaxed slightly as he loosened his grip on her.

"Well, why don't we take care of that problem for you. Does he have his powers yet?"

"No. He is harmless. Not quite a god but also not mortal."

The powers that Caelum was born with had been restrained by Lilith to protect him from other gods sensing and discovering him, but that also gave him a weakness of not being a god yet. It meant that he wasn't tied to the universe like they were. Magnus smirked evilly.

"Good."

Before she had time to understand what he meant, Magnus flashed over to the bed and plunged an Atlantean dagger right into Caelum's chest. The Atlantean dagger was forged of steel from Atlantis and was the only weapon capable of killing an Atlantean creature. It was sharpened with the blood of a primordial god and could even cut a god if used correctly, but it wasn't powerful enough to kill one. But Caelum wasn't quite a god yet.

"No! What have you done?" Cassiopeia screamed.

"I've ended the prophecy. Now there is no danger to Atlantis or to our family. I did this to maintain order and power in our pantheon. To keep us safe. You should be grateful you're now safe too."

Magnus wiped the blood off of the dagger onto the sheets. She fell to her knees as the blood pooled onto the white sheets around her brother's body. Then they both felt it. As Caelum breathed his last, the walls of Lilith's prison crumbled. Her mother was free to travel through the realms. As the barriers fell, Cassiopeia felt their mental connection return. She felt her mother's pain at losing her child mix with her own pain of losing a brother she never knew. One she hadn't been able to save. Magnus's wrath had been dealt against her for the last time as she was pushed over the edge of submitting to his malicious behaviors.

"You have released Lilith. I am sorry, Father, but I have to choose a side."

She vanished to go to her mother.

Magnus was dead. The Atlantean people were dead, Atlantis destroyed. The pantheon was obliterated. The only two still alive were Cassiopeia and Lilith. Cassiopeia didn't know what to do or think, her mind didn't know how to process it all. She could barely even remember it all happening around her. In less than one day her brother and her entire family had been killed, her country was destroyed by her and her mother, and now their rampage was spreading across Greece. Through all of this she had been at her mother's side. Cassiopeia hadn't felt sympathy for most of the Atlantean gods or the people who abused her brother, but she had never intended on destroying their people or destroying the Greeks.

She felt as though she trying to see through a fog. Her mother was on a quest to demolish all who had ripped her family apart and that included the leviathan that had made the prophecy all those years ago. It was genocide. If they continued on this path, the entire world would fall.

They were now in the Greek city of Araxos. Most of the buildings were destroyed and the people dead. As they went toward the last buildings still standing she saw one was a schoolhouse. Cassiopeia saw the terrified children looking out through the windows up at the murderous goddesses. She could feel her scales tipping. This wasn't justice. The haze that had overtaken her mind faded away as her mother aimed to destroy it.

"*No! Stop!* Not that building, it's just children." Cassiopeia stood in the way of her mother's blast.

Lilith stopped. "They all must pay. Children will grow up to become adults who will become just like the ones who hurt my son!"

"That's not justice. You don't judge someone for their future actions. You judge them for who they are now."

"I don't care!" With that, her mother pushed her out of the way and destroyed the building, killing everyone inside. Cassiopeia felt her heart ache and bleed for their loss. She couldn't do this anymore.

"I won't help you."

"Fine! Then stay out of my way!" Lilith's lack of caring for her daughter hurt Cassiopeia.

"Just remember, in your quest to avenge your son, you abandoned and lost your only daughter."

She saw sadness spread across Lilith's face. "You will understand one day."

As Lilith turned away, Cassiopeia seized the opportunity to end this safely. She reached out and grabbed her mother's arm. She felt her powers surge forward. Her eyes turned from blue to red.

"Lilith, your fate . . ."

Before Cassiopeia could see her mother's life or finish her fate, she felt a sharp pain in her lower abdomen. The pain grew more intense, burning and throbbing. Cassiopeia looked down to see a dagger in her side.

Her mother had plunged an Atlantean dagger into her belly on the left side. She looked into her mother's eyes with shock. Lilith heartlessly pulled Cassiopeia's hand off of her. As Cassiopeia fell backward, she felt two strong arms catch her. She reached her hand down to hold the wound, blood flowing over her fingers. She was in shock. Her world began to spin and turn black as she began to lose consciousness. She saw Lilith look at the newcomer.

"She'll survive, we both know that. You cannot stop me. I will kill the leviathan who did this. The one who uttered the prophecy."

Her mother vanished. The last thing Cassiopeia saw through the enclosing darkness were two intensely concerned lavender eyes.

Cassiopeia awakened in a large sand-colored temple. She could hear water flowing smoothly outside. As she went to sit up pain, radiated from her abdomen and she fell back to the bed. She looked down to see her waist wrapped in bandages.

She had forgotten what had transpired but the memories quickly returned. Getting up slowly, she saw a robe draped across the chair next to the bed. Cassiopeia dressed as quickly as she could and walked out to the hallway, veering toward the voices she heard coming from the left.

The hallway opened into a chamber room with a large round table in the center. On the table was a map of the known world. Set, Anhur, Nephthys, Isis, and multiple other Egyptian gods stood over the table talking. They all looked up upon her entry. Nephthys, Set's wife, walked over quickly to help her.

"You should be resting. Your wound was deep." Nephthys wrapped her arm around Cassiopeia and walked with her toward the others.

"I am fine. I needed to know what was happening. I couldn't just lay in a bed while the world is falling apart outside."

The other gods and goddesses looked at each other in silence. Set spoke first.

"Caelum was resurrected. Rumor says the death of all of the Atlanteans caused a surge of power that resurrected him somehow, but the jury is still out on that one. But his resurrection returned Lilith to her prison in Khaos. Greece is still burning but the destruction has stopped. Your mother—"

"She is *not* my mother anymore." Cassiopeia said firmly.

Set paused, looking at her with sadness in his eyes. "Lilith caused a great amount of destruction."

"I can rebuild Atlantis. It will be hard alone, but Caelum and I can do it."

"Cassiopeia, I'm sorry, but Atlantis has been completely destroyed." He paused, trying to gauge her reaction. Sadness filled his voice. "There is nothing left to rebuild."

Cassiopeia walked away from them and over to the windows to look down at the city below. Cairo. The people who had been safe from Lilith's wrath. Her people hadn't been so lucky. She had failed to protect them. Her mother used her to destroy them. Guilt racked her as tears stared to fill her eyes, but she pushed down her self-pity. She would never let it happen again. She would never let herself lose control of her powers again. She wouldn't let the monster inside of her reign free.

As she stood there processing what had occurred over the past two days a horrifying realization hit her when she thought back to the prophecy.

A prophecy for you, king of the gods of Atlantis. As punishment for trying to destroy peace you will be destroyed. One of your children is not of your blood, and when they reach their peak powers, they will destroy Atlantis and the entire Atlantean pantheon. Your actions will cause your own demise. Your choices will be your unraveling.

The prophecy never revealed which of Magnus' children wasn't his natural child. They had all assumed it was Caelum. Based on her similar features to her father no one thought to question that the prophecy didn't specify which child. Magnus was not her father. Caelum was his son and had always been. She had been the enemy right under Magnus' nose that he had been hunting for those long eighteen years. She was the one who had destroyed Atlantis and the pantheon. Magnus had killed his true son and heir to the Atlantean pantheon while she had been the actual threat in their midst. She had reached her peak powers testing the amulet that Set had given her. Before then she had never unleashed the demon inside of her, always keeping that part of herself caged, but that day she did. She discovered her true powers and, in turn, brought the prophecy to fruition.

As much as she had questions about her true lineage, she knew that there was only one person who knew the truth the whole time and had the answers she was seeking. Lilith. The thought of going to see her mother after all that had happened sickened her. Cassiopeia's anger and hurt toward her mother overpowered her curiosity to learn more. To learn the truth. But she would wait. Being immortal had its privileges. She had ample amount of patience and she would use it to wait until her mother needed something from her or until she had something to use against her to find the truth. She knew that even if she went now to face Lilith, the cunning goddess would just evade the questions and keep her secrets. She had for hundreds of years and Cassiopeia knew that she wouldn't change for a daughter that she seemingly didn't care for.

Cassiopeia lifted her head high as she pulled herself together. Her emotions for her mother had clouded her judgment and caused her people to die. Her love for those close to her caused her to act irrationally. In that moment her heart hardened. She sealed off her emotions and locked up the monster. She turned to back to Set and the others. Set saw as the light in her eyes went out as she became cold and emotionless. Sadness washed over him. War and death took the best of a person, especially when it was the genocide of their own people.

"What can I do to help?" She asked Set and the other gods.

"I think we have it handled. Why don't you go find your brother? You two could use one another."

Nephthys stepped closer.

"Just be careful. You have stitches and I don't want your wound to fester. You should come see me once a week to check on how it's healing. Change the bandages daily."

Cassiopeia nodded to Set's wife, acknowledging her instructions. Set reached out and touched Cassiopeia's shoulder.

"We're always here if you need us."

"I know."

With that, she left to find Caelum.

Alexander was in a small town at the edge of the destruction. He had stood by and witnessed the destruction at Atlantis and then the subsequent resurrection of a god. An entire pantheon was almost completely destroyed by its own means and wrongdoings. Now he had another task to deal with. Caelum. Caelum fell into a category of his own, he wasn't a leviathan, but he also had no pantheon left to teach him how to be a god. A god with no understanding or guidance on how to use his powers was a dangerous thing. So, Alexander had decided to take him under his wing. He was technically now the head of the small, yet still powerful, Atlantean pantheon. A good possible ally to the leviathans.

Alexander looked down from the rooftop he was standing on. Caelum, son of the Atlantean gods Lilith and Magnus. Cassiopeia's younger brother. Alexander watched as Caelum tried to figure out what to feed his baby Vantha demon. It was traditional in the Atlantean pantheon to pair every god and goddess with a demon that was born on or around their own birth, but that didn't change the fact that he didn't have anyone to help him raise the small creature. Because the Vantha demons age differently than the gods, she was currently disguised as a mortal, appearing to be only three or four years old. Alexander would never understand the gesture from Lilith to give him a demon in his current state. Before he could approach the god, he saw Cassiopeia step out from one of the alleys and walk up to Caelum.

"You! You attacked me!" Caelum said to her aggressively.

The baby Vantha hissed at her. It was kind of cute since the powerful demon looked to be a small child, but she had unnaturally red streaks throughout her blonde hair and a savage expression.

Cassiopeia stopped walking toward him. She could feel her brother's powers surging. He had no clue how to control the forces inside of him. She could tell that he still hadn't discovered his specific power.

"It wasn't an attack. I was trying to meet you. If it was an attack you wouldn't have survived." She looked down at the baby demon. "Are you hungry little one?"

She summoned a basket of food, making it appear out of thin air. The fish, breads, and meats barely fit inside. The little demon looked at the basket. Cassiopeia could hear her tiny tummy growl at the thought of eating. Even though she was the same age as Caelum, Vantha demons aged much slower than gods and goddesses. They didn't reach full size or power until they were almost a century old.

"Don't hurt my papa." The baby Vantha demon said before she turned to the basket and began devouring the food.

"Thank you. There was no food on Vēlatusa."

Cassiopeia looked back up at Caelum. He was very handsome, like most gods were. His light blonde hair fell to just above his shoulders, but it looked unkept and dirty. He was tall and muscular but walked very unsure of himself. She could see the potential inside of him to become the brother that she had always wanted, but she was still very defensive and guarded about letting anyone in after everything that had happened.

"You were on Vēlatusa? How?"

"My mother gifted the realm to me. She said it's my birthright."

Cassiopeia was taken aback. She was the eldest. Vēlatusa was her home first. After everything she had done for Lilith behind Magnus' back. After all she had sacrificed, and this was how Lilith spit in her face. First, she stabbed Cassiopeia, and then had given her home away. Normally Cassiopeia would be almost in tears, but she felt nothing from her locked up emotions except a lack of justice. She would continue on alone just as she had been for centuries. She had promised herself that she would try to befriend him, but it wasn't worth the heartache and painful memories.

"I don't need this. I'm fine alone. I've done it before."

Cassiopeia felt someone watching them. She turned quickly to see Alexander standing at the corner of a nearby house. She gave Caelum one last look then turned and walked toward Alexander.

"Did you tell him who you are?" Alexander asked, already knowing the answer.

"No. I don't need him. I don't need family. I should leave you to it. You will do a better job of training him anyway."

Alexander looked surprised at her blunt rejection of her brother, but it wasn't his place to pry.

"How are you?" He glanced at her abdomen.

"I'll survive."

He scoffed at her dismissal. "You didn't completely answer my question." His eyes pierced her. "How are *you*?"

She looked away from his gaze. Glancing toward the destruction, she refocused on her hardening heart.

"It doesn't matter. I will survive. I have before and I will now. Even surrounded by people, I have still been alone for most of my life." She looked back to him and he gave her a look. "Don't worry about me, leviathan."

"I worry about you more than you think."

She could see concern in his lavender eyes.

"Why? I'm an immortal, all powerful, god killer. What is there to worry about?"

"I don't worry about that side of you. I worry about the woman who hides behind all of that."

She hated how he could get under her skin and see through her defenses so easily. She looked into his eyes.

"I liked it better when you wore a mask so I couldn't see your face."

He smirked.

"Why? Am I just too charming for you without one?"

He winked and she rolled her eyes.

"You are much more handsome without one, but no. With a mask on, your eyes can't pierce through me and into my soul."

She watched as his smirk went away and was replaced with different emotions. Ones she couldn't place. He quickly regained himself and returned to his playful banter.

"Wait? Did you just call me handsome? I think I am blushing."

She shook her head.

"Always the jokester. I think instead of hiding behind your power you hide behind your mask of emotions. Either serious and defensive or playful and joking."

He became serious again just as she had expected him to.

"We all have masks we hide behind to keep our true faces safe. To keep our hearts safe."

She looked away and back to her brother. Maybe one day, somehow, they would make amends for the hands they were dealt in life, but she knew that day wasn't today.

"Goodbye, Alexander."

She went to leave and stopped. She looked at him as she thought for a moment.

"How were you there when I was stabbed? How did you know?"

"I'm a leviathan. I can see things that others can't."

It wasn't a complete lie, but she couldn't know the truth.

"Thank you."

He let out a small smile and nodded to her. He could see her internal pain as she went to walk past him, and he grabbed her arm, gently stopping her. She looked up into his eyes.

"You can't keep running from your emotions. One day they will catch up to you."

"Watch me."

She pulled her arm out of his grasp and flashed out of the village.

Chapter 4

Building Relationships
BCE

One loyal friend is worth ten thousand relatives
—Euripides

Cassiopeia had gone to Vēlatusa to see Caelum, but he wasn't there. The demons that guarded the realm informed her that he was sparring with Alexander on the leviathan's private island, so she traveled to Isle del Alexandrius to see him. Their relationship still had tension, but Caelum had reached out in an attempt to mend things and she had accepted his offer. He was the only true family that she had left, and he had never tried to, or intended to, hurt her.

Cassiopeia assumed that Caelum wanted to talk to her about the Council of the Gods. Three thousand years earlier, shortly after the fall of Atlantis, the leviathans constructed the Council of the Gods to attempt to prevent future destruction to the degree of what happened in Atlantis. The different pantheons reluctantly agreed, both wanting to seek the protection of the leviathans as well as avoid their wrath. As the head of the leviathans, Alexander led the council. Cassiopeia had, for the most part, wiped her hands clean of pantheon business, only getting involved when her brother wouldn't. Otherwise she had been spending most of her time in Egypt with Set and Nephthys as a guest. The rest of her time was spent traveling and exploring different cultures.

When Cassiopeia appeared on Alexander's island, she could see Alexander and Caelum sparring further down on the beach. They were in battle mode as they swung at each other with full force. She watched their careful dance of swords as they moved along the sand. They each gave her a brief glance but continued their fight. After a few minutes of watching, Alexander finally pinned Caelum to the ground with his sword. When he turned around to face her his smile was wide at his victory. It was infectious, and she felt herself smile back.

"What brings you here, my goddess?"

She shook her head lightly at his endearment.

"Maybe I just came to enjoy the show."

"Why don't you join us?"

"I don't think so. Ah!" Before she could say more, he smirked at her and flashed next to her, scooping her up over his shoulder. "Hey! Put me down!" she yelled at him, while hitting his back and shoulders with her fists. They both knew that if she really wanted to get free of his grasp, she could easily flash away. But a part of her was curious about what he was doing.

"Nope," he said calmly as he walked with her back over to where he and Caelum had just sparred. He gently set her back down. Cassiopeia glared at him before punching his chest one final time. Unaffected by her blow, he chuckled.

"Let's see what you can do, little goddess." A sword appeared in his hand and he held it out to her.

"I haven't fought in years."

"Sword fighting is something you can never forget. You may be a little rough around the edges, but it is something your body never forgets how to do. Come on! I know you were trained, so let's see it."

"Caelum called me to talk, not fight."

"Words can wait. This is much more entertaining," Caelum said with a smile.

She glared at Alexander for another moment before looking at Caelum. She had only seen him a few times in passing since they had parted ways after Atlantis, but now he talked easily with her, as if they had always known each other.

"Fine but I want no judgement. I haven't picked up a sword in over a thousand years. Deal?"

"Yes, my goddess. No judgement here." Cassiopeia noticed Alexander's eyes light up playfully at the sound of her agreement.

She took the sword, its weight heavy in her hand, and gave a few, very rough practice swings. As she went to step forward, her dress hindered her movements, so she changed her outfit into light practice armor. She looked at Alexander and nodded, letting him know she was ready.

Alexander knew to go easy or this was going to be a very short sparring session, ending with her being angry at him. She did a few test jabs and lunges and after a few minutes of lightly going back and forth he watched as her body began to remember what to do. Her moves became quicker and more precise. She was still rusty and not as skilled as he was, but it was all coming back to her quickly.

Alexander upped his game again, making his blows stronger and more precise to match her increasing skill. They danced around each other quickly as she got back into the rhythm of fighting but, in one fluid, swift motion, Alexander knocked her wrist to the side and flipped her to the ground where he pinned her beneath him. She could feel his hip bone pressed against her thigh and she also felt something else. He looked down at her playfully, only inches from her face, with a grin.

She smirked back. "It seems like someone is happy to see me," she said.

His expression quickly changed, as if he was looking at someone else. She took advantage of him dropping his guard and twisted her hips slightly to thrust her leg up directly into his groin. His face contorted in pain as he groaned, falling against her and rolling to the side. She flipped herself with him and straddled him across his abdomen with her sword at his throat.

"Never let your guard down or get distracted in the middle of a fight. It's the number one way to lose."

"That was low," he gasped, his face still contorted in pain.

"Yes, it was. A very *low* blow," she laughed. Alexander huffed and just looked at her. He still had that strange look on his face. As if he was unsure of who she was. His lavender eyes drew her in and mesmerized her as always. She got lost in their depths, completely forgetting where they were or why she had even come there in the first place.

"Are you two going to sit like that all day?" Caelum's words snapped her out of her trance and Cassiopeia suddenly remembered that she was straddling Alexander. Her eyes widened slightly, and she blushed as she stood. She held her hand out for him, but he didn't take it, popping to his feet. She chuckled as she watched him adjust his groin one last time, glaring at her.

Cassiopeia looked at Caelum. "I came to talk to you, Caelum. You sent me a message that you wanted to talk."

"Yes. I . . . I wanted to . . . to better things between us. There is no reason that we should have tension and malice toward each other due to the actions of others." He paused and looked at her, seeing if she wanted him to go on.

"I agree. Continue."

"So, as a peace offering . . ." He glanced at Alexander, but the leviathan's face was blank. Caelum walked over to her side and took her hand in his. "I renounce my title as head of the Atlantean pantheon and pass it to my sister, Cassiopeia of the Atlantean Pantheon."

"As I have witnessed, let it be done," Alexander said.

Her eyes widened as she felt the shift in leadership. It felt like warm water flowing through her body as her connection to all of the power of the Atlantean pantheon poured through her. She gasped and went to step away, but she couldn't find the strength to pull her hand from his. As slowly as it had washed over her, the feeling ebbed away, but she could still feel the additional power coursing through her. The new connection to the source of Atlantean power, to the universe. Caelum let go of her hand. She looked at him, dumbfounded.

"Why?"

"I want to mend things with my sister, and this is the first step. It was always supposed to be yours. It was your birthright, and Lilith took it away from you. She should have never given it to me. I am not the firstborn and I don't know anything about running a pantheon. I know that there is only you and me—technically her, too—but there are politics and other things involved that I don't understand. I know I could learn, but I would prefer to be a guiding voice in the background. I'm not a natural leader, but you are. You have basically been running our pantheon for the past thousand years on your own whenever a situation has arisen, and I have no desire to do that. You deserve it after everything that Magnus and the others put you through. After all you have lost."

She could feel her emotions surge forward. Feelings she had pushed down long ago. They had both been thrust into a war that neither of them wanted and then put into positions where they were pitted against each other. Even though she was raised to hate him, she never fully did. Her resentment of him stemmed from her hatred for her mother favoring him, which clouded her judgment on his true innocence. It had caused him to push her away as well, because he had just seen her as a pawn for her father.

Caelum looked at her, as if worried of her reaction. Her face was unreadable. He went to speak again, but before he could, she pulled him into a hug, holding him tightly. Caelum was surprised, but he hugged her back. She released him and just looked at him.

"Thank you."

Alexander cleared his throat.

"I would still like for both of you to hold a position on the council.

Most pantheons have two leaders for their pantheon at the table, but they get one vote and, even though only one of you is the true leader, you both are equally as important and in charge of your pantheon."

"I agree," Cassiopeia said.

"Me too." Caelum smiled at Cassiopeia.

"Good. The next council meeting is in one week. We meet once a year, or more frequently if an emergency meeting is called. Not all of the pantheon leaders always show up, but if they don't, then they automatically lose their say in any votes—unless they established a valid reason with me in advance. If you are late, don't show up, because I will kick you out, angrily. Even though you all get votes, my say is final. If you need to call an emergency meeting, then you must reach out to me and I will set it up. Do you understand and agree to the rules?"

"Yes, Alexander," Cassiopeia and Caelum answered in unison.

"Good." He seemed very pleased with what just occurred.

"So, I guess that means I will be moving back into my quarters on Vēlatusa," Cassiopeia said.

"Of course! I haven't even been into that wing of the temple. That place is huge. It will be nice to have someone around other than demons."

She laughed. This was a very interesting change for her, but she was happy about it. She had pushed him away for too long over the fear of what her other family members had done to her in the past. It was time for her to move on and begin to mend her wounds. They both knew that it wouldn't happen overnight, but they both were willing to try. They were more alike than either of them realized and had both been used and abused by their pantheon. Now they could use their commonalities to become stronger and support each other. It was just the beginning of their family and their pantheon recovering and growing back into what it used to be.

Twenty years had passed since Cassiopeia had become the leader of the Atlantean pantheon. She had stepped into her new role gracefully and successfully, their small pantheon thriving. She had kept them away from most conflicts and only became involved if it was necessary. They had a strong alliance with the Egyptian pantheon, due to her years of friendship with Set, and that had granted them protection from most of the larger pantheons.

Cassiopeia flashed to Isle del Alexandrius. She needed to talk with Alexander. There had been some attacks directed toward the Atlantean pantheon, which resulted in the deaths of two Vantha demons. She knew it could have been a misunderstanding, as Vantha demons were well known for their aggressive desire to fight and for jumping to conclusions, but the attacker had left no evidence of who they were or why they did it. She wanted Alexander to call a council meeting to discover the perpetrators and either have them explain themselves or deal out a punishment. When she arrived in the council room, she could hear the sounds of the ocean waves crashing. She looked out the large windows that faced the sea. Alexander was usually relaxing out in the water, surfing the waves, but neither he nor his surfboard were anywhere in sight. She turned around and walked down the hall toward the main area of the home where Alexander lived.

"Alexander?" she called, lightly.

Just as she was about to round the corner at the end of the hall, Alexander plowed right into her, grabbing her shoulder and placing his hand roughly over her mouth. Her eyes widened in surprise and began to glow angrily as her hand flew up to grab his. He looked at her, his eyes also bright, his expression furious and worried. He pressed her roughly against the wall, behind the curtains that fell from the ceiling to the floor. Suddenly she heard voices coming from the living area at the end of the hall. Alexander tensed as he pressed more tightly against her, looking toward the voices.

"I thought I heard something," one of the voices said.

"Shut up and stop following ghosts! The leviathan isn't here, and we only have a limited time to find the artifact. So, hurry!" another hissed in a half-whisper.

The voices slowly grew more distant. Alexander turned his head to look down at Cassiopeia but didn't move away. He slowly lowered his hand from her mouth and put one finger over her lips. She nodded in understanding. No talking. Whoever was here must have sensitive hearing because she had lightly said his name before, but they heard her. Alexander kept his hand on her shoulder and leaned away to look down the hall. After a few moments he relaxed slightly and looked down at her, his eyes no longer glowing. He looked at her, confused about why she was here. She opened her mouth to tell him her reason for coming, but abruptly closed it when she remembered: silence. He smirked at her expression then put his hand on her neck, his fingers tangling lightly into the hair on the back of her head and his thumb resting on her cheek. She went to move her head away, but he held his hand firmly against her and closed his eyes. A moment later he reopened them.

Can you hear me?

She gasped quietly as she heard his voice in her head, her eyes widening again.

Yes! What? How?

Her mind began to race at this new connection, and he winced.

Slow your thoughts. I can't follow, and you are going to give me a headache. Just focus on what you want me to hear. The how is not important. You need to leave, it's not safe here.

She huffed and shot him a look.

You need my help. You obviously cannot take them alone or you would have already. Let me help you fight them. Stop being stubborn.

He narrowed his eyes at her.

You're the stubborn one that won't just leave me to my problems. I don't even know what pantheon they are from. It's not safe. You need to go.

He felt her reaching out carefully with her powers toward the intruders. He could see through her mind the strings that held their life force, binding them to the earth. She had become stronger over the years, her powers developing and expanding. As a goddess of fate, she was connected to all living creatures on the planet and she used that to charge her powers. As her powers grew, it also allowed her to see all of their life forces connected to the earth and she now could easily take life by just pulling on one of the strings. Over the years, killing immortals had become nearly completely painless. It was almost an easy task for her, but one she never enjoyed doing. Alexander felt as her fingers twitched when she strummed their life strings and watched confusion flash across her face. He heard one of them coughing from the other room.

Stop! Too much, he thought.

He projected to her mind and watched as she pulled away from them. She looked at Alexander with confusion.

They are from the Lumerian pantheon. Demon, I think. Probably demigod. How? I thought all Lumerians were extinct, except for you. Aren't you worried that they are going to find the artifact that they are looking for?

The Lumerian pantheon had been destroyed, much like the Atlanteans, except none had knowingly survived the destruction. Even the other pantheons didn't know the true cause of their demise. As far as she had been told, Alexander was the last of his people. She saw his lip twitch into a grimace before he relaxed it.

No, because it's not here.

The voices began to head toward them. He pressed back against her as he looked in their direction.

It's too dangerous. You need to leave, please, Cassiopeia, he pleaded silently.

I'm not going to leave you to get hurt, or worse killed. You have helped me in the past. Let me return the favor. You know how powerful I am. I can help you.

She could see the indecision on his face. She thought he was going to send her away, but finally he replied.

Fine. But you must promise me that if I tell you to leave me you will leave. No exceptions.

She nodded her head.

I have an idea, but you aren't going to like how it starts. Alexander began to explain his plan.

"Alexander!" Cassiopeia said loudly as she walked down the hall and into a large living room style space. "Alexander, I need to talk with you!"

"Why, hello little goddess," a deep voice said behind her.

She whipped around quickly to see a very handsome man standing there. He was huge and built like a wall. He was at least seven feet tall and rippled with muscles. There was a long scar that ran from his lip down his jaw and neck, disappearing from sight at the top of his shirt. Even with his attractive allure and his nonthreatening voice, his expression was intimidating, and she could feel a lethality radiating off of him. She saw another, equally attractive but slightly smaller man walk into view from behind him. They were a good twelve feet away from her but still she felt uncomfortable around them.

"I was looking for Alexander but he's not responding. Who are you?"

They looked at each other and smirked.

"We are . . . acquaintances of his. He sent us here to get something for him. Maybe you can help us, little one."

"Yes! You can be of great help to us." The other one almost hissed out the words.

"I don't know how much help you think I can be. Alexander is a very secretive person." There was a thud from upstairs. "Maybe that is him? Are there more of you?"

The larger man narrowed his eyes at her.

"Why would you want to know how many of us there are?" He looked toward the stairs and let out a high-pitched hiss. Cassiopeia flinched as the noise pierced her ears. She took a step away from them. The smaller one looked concerned when there was no answer from upstairs. They glared back at her.

"What game are you playing, goddess?"

"No games. I came here looking for Alexander."

A hiss erupted from the larger man and the smaller one's face began to twist and contort. She watched in horror as he transformed into a large scaly demon. One would have thought he was a dragon except for the fact that his posture and anatomy was very human like. He had long sharp talons where his fingers used to be. Wings sprouted out of his back, and long black horns emerged on his head. His face was very lizard-like, his forked tongue flicking in and out.

As he stalked toward her, she reached her powers out and grabbed his lifeline. It felt different than before, stronger.

"Alexander," Cassiopeia called tentatively.

Another thud came from upstairs. The big one turned to go up and she pulled the life force of the one approaching her. A small cry escaped its lips before he fell to the ground dead. She felt a wave of exhaustion wash over her, but then she saw powers flowing out of his body. Her suspicions were right. They were demigods. She didn't know what their other half was, but she didn't care as she felt his power wash over her. Instead of filling her with strength, as usually happened when she killed a god, she felt power and demonic rage. She quickly realized that some of the demon powers had been entangled with the god powers. She found herself having to fight her own internal demons instead of being able to focus on the being in front of her. He looked surprised and angry.

"Impossible," he hissed at her, as he began to transform into one of the strange creatures.

Cassiopeia shot a god bolt at him to slow him, knowing that if she killed him outright, she wouldn't be able to handle the surge of his demon too. He easily dodged it and lunged toward her. To her sudden surprise, Alexander appeared directly in front of her and slashed his sword at the creature. Cassiopeia stumbled backwards. Her insides were at war with each other. She focused on herself while Alexander handled the creature. She could feel her body fighting off the demonic energy. Just as quickly as the energy had affected her it subsided and vanished. Her powers went quiet for a moment before surging forward again at full strength.

Cassiopeia turned to see Alexander still fighting the beast. She knew she couldn't kill it without risking the same reaction as what happened with the other one, but she could help him a little. She reached out with her mind and found the demon's life force. As she tugged it lightly, she watched as the demigod demon become more sluggish. She saw a black goo begin to drip from his lips. He seemed confused as he fought Alexander but then he looked over to her.

Shit! she thought, *he knows I'm doing something to him.*

His body slammed Alexander into the wall before he quickly changed direction, heading directly toward her. She tried to flash away but nothing happened. She gripped his life force, not knowing if she could fight off another demon's powers but knowing that a chance was better than death. Just as she was about to sever the lifeline, she saw Alexander flash to the creature and bring down his sword. The demigod swiped its talons at him but was unable to stop the blow. Alexander's sword came down onto the back of its neck. The creature crumpled forward. She watched in disgust as its body stopped, but its head rolled toward her a few feet, stopping in front of her. She grimaced at the gruesome carnage in front of her, as more black blood oozed out of the decapitated body and onto the floor. Alexander flashed next to her.

"Are you okay?"

"Yes. I think so." She saw that he swayed a little as he stood. "Are you?"

"I'll be fine."

"You don't look fine."

She turned to him and looked for a wound, but he was covered in black blood and other substances she didn't want to think about. She could see a rip in his shirt. She went to reach out to look but he grabbed her wrist.

"I said I will be fine."

She glared at him. "Let me see."

"No." His voice was getting weaker as he swayed more. "You should leave."

"No," she said firmly before she flashed his shirt off of him. There was a large gash on the left side of his abdomen. It was only a few inches long, but she could tell that it was deep. One of the demon's claws must have stabbed him when he was fighting, probably when it threw him against the wall.

"I'll be fine," he said again, but his words were now a mumble. "You need to leave. There may be more . . ."

"No, you won't! Oh my gosh, Alexander!"

Cassiopeia pressed her hand against the wound, trying to apply pressure, but he stumbled backwards at her push. She watched as his eyelids started to droop.

"You can . . . heal me . . ." He was slumping forward.

"No, no, no . . . damn it."

He was starting to fall but before he could hit the floor, she flashed them to Vēlatusa. Cassiopeia shoved him back as he fell so that he landed on her bed. He was out cold. Knowing they would be safe there, her panic began to set in as she watched him dying. She climbed onto the bed next to him and applied pressure to the wound.

She was confused by his words. How did he know that she could heal herself? She had never told anyone except for her mother. He was always so cryptic, and his amount of hidden knowledge always surprised her. She watched the color draining from his face as his abdomen filled with blood that poured out onto the sheets. She knew she had to do something. She had never healed anyone other than herself before and never a wound this large. She usually only healed scrapes and bruises, but she was his only hope. Pulling at her powers, she focused as if she was healing herself. She could feel the power flowing out, but it wasn't enough. Her hands were beginning to glow, but if she healed him this slowly, he would die before she was done. She focused harder and pushed everything she had into her hands. He couldn't die. He was her friend. Even though they weren't close, she had always felt a strange connection with him. One she could never explain. She could feel in her soul that he was important, and he needed to be saved. Her hands glowed brighter, and she could feel her powers stitching his body back together. But she was feeling weaker and weaker with every passing second. Her eyes began to droop as her body told her to sleep, but she fought it off as she pushed to save him. The wound was almost completely healed as she felt herself slipping into unconsciousness. She could see the color returning to his cheeks and feel his pulse strengthening. She knew that even if the wound was still there, his body had been healed enough to survive. She pulled her powers back, but it wasn't enough to stop her from passing out onto the bed beside him.

Alexander awoke to feel someone lying next to him. It took a moment for him to return to his senses and remember what had happened. Looking down, he saw a waterfall of blonde hair spread out on his chest and on the bed next to him. Cassiopeia was sleeping, her head on his chest and her body pressed against him. Her left hand was still on his abdomen, right next to the almost completely healed wound. She had saved his life, but at what cost? He tried to sit up, but pain radiated throughout his torso, and he groaned in pain. Deciding that it was better to stay where he was, he put his hand on her cheek to check on her. She was breathing softly but overall unharmed.

"Cassiopeia?"

She made a noise but didn't awaken. Now he was concerned.

"Hey, wake up."

"What . . ." she mumbled.

"Look at me."

She mumbled something again, but he couldn't make it out. He placed his hand on her chin and tilted her face up to look at him. Her face looked so peaceful and serene but also drained. Her skin was whiter than usual and very ashen, its usual glow gone.

"Cassiopeia." His tone was blunt and stern. Her eyes flickered open as they tried to focus on his face.

"I am so tired. Let me sleep."

"No, you are drained. Your powers are drained. You need to recharge."

"There's no one here for me to pull power from. Just let me sleep."

Alexander took a deep breath and thought quickly. He knew that if she didn't recharge her powers she might never wake back up, or if she did, she would be too drained to recover and would become mortal. Creatures that were linked to the universe needed to recharge in order to maintain that power in their bodies. Just like how mortal beings need to eat to have energy and life, gods have to charge to have energy and life. If they exerted too much power, they wouldn't be able to recover, essentially making them mortal and eventually leading to death.

Alexander pushed down his pain and scooted himself up so that he was slouching against the headboard. He grimaced through the pain, but he needed to have more leverage to get her out of bed and to the Earthly realm.

"Look at me. Don't take your eyes off of my face, do you understand," he told her.

She groaned but continued to look at him through her drooping eye lids. He felt her hand move up to his collarbone as she looked at him. "You have beautiful eyes."

Normally he would have smirked at her or made a funny remark, but he was too worried to be playful.

"Thank you. Keep looking at my beautiful eyes, okay?"

"Mmmhmm . . . can I sleep now?"

"No! No, keep looking at me. You need to go to Earth and recharge."

"I . . ." He watched as her eyes tried to focus on his. "I can't."

Alexander was hoping she would have enough energy to take herself there, but she didn't. Taking a deep breath, he concentrated his remaining strength and flashed them to a secluded wooded area in northern Europe.

"Trees . . ." Cassiopeia opened her eyes briefly.

He felt how drained he was as well, but his powers would return with time, a perk of being a leviathan. Hers wouldn't.

"Yes, trees. I need you to focus. You have to charge your powers."

"No, I have to sleep."

He watched as her eye lids drooped. "You need to focus!"

He was getting desperate and he needed to bring her mind back to reality. Obviously yelling and being stern wasn't going to work. He needed to do something to shock her out of it.

"Cassiopeia, please," he pleaded with her, softly.

"Alexander, stop being mean."

He huffed at her, then had an idea. "Look at me, please."

Her eyes barely opened to gaze at him. He put his hand on her cheek and pulled her face to his, kissing her roughly, watching as her eyes widened in surprise.

His lips were softer than she had expected. There was an urgency behind his kiss that pulled her out of her drowsy state as her heart rate increased. She was surprised and taken aback by his forwardness, but she didn't want to pull away. She leaned closer to him and watched as his eyes closed and his kiss became more tender. The smell of sandalwood and jasmine filled her head. After a moment he gently broke their kiss and pushed her away. She felt breathless, blown away by such a simple kiss.

"Cassiopeia, you need to charge your powers." His voice was soft, like a gentle caress.

Cassiopeia was still dazed from their kiss and felt her exhaustion wash back over her like a wave. Her eyes widened when she realized how weak she was. She nodded as he pushed her hand into the dirt of the forest floor. She didn't know how he knew how she charged her powers or what she needed to do, but she was too weak to care. She reached out what little strength she had left and pulled the power of the earth into herself. She strummed at the life strings of the nearby forest creatures, not hard enough to sever them, but enough to feed off their energy. As her powers strengthened, her reach grew to the nearby villages and cities until she could reach out to almost every being in the Earthly realm. She sat there for a few minutes charging her powers as Alexander rested his head back against the tree. He could feel that his body wanted to go back to sleep to rest, but he wanted to make sure she was safe first. She had risked her life to save him, so the least he could do was repay her for that. She moved her hand to his chest and he felt her pushing some of her energy into him. He closed his eyes and savored the feeling, as they flowed into him and his strength returned. After a minute or so, the warmth that was filling him stopped. He was still weak and exhausted, but he didn't feel completely like death.

"That's as much as I can give without pushing too far," she told him.

"It is more than I could have asked for, thank you." When he opened his eyes and looked at her, she looked much better. Her skin was almost glowing, and her eyes were bright.

"How did you know how to charge my powers?"

He smiled and chuckled lightly. "Let's just leave that to me being mysterious and all powerful."

"Is that also how you knew I could heal you?"

"Yes. That one I wasn't actually one hundred percent sure about, but it worked."

She shook her head at him. He watched as she looked at him. Her face became blank and she looked away.

"You kissed me," she said softly, her voice barely above a whisper.

"I had to get you to focus. You were going to become mortal and die."

"Would you have been upset if I died?"

He put his hand on her chin, tilting her head up to look at him. She could see the seriousness in his eyes.

"I would have been devastated. Completely destroyed. Can we not even talk about the possibility of that?"

She nodded her head, but her blue eyes swam with emotion. Before he could react, she leaned forward and recaptured his lips. Alexander moaned lightly at the feel of her lips pressed against his. He felt her place her hand on his cheek and the nape of his neck, pulling him closer and deepening their kiss. Their lips were full of passion and desire and their tongues danced against each other. The sweet taste of her filled his mind and consumed his thoughts. His fingers tangled into her hair as he pulled her closer. He wanted her more than he could ever admit, but he knew deep down that she wasn't his. She couldn't be. Reluctantly, his reality came crashing back down and he pressed his forehead against hers, separating their lips but keeping her close.

"Alexander . . ." She spoke softly, her voice cutting into his heart.

"We . . . we can't. I can't."

Cassiopeia looked at him to see that he had his eyes squeezed shut, as if his own words pained him. Her heart wanted to argue, to disagree and push the point, but in her mind, she knew he was right. He was a leviathan and she was a goddess. They were supposed to be mortal enemies. He was created to kill her kind and she was raised to fear his. He was also head of the council and she was a member. Other gods would see it as an unfair conflict of power and they would lash out toward both of them. Even though she knew there was no way that they could be together, her heart still wanted him more than her words could ever explain. He was the only creature she had ever met who had been able to calm the monsters inside of her and make her feel at ease. She took a deep breath as she remembered the last time she had let emotion guide her decisions. Her pantheon and her people had paid the price. She had told herself that she would never make that mistake again, and she had to stand by her oath.

"I know. I understand," she said quietly.

She watched as his eyes opened to look at her. There was so much regret and pain in his expression.

"Maybe one day. When the world is less complicated."

She nodded and kissed him again but much more gently. As if she was saying her final goodbye to him. She could feel the hesitation in his touch this time. Cassiopeia pulled away and sat back on her knees. She looked down to his wound and he winced as she gently touched it.

"You can't go home; in case those things return. There are plenty of spare rooms in Vēlatusa you can stay in until you are stronger."

"I shouldn't."

"At least for a few days, until you can get up and walk without moaning and groaning like an old woman."

He chuckled and then winced at the pain it caused.

She raised an eyebrow at him. "You don't get to argue with me. I almost died healing you, so the least you can do is humor my worries."

He sighed and she thought he was going to try to fight her on it some more.

"Fine."

"Really?"

"Do you want me to change my mind?" He gave her a look.

"No," she said quickly. "I just didn't think you would give in so easily."

"I'm not really in a position to try to argue. I'm too tired."

He smirked at her and she gave him a small smile before flashing him to Vēlatusa.

Cassiopeia was enjoying having Alexander around on Vēlatusa. It gave her something to do, someone to tend to. While she would bring him food and help him stretch and move around, she made sure to keep a distance between them. She knew the true dangers if they became involved in a relationship. Just him being here to heal made Caelum uneasy. Caelum kept Alexander's presence very quiet amongst the demons, not wanting to risk another attack from someone trying to get to him.

Alexander healed quickly. He had been asleep for two days before he finally awoke and began to gradually move around. Today was day four and he was still injured, but he could move around his chambers without assistance.

Alexander looked up as he heard a knock at the door. Cassiopeia stood there with a tray of food.

"Morning!" she said cheerfully.

"Good morning." He gave a small smile.

Alexander knew that he was enjoying her company way more than he would ever admit, and the thought of leaving hurt him because he knew it would hurt her too. But he had to go. He had to figure out who had sent Lumerian demons after him and how they got there. If they did track him here Cassiopeia would be in danger again, and Alexander couldn't bring himself to do that to her a second time.

She set the breakfast down on the side table. Alexander looked at it but didn't reach for it. He watched her expression change as the realization of him leaving washed over her. She did a good job of hiding her disappointment and sadness, but he saw through her mask, just like he always could.

"Oh," she said.

"I have to leave. I need to warn the other leviathans and figure out who sent demons after me."

"Lumerian demons."

"Yes."

She looked away from him, unable to bring herself to look into his lavender eyes, knowing they would unravel her. They couldn't be together. It was too dangerous. She had found herself saying that over and over in her mind for the past four days.

Alexander didn't want her to push him away because of what had happened between them. "I don't want what happened in the forest to change our friendship. I greatly value you being around and accepting me. You do mean a lot to me."

"I know, but sometimes I want you to care more." She rarely showed vulnerability, but with him it was always different, he made her feel different. When Cassiopeia glanced up from her hands, she could see that her words had cut him deeply. Guilt filled her.

"Never mind. I didn't mean . . ."

"No. No, no." He took a deep breath as he pulled her to his chest. "Cassiopeia, I don't push you away because I want to. There are things that I know about that I can't change. There is a reason why I know so much about your powers and why I know other things, too. Don't think that I push you away because I want to. I lo . . ." He cut off his words quickly with a sharp intake of air before continuing. "I care for you more than you could ever understand. I wish I could protect you from all the things that hurt you, but all things must happen for a reason."

Cassiopeia lifted her head from his chest and looked at him. She stared into his mysterious lavender eyes. The emotion in his words touched her, and as much as she wanted to argue with him, something deep inside of her told her that no words would change things. They were never meant to be, even if it hurt both of them to let go. She placed her hand on his cheek before she stepped away from his warm, comforting embrace.

"What happened in the forest doesn't change things. I will be here if you need me as an ally, as I know you will be there for me. You are right. Things happen for a reason and we come from different worlds. Maybe one day the world will change and something might come of it, but there is no point in holding out for false hopes. I do care for you Alexander. If you need help, please reach out. I will be here."

He gave her a small smile. "I know, and I won't hesitate."

She smiled at him. "Goodbye Alexander. Stay safe."

He smiled back, but it didn't quite reach his eyes. "Always."

Chapter 5

Demetrius

3583 BCE

The best kind of relationships begin unexpectedly, when you get that astonished feeling, and everything happens so suddenly. That's why you don't look for love. It comes to you just at the right time, the time you never thought it would have.

—Anonymous

"We should try this strategy! It will work," Demetrius said proudly.

Cassiopeia rolled her eyes and turned toward the young demigod. "Who invited the child to this meeting?"

The other gods snickered. They were in a large war room chamber on Olympus. The Greek mortals were planning an attack against a large Persian force and Zeus had asked for Cassiopeia's insight. Normally she would have said no, but Athena had asked her personally as a friend. She knew she shouldn't have befriended a Greek. Now she was in a chamber with gods and goddesses of war and wisdom, dealing with their inability to cooperate.

The demigod, Demetrius, glared back at her. He was rather handsome, but he had been retorting her every idea the entire meeting and they had only been here for less than an hour. He had soft golden blond hair and bright, piercing sky blue eyes. Currently he had a scowl across his handsome face, his eyes swirling with anger.

"I did," a female voice said.

Cassiopeia looked toward the entrance of the chamber. Athena had finally arrived. She was tall and muscular, with curly golden hair that almost reached her waist and sharp green eyes that were full of curiosity and wisdom. She walked with a very empowering, lethal presence. Cassiopeia looked back to the table, her jaw clenched.

"You're late," Cassiopeia said, irritated.

"Take it up with my boss."

Cassiopeia took a deep breath. Zeus managed to annoy her every time she visited. Looking at Athena out of the corner of her eye Cassiopeia spoke.

"Zeus knows what time I arrive and what time I leave. I am not changing my schedule because he gets a stick up his ass and needs you to pull it out for him . . . and you can tell him I said that."

"I will happily relay the message. That is why I sent my son in my place, hopefully something productive was done in my absence."

"You sent a child in your stead so, no, nothing productive was done."

Demetrius scoffed. "Who do you think you are? You cannot speak to people like that!" To him Cassiopeia was intolerable and rude. He stepped toward her.

Cassiopeia looked at him glaring, ready to end him on the spot.

Athena stepped between them. "He doesn't know. All he knows is that you are an advisor, I didn't tell him or the others more because you wanted secrecy."

"You should teach your children manners before they get themselves killed."

He went to retort again but Athena glared at him in warning. "He is normally more hospitable and insightful."

Demetrius was tired of being pushed into the corner. "I gave a perfectly good battle strategy and you shot it down for no reason! If we send one thousand troops from the east and five hundred from the north, with the fleet off the coast then they will have to go west. They will be trapped between the two water masses and we can pick them off with the fleet. Minimal troop losses."

Cassiopeia nodded in agreement.

"Yes, they will. They will be trapped perfectly—on land that is not in your domain. Therefore, you will have no authority to kill them."

"It's what's left of Atlantean lands it's in no one's domain. Who would care?"

Cassiopeia looked at him and smirked, anger boiling under her skin. She spoke coldly. "*I* would care. It's what remains of the Atlantean lands, aka *my lands*. And to send troops to *my* lands you need *my* permission."

After Atlantis had fallen, the Egyptian pantheon took pity on her and her people, who had no lands of their own to go to, so Set had gifted a stretch of land that bordered the Mediterranean just north of Arabia. Most of the Atlanteans had left that land to assimilate into the other cultures but the mostly empty land still belonged to the Atlantean pantheon.

Cassiopeia scoffed at Demetrius. "Funny thing about war meetings. They usually have an intended purpose, especially when there is an unknown visitor, and especially when Athena is late because Zeus threatened her about this deal having to go through and doing whatever she needed to get it done. What they don't usually have is a young, cocky, inexperienced demigod screwing it all up."

Demetrius didn't respond. He didn't know what to say, realizing that he had screwed up badly. His mother had sent him here to be diplomatic and he let his strong-mindedness and drive to achieve get in the way of just amusing her for a few minutes. The other gods stepped back in fear, looking surprised. They hadn't realized who Cassiopeia truly was either. Her reputation for being able to kill other gods and destroying her pantheon preceded her.

Athena spoke. "Cassiopeia, I asked you to come as a friend, to hear us out. I hoped you might come up with a solution that does not involve the Atlantean lands, but I don't feel that it is necessary for you to be rude in our home. I thought you two would get along. Demetrius' father is general Priamos. He has been trained under him personally."

Cassiopeia could see Athena's pride in her boy. She had met general Priamos multiple times before. One of those times she had used her powers to judge him in front his troops, granting him life. He was a good man for what his job entailed, always caring for and showing kindness to his men. When Priamos was on mission, his men came first. He had never married and probably never planned on having children, but Athena had gone to his bed and gave him the son he had wanted.

"Just because his father is a good man doesn't mean he is." Cassiopeia thought for a moment. "I'm assuming he will be leading the troops that will be cornering the opposing army?"

Athena nodded. Cassiopeia was quiet before she finished her thought. She looked at Athena. "Let me judge him and if he is like his father then you can use my lands, hell, I will even donate my fighting services."

Athena responded quickly and looked at Demetrius. "No."

Demetrius saw an opportunity to fix his mistake. "Wait! It's my choice. Yes."

Cassiopeia smirked. Athena looked at her, worried that her son was about to sign his own death warrant. Demetrius had no idea what he was agreeing to. He had heard rumors of the powerful Atlantean but didn't know the extent of her powers. Cassiopeia flashed to Demetrius and placed her hand on his arm. She was waiting for his permission when she felt Athena's sword aggressively jab her side, warning her to back away.

"Back. Off," Athena growled.

Cassiopeia didn't stop, looking at Demetrius. "Let him make the choice. If he wants to be a big boy, then let him. Maybe he can correct his error."

Cassiopeia knew Athena's worry, but she also knew she wouldn't kill her son right in front of her—she wouldn't hurt her friend like that. She was cold inside, but not that cold.

He didn't break eye contact. "Do it. For a better chance for my men, I will risk myself," he said bravely.

Cassiopeia turned her head toward Athena, eyebrows raised. She could see the worry on Athena's face, but she felt the sword get pulled away. Looking back at Demetrius, her eyes began to shift from blue to a glowing red.

She saw his past and how Athena had been there for him as much as she could. She cared for his father and had tried to raise him around her own duties. He was trained to fight young and learned about strategy. His education was that of a nobleman, but he never became cocky. He treated his men how he treated his friends, and he truly cared for them. He had risked his life to save others. He was a good man, just like his father, and he deserved life.

Cassiopeia pulled her hand away and Demetrius gasped at all he had just seen. She turned and walked away from him, looking at the table, as if assessing what to do or say.

Athena looked worried as Cassiopeia looked to her and then to Demetrius. "I will meet you at the war camp in two days. *Don't* be late this time."

With that, she flashed out of the room with a newfound respect for the son of Athena.

Demetrius and his mother rode into the war camp together. The men greeted them with praise and excitement. They stopped at the war tent first, where all of the plans for battle would be made. Cassiopeia was already there, having arrived very early in the morning. She turned to look at them as they entered, giving Athena a small smile. She could be more relaxed around her friend now that they weren't being watched by the other gods and goddesses of Olympus.

"I think the plan has been beat to death. There is no way the Persians can win, especially with my backing. Zeus owes me one. A big one," Cassiopeia said.

Athena laughed. "As if he would ever admit to that. I have a surprise: Priamos will be here before nightfall he wanted to see you again!"

Cassiopeia smiled, happy to be able to see her old general friend again. "I would like to see him again as well. Before that though, I wanted to ride into their camp and talk with the king today. If we can convince him to cede, then we may not have to have any battle tomorrow."

Demetrius stepped forward. "May I go with you?"

Cassiopeia looked at him sternly. He was leading this, so he should be there for the negotiations. "I don't see why not. Just let me do the talking, I've found you tend to piss people off." Cassiopeia smirked at him. "I leave in thirty minutes."

He ignored her side comment and nodded, quickly leaving to put his things in his tent so he could accompany her. The two of them left with no soldiers or guards, Cassiopeia told him they didn't need any and that it just made them look less threatening.

They were greeted at the outskirts of the enemy camp by guards and taken to the king's tent. It was a huge structure with multiple compartments. They walked into the main area and were greeted by the royal ambassador, who escorted them to the king. He was sitting on a throne in the far back compartment of the tent, which was set up similar to a throne room. Cassiopeia could see the pride and arrogance radiating off of the over-confident king. The fact that he had his men carry a full-size throne to his war camp told her everything she needed to know about him.

"I was told the Atlantean goddess would be staying out of this conflict, but here she is being the messenger dog for the Greeks."

"Well you certainly have no refinement. Is that anyway to greet a goddess and a demigod?" Demetrius was surprised that she included him in her greeting.

The obnoxious king spoke again. "You are no goddess of mine, and you don't scare me. I'm marked by my true gods, so you can't harm me." He lowered his collar to show her part of the branded tattoo. When the gods wanted to ensure the protection of a mortal, they could mark them with their sigil. It meant that killing him outside of battle would mean war between the Persian gods and the Atlantean goddess.

He continued with his crass words. "Do you come here to surrender? Are you my present?" he said with a wink. Cassiopeia actually felt herself become disgusted and nauseated.

Demetrius could see her beginning to become frustrated at his rudeness, so he spoke. "Your highness, we are here to accept your surrender to save your men's lives."

The king laughed. "Are you out of your mind?! My men outnumber you two to one! I have the support of my gods! I do not fear you!"

"You should." Cassiopeia was done with his arrogance. Yes, she couldn't kill him, but his gods hadn't marked everyone at the camp.

"You are a killer of your own people, goddess. If anything, the Greeks should fear having you on their side. Hopefully you'll betray them just like you did with your own family, and then I won't have anything to worry about. Hell, I'll even let you come to my bed afterwards."

He continued to laugh. Demetrius felt a wave of anger wash over him at the way the king spoke to her. His god blood could feel Cassiopeia's powers radiating off of her body. He watched her clench and unclench her fists.

Demetrius spoke again. "So . . . that's a no on the surrender?"

"Get out of my sight! Why don't you talk to the Atlanteans about surrender."

Demetrius saw her jaw twitch. Cassiopeia stopped clenching her fists and opened her hands. He heard the guards by the entrance begin to cough. Then all the guards in the tent started to cough. The king looked around the room at his men.

Cassiopeia spoke with an evil cold undertone in her voice. "You stupid, stupid mortal. I may not be able to touch *you*, but none of your guards are marked. I don't give two shits about your Persian gods. I am a primordial goddess with enough power to burn this camp to the ground myself." The men were now struggling to breath. One began to vomit blood. "I will see you tomorrow. Hopefully you will have learned some manners, and we won't have to go through this display again."

She turned and walked away. Demetrius followed, wide-eyed, as the guards dropped like flies around them. As she took her last step out of the compartment, Demetrius heard all of their necks snap, their bodies falling to the ground in sickening thuds.

As they mounted their horses and began to ride back, Demetrius looked at Cassiopeia. He could see pain in her eyes, as the king's words had hurt her, but he didn't like how she had handled it.

"Was that necessary?" he asked.

"Excuse me?"

"Did you have to kill those men? They weren't being insolent, their king was."

She stopped her horse and turned to look at him. "Those men would have been fighting tomorrow. They would have defended their king with their lives. They would have cut down your troops. I just saved some of your men's lives!"

"You could have just snapped their necks. You didn't have to make a whole display of it."

She was livid. Who was he to judge her methods? "He needed to learn that his actions have consequences. Being polite is part of common decency. Who was he to talk to me like that? He is a speck of dust in the grand scheme of things."

"Why do you hide your emotions behind this veil? You act like nothing hurts you, like no one can touch you. What does that get you? It gets you a reputation for being cold and heartless. You killed them because he got under your skin, because he mentioned your people. Because he made you feel."

She flinched slightly. "At least if people think I'm cold and heartless they won't try to befriend me. Then they can't hurt me. They will stay away because they fear me. You saw the other gods and goddesses at the war meeting. The second they realized who I was they stepped back in fear. They stayed away."

Cassiopeia turned her horse and began to head back to the camp. She didn't want to talk with him anymore. He was so frustrating to her. She didn't understand how one demigod could get under her skin so much. As they rode back, Demetrius was thinking the same thing about her.

When they returned to the camp, Priamos had already arrived. Demetrius dismounted quickly to go greet his father. As Cassiopeia entered the war tent, she could hear the two men talking and laughing. When Priamos saw her, he smiled and raised his hands, pulling her into a big hug. He looked older than the last time she had seen him, which she realized had been almost twenty years earlier. He was still fit and muscular, but he had grays running through his blond hair and beard. She could see wrinkles around his mouth and at the edges of his bright blue eyes, the same eyes as his son. It was one of the many things that showed her how time moved on without her.

"How has my Atlantean beauty been? Will you be joining us in the battle tomorrow?"

"I have been well, but I will not be participating in the battle. I will just be overseeing."

"No!" Priamos looked truly saddened. He turned to look at his son as he draped his arm over her shoulder. "You have never seen a better fighter before . . . except for your mother, of course." He smiled sweetly at Athena.

Athena shook her head. "She has even bested me."

Demetrius was surprised. He had never pictured Cassiopeia as a fighter, just a goddess who hid behind her powers.

"Tonight, we are going to have a small celebration for our temporary alliance and our impending victory tomorrow," Priamos said.

"I shall be there, Priamos." Cassiopeia said.

As Cassiopeia walked toward the dining tent, she quickly realized that Priamos' and her definitions of a small celebration were *very* different. Officers and soldiers, who were all trying to let off steam before the battle tomorrow, packed the main dining tent and spilled outside. She walked through the crowd of men easily, as most quickly moved out of her way, and entered the tent. Inside was just as bad, except now there was food and fresh wine. Somehow Priamos had gotten whores and musicians to come into the camp. There were women dancing around half dressed, tempting the soldiers. She saw Priamos, Athena, and Demetrius sitting at the main table at the end of the tent. As she walked to them, she could see Demetrius watching her. She had on a simple white peplos and belt that fell to just above her knees and her hair was braided and pinned up. Priamos stood when he saw her, grinning.

"Cassiopeia! Welcome, now, I know I said small but... the men get what the men want!"

She heard the men around them cheer at his words. She just smiled shaking her head. Priamos' enthusiasm and excitement about life was contagious and intoxicating.

"Where can I get wine? And food, I'm famished."

Priamos clapped his hands and a servant came with a tray of food and wine. He poured it into her glass and went to water it down, as was traditionally done, but she waved off the water. She ate and drank, watching the men enjoy themselves. She laughed and talked with Priamos and Athena about the changes in their lives over the last two decades, but Demetrius just observed them, staring mainly at her. He didn't know why she aggravated him so much, but he also felt drawn to her, like she was a strategy, a puzzle, that he needed to solve.

After a few hours of the party, she had made her rounds around the tent, talking with the men and getting them psyched for the battle in the morning. Demetrius saw her near the front of the tent as she grabbed her goblet and walked outside. He followed, curious to see where she was going, and also to make sure she didn't kill a drunken soldier who had wandering hands. As he walked, he could feel the nice light fog of drunkenness that hovered over him.

He found her near the edge of the encampment, leaning against a tent, looking out at the enemy camp in the distance. She turned her head slightly toward him, sensing his arrival. He could tell she was intoxicated by how she was standing. He watched curiously as she used her powers to fill her goblet with wine and something else.

"What did you just mix your wine with?"

She laughed. "Pomegranate juice. It makes it sweeter, so you don't have to water it down. I highly recommend it."

He could hear a slight slur in her voice, and he could tell her Atlantean accent was thicker and more dominate than usual. It had a nice flow to it, as if she was singing her words.

His inhibitions lowered, and he spoke before he thought. "That sounds gross."

She laughed out loud this time. "Don't kick it until you try it."

Cassiopeia held her goblet out toward him. Demetrius reluctantly grabbed it and took a swig. She watched him intently the entire time. He nodded and took another sip. She smiled at him.

"I retract my last comment, that's not bad." He chuckled. "Why are you out here?"

Her expression became serious again as she looked out toward the other camp. "Just thinking about tomorrow. About the men who won't be going home."

"You should really fight. We could use a good warrior. We can spar tomorrow before the battle if you want. I like to warm up anyways."

Cassiopeia looked down at the ground.

"I don't spar. I tend to kill people when I do. I just can't stop. So I only fight when it's life or death, then I can relax and enjoy the fight. I haven't had the . . . kindest life. Fighting for me is a survival thing, not a fun game."

He paused at her words. "I understand, but you should at least consider fighting in the battle tomorrow." He placed his hand on her arm. "We could use you."

"I'll think about it. Will that make you happy?" She smirked at him. He smiled back. "Yes."

She looked at the moon in the sky. "I should be going."

"Of course."

Cassiopeia looked back out one last time and Demetrius found that he wanted more of her wine concoction before she left. His current lack of decorum took over and he reached out, grabbing her goblet from her before she turned to leave. Her eyes widened in surprise as he took a swig, smiling at her.

"Hey!" She reached for it and he held it away from her. Cassiopeia realized that when she reached for it again, she was only inches from his face.

Demetrius had realized it too, his smile dissipating as he looked into her eyes. She looked from his stunning blue eyes to his lips and back to his eyes before she watched him lean into her and captured her lips with his. He moaned as he felt her kiss him back, leaning her body into his. She pressed against him, savoring the feel of his hard, muscular body. Demetrius tangled his fingers into her hairs at the nape of her neck as he deepened their kiss, their tongues moving in sync with each other. They broke the kiss, and their breathing was heavy.

Cassiopeia spoke first. "Do you want to . . ."

"Yes." He pulled her back to him more forcefully, kissing her lustfully. He dropped the goblet to wrap both his arms around her body.

Cassiopeia flashed them to her tent. They kept kissing as she reached down to remove his belt, him doing the same for her. She heard his belt hit the ground and felt his hands roaming around her body. He pulled away from her mouth and began kissing her neck fervently. He grabbed her peplos and pulled it over her head as she lifted her arms up. He reached down and untangled the fabric beneath, letting it fall to the floor. He looked down at her completely bare body. It gave her a shiver through her body to be so bare to him while he was still clothed.

Demetrius stepped toward her and kissed her again. She felt the pole from the tent press into her back as he pushed her gently against it. As he lifted the bottom of his chiton and raised her leg up, she could feel him rubbing into her core. She knew she was ready for him as she lowered herself to meet him. They both groaned in unison at the feeling of each other. He thrusted against her as she raised her arms to hold onto the pole, feeling the waves of pleasure wash over her with every motion. He lifted her other leg, so he was holding her completely off of the ground, supporting her weight in his arms. She couldn't hold back any longer as she felt a wave of euphoria wash over her entire body. He kissed her neck as she cried out in pleasure.

Demetrius waited until the last quivers of her orgasm escaped before he carried her over to the bed, separating their bodies for a brief moment to turn her around. Cassiopeia laughed lightly at his demanding, aggressive urgency, as she was usually the one in control. But this lack of control was turning her on more. He grabbed her hips and thrust deep into her. She moaned loudly at the sudden rough penetration. As her pleasure was increasing, she fell from her hands and knees to her knees and shoulders, her hands grasping at the bedding. He leaned forward, pinning her body to the bed. Demetrius slipped his hand beneath her, moving it down to her core. He smirked when he knew he had the right spot as he felt her tense and tighten under him. He increased his speed, as he could feel his climax coming, but he wanted to hear her cry out again. She could feel her pleasure building quickly as he stroked her. He heard the tent begin to shake from her powers surging. Right as he didn't think he could last any longer, holding back as much as he could, he felt her clench and cry out and he relaxed to join her in climax. The tent stopped shaking, Demetrius rolled off of her to lay on the bed, still breathing heavy. Cassiopeia leaned over and draped her leg over his.

She laughed lightly. "That was nice. Very nice, actually."

He laughed at her indisputable, but simple comment. "Yes, it was."

Cassiopeia got up to clean herself and when she came back, she slipped onto the bed next to him, lying on her stomach. Demetrius didn't know if he should stay or leave. What he did know was that just looking at her bare back and buttocks was making him stir again, but he knew he shouldn't. They needed sleep for the battle tomorrow. They were of no use to anyone if they were exhausted from sex. Demetrius could feel a drowsiness beginning to fall over him as he laid there. Cassiopeia shifted slightly toward him, and her legs brushed against his and stayed there. That was his sign that she wanted him to stay as he slipped into slumber.

Chapter 6
The Battle
3583 BCE

If you love somebody, let them go, for if they return, they were always yours.
—Kahlil Gibran

Demetrius woke the next morning to an empty bed. It was still early, the sun hadn't even crested the horizon, but Cassiopeia was already gone. He dressed quickly and left for his tent to put his armor on for the battle.

He could hear many of the other men beginning to stir as he got ready. The camp was slowly awakening. Grabbling his sword and sheath, he headed toward the war tent, putting it on as he walked quickly. When he entered the tent, he could see that Priamos, Athena, and Cassiopeia were already there, along with some of the other generals. He noted that he was not the last one to arrive, and that made him feel better.

He wondered why she had not woken him. Had she been upset about the night before? Demetrius rubbed his face to clear his head. He needed to be focused for the battle, not wondering if some goddess thought he was good in bed. As he looked down at the table, he saw her look up at him. His stomach fluttered and his mind began to race once again.

Damn, he thought, he was screwed.

She had somehow entangled herself into his mind. Demetrius began to talk about the strategy and get all of the plans in order, trying to distract himself. They all agreed with the final plan and began to leave.

Demetrius heard Cassiopeia speak to Priamos. "I will need to borrow a horse if I am to participate today."

Demetrius was surprised. "You are fighting?"

Cassiopeia looked to him with a small smirk but didn't answer as she left the tent.

Athena spoke. "Yes. Whatever you said to her last night changed her mind about fighting. Good job Demetrius!"

Normally he would be proud of his mother's praise, but instead he felt like she was thanking him for sleeping with Cassiopeia.

"Of course, Mother."

Demetrius turned and left the tent. As he rode to the front line, he saw that Cassiopeia was already there. He rode up next to her. In her golden battle armor, with a golden helmet that had a mohawk of red feathers, sitting atop the white horse his father had given her, she looked fierce. She glanced at him before looking back toward the opposing army.

Demetrius wanted to confront her about changing her mind to fight, but he didn't want to have her change her mind back. He could see her small smirk out of the corner of his eye. She turned her head to look at him up and down, before looking back out to the battlefield.

"No, I didn't change my mind because we had sex. I changed my mind when I heard the men praying this morning and saw them writing their final letters to their families. Yes, what you said yesterday impacted my decision as well, so that's why I told Athena you changed my mind."

"So, you lied to her to make me look good?"

"No, I told her because you planted the seed of doubt into my mind to even give me the idea to fight. You were the one to put the pieces in motion. The men were just the final piece that made the wall crumble." She paused. "You really shouldn't doubt yourself so much. You are going to become a great general one day, just like your father. You just need to work on your decorum toward those around you. Not everyone can handle a blunt, straightforward person, even if that's what is needed."

He was taken aback by her words, as he smiled slyly at her. "Did you just complement me?"

She laughed lightly. "Don't go getting a big head, Demetrius."

He felt his stomach flutter slightly at hearing her say his name. Before he could retort, he heard his parents ride up to them. Athena looked like a proper warrior goddess in full armor and helmet. His father also looked like a proud warrior on his horse next to her.

Cassiopeia spoke to them. "I was going to ride down first. I wanted to give them one last chance to surrender, maybe even offer single-warrior combat to end this quickly."

Athena nodded but looked to Demetrius. "It is not my call. Ask Demetrius. His is in the lead on this battle."

Cassiopeia looked at him, waiting for his response.

"I will ride with you," he said.

She nodded in agreement and they both rode down with the white flag to the center of the battlefield. When they came to a stop, two Persian gods, twins, flashed in front of them.

"I am Ahura and this is my brother Angra."

"Have you come to surrender Atlantean?" Angra asked slyly.

Cassiopeia looked surprised by their straightforwardness. "If we're going to be blunt, I came to save your people. One-on-one combat. Winner takes all . . . oh, minus the king. He's dying today no matter what. He pissed me off."

The brothers laughed.

"Who is your champion? The demigod of Athena? We would destroy him."

She could see Demetrius become enraged at his words, but she didn't act phased. "I will fight one of you. No god powers, just one sword per person."

Demetrius looked at her. She was stoic, waiting for their answer.

"You may be able to kill a god, but we can't. How can we kill you?"

She smiled. "I was hoping you would ask," she looked over in the distance to the right. "Do you see that figure over there?" They nodded. "That's a leviathan. He will be judging our battle and if you win, he will strike my death blow."

The Persians seemed surprised by her being so prepared.

"Give us a moment to speak."

She nodded and backed her horse a few paces.

Finally, Demetrius spoke to her. "Are you crazy? Why would you risk your life for a battle that doesn't involve your pantheon? What if they don't keep their word?"

Her eyes widened slightly but he could see her amusement behind them. "No, I'm not crazy. The battle involved my pantheon as soon as I agreed to help. And if they don't keep their word, then we fight anyway. I doubt they will go through with it. But imagine if those men watch their gods fall to the sword of another god. Will they fight as fiercely? If anything, it will cause their men to lose heart."

"Or you could be cut down. Then the same would happen to our men."

"As much as I appreciate your concern, I am very skilled with a sword. But if you say no, then we can retract our request and ride back to the men. As Athena said, this is your command and I will respect your decision."

He looked to the Persians talking quietly amongst themselves then looked into her powerful blue eyes. "If you have no doubts about winning then you can fight. But *any* doubts and we ride off now."

"I have none."

He took a deep breath and nodded to her. The Persians were ready to speak again.

"Angra will fight you. No extra powers other than those that you possess naturally. One sword per warrior. The half-blood and I will be the judges."

"He has a name." Cassiopeia snarled. "I suggest you learn it because come sunrise tomorrow, this battle will have his namesake."

Demetrius was surprised by her aggression in his defense. He had never thought of the honor of having something important named after him. The god rolled his eyes as Cassiopeia dismounted from her horse. She bounced and stretched lightly as she readied herself for the fight. She tugged at the neck of her breastplate as if it was bothering her. Demetrius furrowed his brow.

"One second," her breast plate and shoulder pads flashed off of her and onto her horse's saddle. His eyes widened as he realized she was about to fight with no armor. "That's so much better. You Persians don't mind if I fight with minimal armor. If it's a problem I can put it back on."

"I don't care, let's just get on with this. I want to go home."

The two gods switched swords so that he had the Atlantean sword and she had the Persian one, shaking hands to seal the deal before the witnesses. As she squared up across from him, she gave a sly smile.

"You won't be going home, my dear."

Angra lunged. Cassiopeia dodged, flipping to the side. Demetrius had not understood why his father was in such awe over her fighting until he saw it for himself. She moved like water around the Persian. Even with her quick, sudden motions you could see on her face that she was very relaxed fighting.

The Persian swung, almost slicing her stomach, and she dodged, laughing. "I thought you would put up more of a fight! You should really get your sword properly balanced. How am I supposed to have a proper fight in these subpar conditions?"

This angered Angra. He continued his attacks, with her throwing in a few of her own, but she avoided his every swing. He watched her face change as she was beginning to get tired of her own game, becoming more determined. Her blows and movements became swifter and more assertive. When the Persian lunged out and scratched her arm with the sword,

Demetrius saw in her eyes that she was done. In three quick motions she had the Persian on his knees in front of her as she slit his throat. Ahura cried out as he watched her kill his brother. She let go of his body, letting it fall to the ground with a hard thud. She hadn't even broken a sweat. As Angra took his last breath, Demetrius watched as black dust flowed out of his body and into the air above him. He could see, based on Cassiopeia's expression, the discomfort for this part. The dust flowed toward her and into her body, her eyes beginning to glow brightly as she vaguely grimaced in pain. Once all the dust was absorbed, her eyes returned to normal and she became stoic. She threw the Persian sword onto the ground and retrieved her own. Cassiopeia glanced at Demetrius, breaking him from the trance that her fighting had put him in.

"Surrender your men, as were the terms of the agreement."

The Persian god didn't look up from staring at his brother's body. His eyes filled with sorrow and anger. "No, you will pay for this!"

"You shook on it!"

"No! *He* shook on it. I owe you nothing!"

Demetrius nudged Cassiopeia's horse toward her. She flashed her armor back on and mounted.

"Let the battle begin. But let it be a note of your character and lack of honor. If I find you on the field, you will meet the same fate. Mark my words."

Ahura didn't respond as Cassiopeia and Demetrius turned around and rode to their troops. They informed Athena and Priamos of what happened. By the time they had reached them, the Persian army was already readying for the fight.

They attacked, riding forward swiftly. As the Greek army rode in, Cassiopeia could feel Angra's powers mixing with her own, filling her with discord, chaos, and rage. She let those feelings wash over her and blacked out for most of the battle. Demetrius focused on his own opponents, but he saw her in the distance occasionally, cutting down men as if they were made of air. He could feel himself stirring just watching her, as his testosterone and adrenaline were raging from fighting.

Athena was next to her, fighting just as swiftly. They were a lethal combination of skill and swordsmanship. He watched as Athena threw her shield up as they twisted around each other, Cassiopeia catching it on the other side. For them, this wasn't life or death. This was a dance, a game. Yes, they fought for the men, but they also fought because they wanted to, because they were good at it.

Demetrius hadn't said anything monumental to her to make her change her mind about fighting. Cassiopeia had seen her friends and needed to decompress, so she changed her own mind. She decided to fight. Demetrius watched as they pushed the Persians toward the Atlantean lands. Cassiopeia was using her powers to ban the Persians from her lands, and as the feet of the Persian soldiers touched the Atlantean soil they burned into ash. When Cassiopeia turned toward him, he could see her eyes were red. Her hair had also turned white. She was no longer using her weapons to kill men, just her powers, as she reached out and grabbed them, dictating their death. After a few hours of fighting, the Persians finally held up the flag of surrender. The Greek soldiers cheered for their victory. Demetrius watched as Cassiopeia grabbed a nearby horse and mounted. She reached down to Athena, who joined behind her. They rode through the battlefield, the men cheering them for giving them a victory. Demetrius knew his mother was soaking up the praise, but in his heart, he knew that Cassiopeia was not truly enjoying it. To her this was a job and it was done. She hadn't done anything other than what the gods were supposed to do: stand by their people's side and help them. They rode back to the camp and he stayed behind to help the injured men around him, knowing exactly where he was going to go after.

Cassiopeia was back in her tent removing her armor. She knew she could just flash it off, but for some reason she had always found it soothing to remove it by hand. It was therapeutic after all of the destruction, something that she had to do slowly to help ease her mind back to reality.

Cassiopeia had all her armor off and was just unbuckling her vambraces and setting them down on the table when she heard someone enter her tent. She turned to see Demetrius standing there. His blue eyes were dark and filled with burning desire. She knew exactly what he wanted as he walked swiftly across the tent to kiss her roughly, pinning her between him and the table. She groaned as she could taste the saltiness of him on her lips. She could tell by the demanding need of his lips that he didn't want anything but sex, emotionless and raw. She could feel the cold steel of his armor between them as he pulled her roughly against his body. Demetrius didn't care as he lifted her under-armor peplos, exposing her lower half to him. Cassiopeia undid his belt and unclasped his armor, moving his under-armor out of the way. She could feel through the light cloth that he was already hard and ready. He pushed her back, laying her on the table as he lined himself up and plunged deep inside of her. She cried out as he felt her buckle against him. He held her hips as he thrust against her, feeling waves of euphoria wash over him. He knew she was feeling the same as she gripped the edge of the table, her knuckles white. Demetrius leaned down over her, feeling himself getting closer to climax with every motion. He could feel her tightening around him about to reach her end as well.

She began to moan as she was reaching her peak, and he growled into her ear. "Say my name."

"Demetrius." Cassiopeia moaned it as she reached her peak, Demetrius following quickly after as he heard his name escape her lips. They were both panting heavily in exhaustion. She kissed his neck and dropped her head back to the table.

"Wow." She had never combined her pent-up energies after fighting with sex. It was something she wished she had discovered long ago. "That was . . . wow."

Cassiopeia didn't know what else to say. She could see a smile of triumph on his face. Demetrius looked at her out of the corner of his eye, then leaned over and kissed her deeply. He pulled away, stepping back from her, but he enjoyed getting to see her splayed across the table, spent. He groaned. She smirked at him.

"I'm sure we have time . . ." she winked.

"I know we don't. Technically I shouldn't have come by for this, but I couldn't resist. I needed to *claim the land.*"

Cassiopeia laughed lightly, but behind it was a small sadness. She was going to wait to tell him, but this was probably the last time she would see him. She sat up on the edge of the table.

"I'm leaving soon. I did what I agreed upon."

She could see a sadness in his eyes, but he quickly hid it.

"You don't want to stay for the victory celebrations tonight?"

"This was enough of a victory celebration," she smirked at him "I have no reason to stay."

He stepped toward her, his body only a few inches away as he gazed into her eyes.

"You could have one," he said quietly.

Demetrius could see in her eyes that she wanted to say yes. But then her eyes became dark, as if remembering something painful. Cassiopeia knew she couldn't. She could never become romantically involved with a mortal and, of all mortals, Athena's son. She looked away.

"No. I can't. I'm cold and calculating for a reason. When I care for people one of us gets hurt. So now I just don't care." She looked back at him. "I have truly enjoyed our time, but I can't stay."

Demetrius looked away, feeling sad but not destroyed. He looked back to her and nodded in understanding. He put his hand on her cheek and kissed her deeply one last time before he turned and walked away.

Cassiopeia was in her quarters in Vēlatusa sitting in front of her mirror while Sierra brushed her hair. Suddenly, a letter manifested onto her beauty table. She picked it up to see it bore the seal of Athena. It made her smile, as she hadn't heard from Athena in almost two years, since the battle against the Persians. She opened the letter and laughed. Sierra was curious too.

"What is it, goddess?"

"Athena is pregnant again with Priamos. She invited me to the announcement celebrations."

"Oh! Can we go? Please, Cassiopeia, please!?"

Cassiopeia looked at her demon, who was now bouncing up and down, begging. She could tell that Sierra was excited based on the fact that she had used her name instead of goddess. It had been a while since they had gone to a party, especially one that Sierra was allowed to go to as most gods tried to avoid interactions with Vantha demons. And, a piece of Cassiopeia wanted to see Demetrius again. She didn't know what about him drew her in.

Smiling, she nodded her head at the demon. "Yes, we can go. *But* it's a mortal party, too, so you must be disguised as a human."

"Yay!"

She laughed at her demon's overexuberance. "We need to pick out dresses. The party is in one week."

Demetrius did not want to go to the party. He was happy for his mother and father, but he would rather be doing more productive things than celebrating the fact that his parents got laid. Especially when he looked to be the same age as his mother.

He was standing by his throne-like chair next to his parents as they greeted their guests. Demetrius had taken notice of the fact that only a few gods were here, and none of them were major gods in their pantheon. The others frowned on celebrating their demigod children. To them, they were just a side effect from sleeping with mortals, and nothing to be celebrated.

As he watched the guests arrive, he saw her walk in. Cassiopeia. She had on a dark blue, Atlantean-style dress with white edging that went all the way to the floor. He noticed that it had no sleeves and dipped low in the front, showing her cleavage. It seemed to melt off of her body as it fell like silk to the ground around her. She had kohl-rimmed eyes and had darkened her lips. Her hair was pinned up in a very Atlantean style. His breath was taken away at her presence. He thought he would never see her again. She was just as he remembered. Demetrius watched as she moved through the room gracefully and smoothly, like a morning fog rolling in over the hills. People naturally moved out of her way due to the aura she emanated. As she neared the host and hostess, she looked up and made eye contact with him.

Demetrius had changed since she last saw him. His hair was longer, falling loosely onto his shoulders, the top was pulled back to keep it neatly out of his face, and he had an inch or two of growth on his jaw. She had only seen him in his battlefield attire, or with nothing, but he now had on a white chiton with a dark blue himation trimmed in gold. He looked just like a general's son, and he looked good. It always amazed her how different a solider could look at home versus the battlefield.

Cassiopeia moved her eyes over to Athena, who was glowing as usual, her tummy already showing her pregnancy. Athena stood to greet her friend.

"Welcome! I was surprised you decided to come! Usually, you avoid these types of things."

"Yes, well, it has been a while and I was missing my friends."

"It's been longer before."

"That is true. Maybe I came to see someone specifically," she teased. Demetrius felt his stomach flutter lightly as she spoke, but he pushed it down. She had already rejected his advances for something more than sex. "Priamos! How are you doing old friend?"

Priamos laughed. "You pretend you like me, but I know you just tolerate me. What would two beautiful goddesses want with a man like me?"

He winked at her and Athena. Athena went to respond but Cassiopeia spoke first.

"Sometimes what is on the inside matters more than anything. We are your reward for being a good man . . . Athena more so than me." She smiled, winking back.

"I can accept that answer. Go enjoy yourself! The festivities are going on for the next five days!"

Cassiopeia's eyes widened. She hadn't realized this was a whole event.

"I went a little overboard, but who doesn't love a good party? And I won't be able to party much longer, the baby will be here in only a few months." Athena laughed at herself.

Cassiopeia loved seeing her with Priamos. She was always so happy here and relaxed. Cassiopeia still didn't understand why, if Athena cared for him so much to stay with him all these years and have multiple children, she wouldn't petition to make him immortal and marry him. If Zeus saw her joy, surely he would say yes. Cassiopeia would even go to Olympus to petition on their behalf if she was asked. She didn't bring it up anymore though because the last time she did Athena shut it down quickly, saying that he was created as a mortal for a reason and this was how it had to be. Cassiopeia had seen her friend love other men before, but this was going to hurt her one day much more than the others. Cassiopeia looked to Athena.

"I'm going to go mingle. I will meet you in the great hall when you are done greeting your guests?" she said, winking at Athena. Demetrius could have sworn she glanced at him.

Athena nodded with excitement and Priamos spoke. "We shall save you a seat at our table."

He waved for his servant to make the arrangements. Cassiopeia walked away toward the dining hall and Demetrius felt himself stirring as he realized her dress was backless. He could see from the nape of her neck all the way to her lower back, noticing a small gold chain that went across at the top then hung down the center of her spine. It was painful to watch her leave and just stand there to greet the next person. Demetrius waited for a few more people to arrive before asking to take his leave to make rounds in the dining hall. His father allowed it, and he went on his way to secretly find her.

Demetrius felt like a lost puppy as he scanned the dining hall for her face. He walked to the far corner, looking through the crowd as he went, but he didn't see her. When he felt someone standing behind him, he didn't pay any mind until they spoke.

"What are you looking for my lord? Maybe I could be of assistance?"

Demetrius turned toward her melodic smooth voice. She was just inches away from him, with a sly smirk on her face. She was so close he could smell her perfume clinging to the air. It was a unique scent that he had never smelled before, but it made him want to bury his face in her neck and breathe her in. Cassiopeia could see in his eyes that she was who he had been looking for, but he would never admit it. He reluctantly looked away from her and back to the crowd.

"I don't think you could help. I was actually looking for Dionysus. We need more wine and other things."

She smiled lightly behind him. It was a good save on his part, but she was smarter than that.

"Here let me help you look . . ." She leaned forward and he felt her breasts press against his shoulder as she stood on her toes and put her hands on him to see around him. She heard his breathing change as she touched him. "I think he's right there."

She pointed out to the crowd and there was the drunken god. *Damn.* He had been hoping the god was elsewhere.

Cassiopeia moved her head next to his ear and whispered. "If you want to pretend that you weren't looking for me that's fine, but then you should get better control of your breathing when my body touches yours."

Demetrius could feel her breath against his ear as she spoke. It was taking an unreasonable amount of self-control to not turn around and kiss her until she begged him to stop.

"Maybe you should teach me. In private, of course."

His voice was a deep baritone that vibrated through her core. He could hear her smile when she breathed, but then he felt her move a few inches away from him. He turned his head to see her out of the corner of his eye. Her expression was more serious and guarded.

"I may have time for a private lesson after the party, but I would recommend you bring a friend to ease suspicions." She looked at him through her lashes. "I share." Her voice was seductive and flowed like honey. She looked him discreetly up and down, but he looked at her with a deadly seriousness.

"I don't."

For some reason his sudden, raw possessiveness made her want him more. Cassiopeia didn't want to wait hours, but she knew they had to. She already felt slightly guilty about sleeping with her best friend's son, but she couldn't control herself around him—not after what he did the last time they were together.

"Do you see the blonde over there in the purple dress?"

Demetrius spotted her and nodded.

"Bring her back to your room. I will take care of the rest."

He looked back at Cassiopeia.

"I wasn't joking . . ."

"I said I would take care of it. Unless you want your mother, who is looking this way, getting suspicions about us. Trust me, boy."

He hated when she called him that. When he looked at her face, she looked angry and disgusted. He was confused. She shoved him and walked away. When she was behind the nearby pillar she looked back and winked. Demetrius looked over to see Athena looking at him, so he just shook his head and ran his hand through his hair, walking away. Cassiopeia was an enigma to him. She made him crazy—in a good and bad way.

After dinner Demetrius saw her talking to the blonde girl and the girl looked at him, nodding. After that, he easily found the girl and she clung to him the rest of the night. He pretended to be into it, laughing and drinking enjoying the party. The girl kissed him a few times and sat on his lap, but he felt no stirring for her. She wasn't who he wanted.

Demetrius and Cassiopeia didn't talk directly for the rest of the night. He reluctantly escorted the blonde girl back to his room. She was clinging to him on the way to his quarters, but once they arrived and he shut the door, she became completely uninterested in him. He was relieved, but confused. She walked around his chambers looking at his things, as if she was waiting for something.

"Can I get you anything?" he asked her.

"Nope."

Before he could say more, he heard a noise outside the door. The blonde turned to the door and squealed. "Goddess!"

Goddess? Demetrius was so confused. The girl opened the door and began to chirp and squeak in an unusual language. Before she got more than three or four squeaks out, he saw a hand cover her mouth and slip into his room. Cassiopeia glared at the girl, who was now quiet. Once the door was completely closed, she removed her hand. The girl looked sad, speaking quietly and looking down to the floor.

"I'm sorry goddess. I was excited to get back to the party."

"You tell no one about this, and change your features."

He watched as the girl's hair, eyes and outfit changed before him. "What the . . ."

They ignored him. Cassiopeia looked at Sierra sternly.

"No killing people. If Athena tells me that you didn't have perfect decorum, you will answer to me. Understood?"

"Yes goddess."

Cassiopeia nodded and the girl vanished into a smoke and was gone. He must have had a look on his face, because Cassiopeia began to laugh.

"What? You've never seen a Vantha demon?"

His eyes widened more. He had heard stories of how lethal and violent they were. Anyone the Atlanteans chose to unleash them on faced a disgusting and brutal death. They enjoyed killing and eating their prey.

"You let me flirt with and be alone with a Vantha demon!"

"She's my companion. You were completely safe. Probably safer than you had ever been in your whole life."

"I kissed her!"

Cassiopeia rolled her eyes with a smirk on her face. "And she probably thought it was just as gross kissing a human. She's been my companion and friend since I was a little girl. We were born on the same day. She is sworn to protect me with her life and would do so without hesitation. Atlantean gods and goddess are paired up with their companion demon when they are young to build a lifelong bond."

He had never heard of such a thing, but the Atlanteans had been beyond their time and this was one of the reasons why.

He watched as she began to look around his room. Suite would be a better term for it. The ceilings reached up over twenty feet, with stone pillars around the doorways, which had glass paneled doors. The main entry room included a large dining table in the center and a fireplace in one corner. The fireplace was huge and double-sided. It was open to his bed chamber as well, which was large in its own right. There was a massive canopy bed, with curtains tied to all four posts. A large dresser was against the wall, and near that was a portable divider for dressing and a mannequin holding his pristinely polished armor. There were paintings hanging from the walls of different battle scenes. A bookshelf was on the same wall as the bed, and was completely full of books. There was one chair in front of the fireplace, with pelt rugs strewn about in front of it. She then realized that the huge fireplace wasn't just double-sided. It stretched to a third room, the bathing room. It held a large Roman-style walk in tub in the center. Cassiopeia could tell the floors were heated from the steam she could see rising from the water. She walked back into his bedroom and looked at the large balcony on the far wall. When she walked over, she opened the doors. It opened up to a view of the back gardens. She could see some people moseying around the gardens, probably drunk. Walking back inside, she used her powers to quietly shut the doors behind her.

Cassiopeia was still looking around when she realized he was watching her. She blushed slightly, having forgotten why she was here, infatuated with her own curiosity. Demetrius was enjoying just watching her as she walked from room to room exploring. When he saw her blush at him, his heart raced. He knew he didn't just like her as someone to sleep with. He *liked* her. A lot.

She walked over to the bed and fell back onto it. He smiled at her childlike action. She leaned up onto her elbows. He could see the longing in her eyes as they looked at each other. Demetrius walked over to the post of the bed. He knew that, normally, he would feel awkward over the silence, but with her he didn't. While he just looked at her, he saw her eyes shutter down and she hid a yawn. She gave him a look up and down his body making his groin awaken.

"So . . ." Cassiopeia smirked.

Demetrius knew she was tired, but she was doing a good job of hiding it. He rubbed his temples and eyes. He wasn't overly ready for bed, but he didn't want her to feel bad.

"Would you hate me if we just went to sleep? I know it sounds pathetic, but it has been a long day and we have a longer day tomorrow."

"Not if I don't stay tomorrow."

Demetrius hadn't thought about that. He just assumed when she was talking to Athena that she would stay the whole time. She sat up and stood, looking as if he had hurt her feelings.

"I understand, you're tired. I'll go."

"No!" She was surprised by his outburst as he placed a hand on her arm. "I . . . I . . . ugh."

Demetrius ran his fingers roughly through his hair. He wasn't good at this. He usually just slept with women and then forgot about them shortly after, having never courted a woman whom he wanted to have more with before. He looked at her and she still looked confused, but now he could see some amusement in her eyes.

"You're tired." Demetrius said to her. She looked slightly guilty. "I was just trying to be polite and courteous, but I came off sounding like an asshole trying to blow you off."

Cassiopeia looked back at him. Her blue eyes were full of so many expressions he couldn't tell what she was thinking. She leaned forward and kissed him. He wasn't expecting it, especially how she kissed him. There was no lust or craving, it was soft and tender. She was kissing him because she wanted to be closer to him, not to satisfy some itch or craving. Demetrius placed his hands on her cheeks, kissing her softly back. She pulled away and looked up at him, his light blue eyes mesmerizing her, as her eyes flicked back and forth between them. She didn't know what had captured her about him. When she had first met him, she couldn't stand him, but now he filled her thoughts, making her want to feel.

"I would like to sleep, but I could sleep in my own room if you want."

The thought of her leaving saddened him. Demetrius kissed her again, just as she had before, except this time he walked toward her causing her to back into the bed. He could feel a smile form on her lips as he showed her what he wanted. He pulled his lips away.

"Stay."

Cassiopeia nodded and turned around, lowering her head as she pointed to a clasp on the gold chain. "Can you . . ."

Demetrius unclasped it. He watched her dress fall to the floor and she was in just her undergarment, her upper body bare to him. She crawled across the bed and pushed down the comforter, sliding under the sheets. He loved the sight of her in his bed, almost more so that she wanted to be there just to be by him.

Demetrius quickly blew out the candles, lowered the torches, and removed his himation, then his chiton before joining her under the sheets. He suddenly felt flustered again, because he didn't know what to do with himself. Luckily, she took charge, and slid over to him, resting her head on his chest with her arm draped over him and her legs intertwined with his.

He could hear the sleepiness in her voice when she spoke. "Good night Demetrius."

He smiled at the simplicity of it all. "Good night, Cassiopeia."

Chapter 7

Changing Tides
3581 BCE

You don't find love; it finds you.
—Anaï Nin

Cassiopeia woke wrapped in Demetrius' arms. She felt so safe
and protected, an unusual feeling for her. The past four days of
celebration had flown by in a whirlwind of events, alcohol, sex,
and fun. She couldn't remember a week in her life where she had more fun
being around others. Most of her days had been spent secretly flirting with
Demetrius and the nights tangled in his bed. She knew they were playing
a dangerous game, as Athena would never approve of their relationship.

Cassiopeia looked at his sleeping face. He looked so peaceful, so
content and relaxed. As she looked at him, she realized that today was the
final day, then she would leave to go back to Vēlatusa, and he would stay

here. She felt a pit in her stomach at the thought, her heart cracking just thinking about it. Her surge of emotion surprised her. She had done such a good job of locking her feelings away, but he had found a way to wiggle in. As she looked at him, her stomach tightened as she realized she had deep feelings for him. He had broken through her barriers and into her heart. She felt him beginning to stir awake. His sleepy blue eyes opened, focusing on her face, and he smiled lightly, stretching as he woke. He ran his fingers up and down her bare back.

"You know some people think it strange to stare at them while they sleep." Demetrius winked and she gave a small smile. He became worried when she had no retort.

"What's wrong? Please tell me what's on your mind."

Cassiopeia sat up, turning away from him. She was at a crossroads. She could tell him how she felt and stay with him here, or she could leave and end it right now. Leaving would be the safe option. He couldn't hurt her if she walked away. But her heart wanted to stay, to lie back down and stay curled in his arms forever. She realized she needed to clear her head and think.

"I'm going to go for a ride. I need to think about some things."

She got out of bed, and before she had even completely stood, was already in a riding outfit. He was taken aback by her sudden declaration to go.

"I can go with you."

"No!" She realized she answered too quickly. "I need to be alone to think."

"Did something happen? Please talk to me, Cassiopeia." Demetrius got out of bed quickly, walking over to her. She wouldn't make eye contact with him as he placed his hands on her arms. "Talk to me. Please."

Cassiopeia could hear the concern and sentiment in his voice, but it only made her heart ache more. She took a deep breath before looking up at him.

"I promise you I will be back before sundown, probably earlier. I just need to think about some things."

Demetrius still looked worried. He didn't remove his hands from her arms.

"Please, Demetrius."

He nodded, and reluctantly released her arms. He never wanted to let her go, but he knew that if he held her here, she would pull away harder. Demetrius watched as she walked away. At least this time he knew he would see her at least one more time.

Cassiopeia rode her horse down the wooded path in full gallop, twisting and turning quickly to avoid trees. They finally reached a clearing and she stopped, quickly jumping down from her horse. She walked away a few paces and fell to her knees. As her feelings and powers surged, she dropped her head to her hands to collect her thoughts. She had feelings for him, and she knew he had feelings for her. He could just be infatuated with the fact that she was a goddess, but that was unlikely seeing that he was the son of Athena, a goddess herself. Another realization washed over her: she had fallen for her best friend's son. Athena was one of very few goddesses who still allowed Cassiopeia in their company, and she just ruined it. As she was going over her dilemma in her mind, she heard movement behind her.

"I told you to let me think. Why did you follow me—?" she turned as she spoke to find Priamos standing there.

"Go ahead, say the name that you were going to say. I'm curious who's on your mind." He had a sly smirk on his face.

"I'm sorry Priamos. I'm distracted."

"I noticed. His name wouldn't happen to be Demetrius, would it?"

Cassiopeia looked away, not knowing what to say. She was also confused. Looking back at Priamos she asked, "How? How did you know?"

"When my son doesn't want to spar and would rather go to his mother's party, that was the first clue. Then I just watched. He looks at you more often than you think, and you do the same." Cassiopeia blushed lightly. "The final piece of the puzzle was you. When you completely avoid his presence but will momentarily allow his touch but then pull away from it hesitantly. You two dodge each other's company too much." He laughed lightly. "Oh, and I also saw you leaving his room one morning, when he grabbed you and kissed you and you told him that he needed to be more careful because someone could see. That was a big clue."

Cassiopeia was now fully blushing. "I don't know what to do..."

"Do you love him?"

She honestly didn't know. Cassiopeia had feelings for him, but was it love? She had never loved someone in a romantic way before. Priamos could see her internal debate.

"You are a unique being, Cassiopeia. I've never met another creature like you. The only thing you fear is yourself—your powers, your emotions. You hide behind a stoic hard exterior so that you don't have to feel. So that you don't have to trust." He paused, looking out across the field. "He loves you. I don't know if he realizes yet, but I can see that you know it."

"I don't trust others for a reason. Most of the people in my life who I have trusted have either hurt me, or I hurt them. I don't want the same for him." She paused and looked out at the trees around them. "He asked me to stay before I left after the battle years ago. I just ran, like I always do. But the thought of him drew me back, and now I'm in too far and I have to choose between him or Athena. I have betrayed my friendship."

"I'll talk to her. She will understand. Just please don't leave him high and dry. If you are going to leave, then end it and don't come back."

Cassiopeia nodded, understanding his request. She looked to the ground and spoke quietly. "I don't want to leave. I don't want it to end . . ." She paused, her eyes filling with tears as she felt her pent-up emotions surge forward. "I'm finally happy again."

She felt Priamos place his hands on her shoulders, she looked up at him.

"Then don't leave." He thought for a moment. "Stay until the baby is born. It's only a few months, a blink in your life, and if you don't feel anything at the end of that time then you can leave. But give it more than four or five days before you make your decision."

"I want to, but Athena . . ."

"Leave her to me. He may be her favorite son, but I have some tricks up my sleeve. She just wants him to be happy. If she sees how I see him look at you, then she will understand. Now go to him and tell him your decision."

"I will stay until the baby is born."

"Good."

He smiled and she nodded as they mounted their horses and rode back to the villa. When they arrived, Athena was in the main courtyard. She did not look pleased.

Cassiopeia looked at Priamos. "I'm pretty sure that is directed at you."

"I don't know . . . you've been bad, too." He winked at her, she smiled back, blushing lightly and rolling her eyes.

"You two just think you can skip out on half the day? Where have you been?" Athena said angrily.

Priamos walked up to Athena, placing his hand on her tummy and looking at her.

"I am sorry my dear, I went for a ride to clear my head. Then I found this beautiful damsel in distress, who I just had to rescue, and then she said she felt like a party, so I brought her back here."

Athena was not amused. She gave Cassiopeia a look.

"What?" Cassiopeia said with a shrug. "I left by myself and found a man in the woods who claimed he lived here. I told him he was crazy, but he insisted. I guess I was wrong. Or perhaps you just let strange men touch your belly."

Athena rolled her eyes. "Now I know why I used to hate being at camp with the two of you."

They laughed as Athena shook her head and walked away, Priamos beside her. Cassiopeia flashed to Demetrius' room, but it was empty. He must be at the arena for the festivities. She bathed, fixed her hair, changed her clothes, and headed over to the festivities to tell him her decision.

As Cassiopeia entered the noble's booth at the arena, she looked at Demetrius' empty seat. Athena and Priamos were already in their seats as the spar was about to start. When she looked out at the field, she realized why he wasn't in his seat; he was fighting. They had just begun and were still circling each other, throwing testing jabs.

Priamos spoke. "Sit my dear. Enjoy the fight."

Athena said nothing, she didn't even look at her. Priamos gave her a look that told her not to say anything, so she sat. Cassiopeia watched as the two men dodged and jabbed at each other, each trying to land a blow. They were using metal practice swords, which gave the weight and feel of real swords but had duller edges. They still hurt to get hit with and could still cut if enough force was applied or at the right angle. She watched the two men dance with their swords. Fighting was always an art to her. The beauty and grace of two people trying to both touch and dodge each other at the same time always gave her a rush. Her only problem was that she would lose control in the dance and not stop.

As they fought, Demetrius looked up to the stand and spotted her watching. He hesitated. Cassiopeia's eyes widened as she watched his opponent take that opportunity to get in a blow. He sliced his sword across Demetrius' bicep, Demetrius wincing in pain as he pulled away. Cassiopeia stood. She felt Priamos kick her foot, but she ignored him as she stepped forward to stand with her hands on the banister of the balcony. She watched as Demetrius babied his arm for a moment, blood dripping down to the sand. He decided it wasn't that bad and continued the fight, but he was more aggressive now. Cassiopeia couldn't take her eyes off of him as she felt herself filling with concern. She heard movement and turned to see Athena get up and leave. When she went to say something, Priamos stopped her. Cassiopeia realized that she just exposed her feelings to Athena.

"I told her after we got back, and she didn't believe me until she saw it for herself." Priamos said.

"I should go after her."

"No. Give her space and time to digest it. She will forgive you. Technically I don't think she needs to forgive you; I think she just needs to accept it. She'll come around. Oh . . ." Priamos winced as he looked out to the field.

She turned quickly, just in time to see Demetrius pin his opponent to the ground, sword at his throat. Cassiopeia closed her eyes as she felt a sense of relief wash over her. When she opened them, he was looking at her.

She heard Priamos clapping and cheering. "My boy! The champion! As strong of a warrior as me and his mother!"

The crowd was cheering, but she could barely hear them over her own heart pounding. She watched as Demetrius bowed to them and turned to leave the arena, waiting a few moments before she left as well. When Cassiopeia walked into the small medical tent, Demetrius' back was to her, as he was unclipping his left vambrace to lift his sleeve and get to the wound.

"I need you to tend to this quickly."

He thought she was the medic. She heard the metal vambrace hit the table and he turned around, eyes widening in surprise when he saw her. Before he could speak, she walked up, grabbed his cheeks and kissed him. Her lips urgently needed his as her tongue explored his mouth. He moaned at her sudden gesture. Her kiss was passionate, but he could feel her emotional need. She pulled away and just looked at him, her eyes trailing down to his arm. She turned his arm over, looking at the wound. It wasn't as bad as she thought it was. It just bled a lot. She grabbed the bowl of water and a rag and began to clean the area. He stayed silent, watching her tend to him. For some reason, her very simple gesture gave him an intense feeling of intimacy. After she cleaned the wound, she grabbed the gauze and wrapped it tightly, seeing him lightly flinch when she pulled it tight around the injury. She pulled his sleeve back down when she was done and looked up at him. She could see a flurry of emotions in his mesmerizing blue eyes.

He spoke first. "Are you ready to talk to me?"

"I saw Priamos on my ride."

Demetrius didn't respond.

"We talked . . ."

Demetrius was holding his breath, bracing himself for her to leave and to never see her again.

"I've decided to stay until the baby is born—but only if Athena agrees to it, and I will have my own room. No exceptions to either."

He felt his stomach jump and his heart soar at her words, but he kept his face and demeanor stoic. Cassiopeia could see the gleam of excitement in his eyes at her answer.

He nodded his head. "Whatever the goddess requests, she shall have."

She lowered her composure for a moment, smirking and shaking her head, then her serious expression quickly returning.

"We will speak with Athena today."

He nodded and leaned to kiss her again, but before he reached, her someone opened the tent.

"Oh. I'm sorry my lord, I came to tend to your wound. I can come back."

Cassiopeia stepped back from him. "No, it's fine. I have things I need to see to."

The young girl gasped, bowing. "Goddess, it is an honor."

Cassiopeia ignored her and walked out, giving one last look to Demetrius before she left the tent. He wanted to follow but he didn't want to raise suspicions. Inside though, he was jumping up and down cheering at his emotional victory.

As Demetrius walked proudly back to his room to change out of his armor and sweaty clothes, he heard yelling in the main hall. He stopped, hearing Athena's voice. He walked toward the main doors quickly to listen. He heard Cassiopeia as well.

"I didn't expect this," Cassiopeia said.

"So that's why you lied to me? You kept secrets in my own home! I trusted you!"

"Honey, please calm down and sit. Just listen." Priamos tried to calm his angry partner.

Cassiopeia spoke. "I hated him when we met. He was pompous and naive, rude and cocky, but . . . I don't know, something changed. He became different. What was just drunken sex has become something more."

"Do you have feelings for him?" Athena asked.

"Yes."

"Do you love him?"

Demetrius waited nervously for Cassiopeia to answer. He hated eavesdropping, but now he couldn't walk away.

"Honestly . . . I don't know. I've never loved before," Cassiopeia admitted. The whole room was silent. You could cut the tension in the room with a knife. Cassiopeia spoke again. "It's your choice Athena. If you say no, I will respect your wishes and go. No arguments. No fighting. I will leave and not return."

Demetrius couldn't stand in the hall anymore. His stomach dropped at the thought of her leaving forever. He walked into the room and looked at his mother. Her face looked tensed and stressed. As she looked at him, slightly surprised by his intrusion, her expression softened into one of love and heartache. Cassiopeia turned around to see him. He knew he shouldn't intrude, but he was involved too, and he should have his opinion heard.

"Mother, please."

Athena looked torn. She stayed quiet, looking at her son.

Priamos spoke, quietly touching her arm. "This is not a democracy, my dear. You are the queen here and your vote is all that matters."

Athena took a deep breath, looking back to Cassiopeia. Anger returned to her expression, but Cassiopeia could see a tinge of sadness.

"You may stay until the baby is born and then we will speak about it again. I can choose for you to leave at any time—no arguments from either party. You will have your own quarters and your demon may not be on the grounds for extended periods. You are not to take Demetrius to Vēlatusa or off of the villa grounds without my explicit permission. No using massive surges of your powers, but you may come and go as you please. Zeus does not need to know of any of this. It would just anger him. If word gets back to Olympus, there is nothing I can do to protect anyone. Does everyone understand and agree?"

Demetrius nodded his head, a small smile forming at the edge of his lips. Cassiopeia also nodded her head in understanding and agreement. Zeus barely tolerated her friendship with Athena, and he would see any relationship between her and someone from his pantheon as a direct betrayal. He liked to be in control, and he would find any way possible to exploit their relationship if he thought he could use it to control her and benefit himself. That included endangering his demigod grandson.

Athena wasn't done, she turned her head to look at Priamos.

"You too, I don't want to be in another argument over this matter."

He laughed lightly. "I don't argue, I negotiate," Priamos said slyly.

Athena rolled her eyes. She turned to leave the hall.

As she walked past her, Cassiopeia whispered, "Thank you."

"This means nothing. You are not forgiven. Forgiveness is earned and this is a big one. I am agreeing to this for my son, not for you." Athena pulled away and left.

Priamos followed her, leaving Cassiopeia and Demetrius alone in the main hall. Cassiopeia should have felt victorious and happy, but instead she was racked with guilt and hurt. Demetrius closed the space between them. He placed a hand on her shoulder. She went to shrug away, but he wrapped his arms around her, pulling her in. She hadn't been hugged like this since she was a child, just pulled to someone to be held.

She closed her eyes as she rested her head on his armor chest plate. "Why do I feel like I did something wrong? Why am I so racked with guilt? I don't want to be."

"Would you be feeling guilty if you had left? Would you have a pit in your stomach if you had said goodbye and left me forever?"

She pulled her head away and looked up into his light blue eyes. "Yes."

He leaned his head down and kissed her, groaning slightly at the feel of her against him as she ran her hand up to rest on his neck and jaw.

He pulled away reluctantly, looking down at her beautiful face he spoke. "Maybe we shouldn't be so public."

"We can't be public at all. Another god can't see us and take word back to Zeus."

Demetrius went to pull away, but she used the hand resting on his neck to push his head down, kissing him again, deeper and full of need. When she pulled away, he looked around and they were in his room. Her eyes were filled with a heated playfulness. Demetrius smiled slyly, knowing exactly what Cassiopeia wanted to do to him.

The months went by in a blur. Cassiopeia was set up in her own quarters, but by the time the baby was born, she was living in Demetrius' rooms. She hadn't slept in her own quarters in over a month. They weren't forward about it, but they also hadn't been discreet. Cassiopeia had felt a whirlwind of emotions over the past few months, all of which she never wanted to go away. Their relationship had evolved into something deeply emotional.

Athena hadn't said anything about their relationship since the day she allowed her to stay. The two goddesses had spoken on only a few occasions, and only as acquaintances. Athena's baby boy was only a few days old when Athena asked to speak with Cassiopeia.

Cassiopeia walked into Athena's quarters warily. The Greek goddess was still on bed rest for the next few days, tending to her newborn son, who was sleeping in the bassinet a few feet from the bed.

"Athena, you wished to see me."

Cassiopeia knew what this conversation was going to be about, and she already knew how she wanted it to end. She wanted to be with Demetrius. She couldn't even imagine leaving him or being without him in her life. Athena sat up slowly as she looked at her friend. She hated how everything had transpired between Cassiopeia and Demetrius, but she knew that they hadn't done it out of malice or spite. They had simply fallen for each other.

"I said we would speak about it again after the baby was born."

"Technically he's not born until he is named and that doesn't happen until tomorrow."

Athena gave her an irritated yet amused look. "Really?" Her eyebrow raised.

Cassiopeia walked up and sat at the end of the bed, looking at her friend. "I miss you."

Athena looked away, but she also felt the same way. It had been difficult for her to live with one of her closest friends and not spend time with her. "You hurt me."

"I know, and that was never my intention. I didn't want this, but now that I have it . . ."

"You don't want to let it go."

Cassiopeia looked at Athena. "Exactly." She looked down at her hands. "I love him."

Athena reached out and grabbed her hand. "He will only hurt you. He will grow old and you will stay the same as you watch him die. If you have children, you will have to watch them die too. One day you will have to let him go. You need to know that."

"You want me to leave."

"No." Athena looked into her eyes. "I only want you to know the truth before you commit yourself to this journey. It will feel amazing in the moment, but when you step back in thirty or forty years it will be the deepest cut."

A tear rolled down Cassiopeia's cheek. "I understand, and I accept that."

"Then it is your choice. You have my blessings and my friendship. I only have one request. Don't let him denounce the Greek pantheon. I would like to see my son in the afterlife."

Cassiopeia understood. If she wanted him to become immortal the only way was to give him ambrosia from Olympus, which only Zeus could grant. If he renounced the Greek pantheon and swore allegiance to the Atlantean, she could give him elixir from the Atlantean tree of life and make him immortal. But if he took it, then he would go to the Atlantean underworld if he ever died and not the Greek underworld. Athena would never be able to see him again. Athena squeezed her hand and Cassiopeia pulled her gently into a hug.

Athena smiled. "Welcome to the big, fucked-up Greek family." They laughed. "I would like to speak with my son before you tell him your decision."

Cassiopeia nodded her head and got up, leaving Athena to her newborn babe.

Cassiopeia flashed to the arena, standing hidden behind a pillar of the entryway. She watched Demetrius and Priamos sparring. She could tell that Demetrius was holding back on his blows, so as not to injure his father. Priamos was nearing his fifties, but he was still a formidable opponent. A servant walked out into the arena and the two men stopped fighting. The servant spoke with Demetrius and they both left, leaving Priamos alone. Cassiopeia could hear Priamos yelling something about Demetrius not having to make an excuse for needing a break and she smiled. She saw Priamos lower his strong facade as Demetrius left, putting his hand on his sore shoulder. He paused, sensing being watched. When he turned, she had flashed to right behind him.

She smirked. "I thought I felt someone watching me. If you're looking for Demetrius, he just went to go see his mother."

"I saw him leave. I already spoke with Athena."

He gave her a look. "Obviously it went well if you are still here. Or are you saying goodbye?"

"She said she wanted to speak with him first, before I told him my decision."

Priamos looked toward the villa, almost worried. "You know she's going to try to scare him. To convince him to let you go."

"And if she succeeds, then it was never meant to be, and I had a wonderful stay in your home. If he feels the same as I do, then nothing she can say will change his mind. She only made me realize something that I am going to have to do."

He looked confused. "What?"

"I'm going to have to set up a meeting with Zeus. After Demetrius and I talk about it, of course."

Priamos shook his head, knowing she was going to try to get ambrosia.

"He really captured your heart, didn't he?"

She nodded. "Very much so."

Cassiopeia looked up and saw as Demetrius rounded the corner of the entrance to the arena. She could tell he had been running. His hair was disheveled, and she could see a sheen of sweat on his brow. Cassiopeia walked toward him, but he didn't hold his composure as well. Demetrius ran the final steps to her and scooped her up in his arms, spinning as she laughed lightly. He set her down, looking into her eyes, his own sparkling in the sun like two pools of water. He placed his hand on the nape of her neck and pulled her into a kiss. As he pulled away, he pressed their foreheads together.

"I love you."

Her heart fluttered at his words. Even though she knew in her heart, he had never said it out loud before.

She smiled and closed her eyes taking in this moment. "I love you too."

Chapter 8

Future Plans

3578 BCE

There is only one way to get ready for immortality, and that is to love this life and live it as bravely and faithfully and cheerfully as we can.
—Henry Van Dyke

emetrius had been called back to the front lines after his many successful battles against the Persians. He had, over the years, proved himself to be just as formidable an opponent as his father before him.

He rode into the Greek encampment with only a few soldiers by his side. His mother was going to be here for the battle in a few days but didn't feel the need to oversee his planning. Priamos was sitting this battle out, as he had officially retired, becoming a counselor for war advice to men and gods alike. Cassiopeia had been in Vēlatusa when he got called back to the field. She had been gone for a week, planning on being gone for another fortnight, and he knew she would be upset that he left without telling her. But at the same time, he didn't want her to worry and sit over him the entire battle. He was his own man and he could do this on his own. She would find his note, or his father would tell her where he was when she returned—if he was still gone. Demetrius was hoping to be back long before she came back. He stopped in front of the main war tent and dismounted from his horse, walking inside. His advisors and captains were already there. He looked over their plan, changed a few details and discussed their current situation with them. Most of the men were curious whether his mother was going to be fighting with them.

"It would be a great advantage to have Athena by our side."

"It would really raise morale."

Then he heard a comment that made his heart jump and his stomach twist.

"What about the Atlantean goddess? I heard she fights like no other."

"And she's got a body that just begs to be touched."

The men around him laughed, but he felt his blood begin to boil at their crude comments.

"That's enough! If one of the goddesses decides to fight alongside us, then so be it. But if they do, you will treat them with the *utmost* respect. Am I understood?"

The men picked up on his deadly serious tone, nodding around him.

"We shall recheck the numbers tomorrow and finalize the plan before the battle," Demetrius said dismissively.

They all dispersed, and Demetrius headed toward his tent. No one knew of his relationship with Cassiopeia. They had kept it very secret, not wanting Zeus or any of the other gods to discover it. They had decided to wait a few years before going to Zeus to try to get the ambrosia. Just because his mother had accepted their relationship, it didn't mean that the other gods would approve. Those that didn't like their union could be a threat, using him against Cassiopeia. They had both been itching to become public with their relationship but knew that, with him as a mortal, the risks outweighed the benefits. So, they waited as the years passed.

Demetrius' tent had been set up for him before he had arrived. There was a large simple bed, a wide table to be used as a desk or for dining, and a small vanity with a washing bowl. He knew if Cassiopeia was here, she would be complaining that there was no full-size tub. He smiled just thinking about her. They had become so much closer and stronger together over these last few years, the best of his life. He woke almost every morning to the woman he loved and went to bed at night with her by his side. She wasn't too overbearing, but she also didn't stay distant. They were two sides of a coin that perfectly balanced one another.

Demetrius changed from his travel clothes to something more comfortable and nicer for the evening's festivities. He didn't throw parties as extravagant as his father, but he did allow musicians and dancers for his men to enjoy, to help relieve the stress before the battle. Before, he would have partaken in enjoying the women as well, but he had his heart and body set aside for another who wasn't here. Demetrius went to the main dining tent, following the sound of the music and drunken laughter.

Cassiopeia appeared in their quarters at Priamos' villa early with a surprise for Demetrius. One they had been worried and talked about for a long time. She had only been gone just over a week, but she couldn't get her mind off of him. When she called out his name there was no response.

He must be out, she thought.

Looking over at the mannequin that usually held his armor, Cassiopeia noticed that the armor was gone. She was about to go to the arena when she saw a note on the table. Opening it, she read that he had gone to lead a battle and left her a heartfelt letter. Cassiopeia could feel her eyes flash to red before she regained control. She heard Priamos' voice carrying up from the garden.

Priamos was walking through the gardens with his son, Markus, who looked like a small version of the general. The little boy was growing so quickly, Cassiopeia didn't realize where the time went. She flashed down to the gardens but stayed back, watching Priamos interacting with his young son. Markus was only three years of age, but she could already tell that he was smart and quick like his father and mother.

She suddenly felt a desire to have that, to raise a baby into a child and then into their own person. Cassiopeia had never had a want or need for a child. Being a mother never interested her, but she felt something inside of her changing. She had a sudden curiosity about what it felt like to feel a tiny life growing inside and watching the small being that she created grow. Would her children look more like her or Demetrius?

As she was daydreaming about the future, she heard Priamos clear his throat. He was only ten feet away from her.

"Are you going to stare at me all day, or did you come to speak? In all honesty, I don't mind either interaction—but the staring is getting a little unnerving."

Blushing slightly, she held up the letter with a very irritated look on her face.

"I see you found his note," Priamos said. "He left a few days ago. The battle should be in two days, about midday. Unless their plans changed."

"He left and didn't think I would want to talk about it first?"

Priamos gave her a look. "You fell in love with a military officer, a fighter. Did you really expect him to sit by the fire waiting for your return every time you leave? He told me to tell you to go to him if you returned before he was back. He didn't go to this battle to get away. He went because he wanted to, because the music of battle called to him. You of all people should understand not wanting to be tied down in one place."

Her expression didn't change. She was now angry at the fact that she knew Priamos was right. Little Markus ran up to her, excited to see her.

"Cassa!"

"Hello, little man."

She smiled at him as she knelt down, his excitement causing her to forget her anger, and pulled him into her arms. He hugged her back but quickly was ready to go explore the next thing and pulled away to go running down the path on to his next mission of exploration.

They laughed. Cassiopeia turned to Priamos. "Do all children have this much energy and curiosity?"

"Energy, yes. Curiosity varies from child to child. Demetrius would never wander far from me or his mother. Markus, on the other hand, has no fear of the unknown."

She smiled and they followed after little Markus, enjoying the moment.

Cassiopeia continued their previous conversation. "So, I'm being foolish and unreasonable by being upset." It was a mixture between a question and a statement.

"No, you are being his partner, someone who worries about him. I, of all people, understand how you feel. Here *I* am sitting by the fire waiting for his return." He winked at her, laughing lightly.

"Is Athena with him?"

"I don't believe so. She was talking about joining him the last time we spoke, but she said she had other duties she needed to take care of first."

As if hearing them speaking of her, Athena appeared next to them. She looked like she had been in a hurry and looked at Cassiopeia suspiciously. "What were you doing on Olympus?"

Cassiopeia rolled her eyes. "I find it interesting how Zeus tells me not to speak of our meeting to anyone, but somehow the word always gets around the mountain."

"You didn't answer my question."

Cassiopeia held her hand out and manifested the small jar that Zeus had given her. The second Athena laid eyes on it she knew what it was. Ambrosia. Priamos only had to look at Athena's expression to know as well.

"How?" Priamos asked.

"Honestly I don't completely know. He asked for a meeting and he said that he wanted peace between our pantheons and, to show a sign of good faith, he gave it to me. He said he would ensure the ambrosia was delivered every week on the same day at the same time."

"You trusted him?" Athena asked in disbelief.

"No, I didn't, but then he swore to it before me and Hera. I didn't tell him about Demetrius. He already knew."

Athena looked away, confused.

"Why?" she whispered under her breath.

"Every week on the same day, at the same time, ambrosia will be delivered—for as long as Demetrius lives. That was what he swore on his life. Demetrius has been accepted as an earthly member of the Greek pantheon, to defend their power on Earth but not to exceed those duties. Zeus seemed upset about it. As if he was being forced but, Athena, does it matter why? We have talked about this for years. This is what we hoped for but thought would never happen."

Athena looked at Priamos.

"You can have your son forever. I know in your heart you want this." Priamos said quietly.

Athena looked over to Markus, who was unaware of the intensity of their conversation. Cassiopeia could see pain in her eyes.

"There is enough for two. Demetrius doesn't need to take it every week. Every other week could suffice."

Because Demetrius wouldn't be a full god, he wouldn't have any way to recharge himself. Therefore, he would have to take ambrosia every few weeks to keep his newfound powers and immortality. That is why it was incredibly important for Zeus to agree to deliver it for the rest of Demetrius' life.

Priamos shook his head at Cassiopeia. "It's not that easy. I never wanted to become immortal. I have seen the burden that it has taken on you two and I never desired to feel that weight. As for Markus, he may choose differently when he is older, but I will raise him the same way Demetrius was raised, without the hope of ambrosia to lengthen his life. If this is what Demetrius wants, which I truly believe that it is, then I am happy for you and my son. One day we can have another discussion about Markus—if that is still an option."

Athena nodded in agreement.

"I feel the same. Zeus truly swore it?"

"Yes, I felt the magic bond him to it. But, it is still Demetrius' choice if he wishes to take it."

"Well, let's go to Demetrius to deliver the good news. We can celebrate by fighting the Persians in two days."

Athena held her hand out to Cassiopeia and pulled her into a tight hug. Their friendship had become more than just that of friends. They had truly become family. They had a bond that they would keep forever.

Athena released her. "You should tell him alone. It's something that is personal between the two of you."

Cassiopeia nodded and Athena flashed her to the war camp to search for Demetrius.

The men told Demetrius that they had a surprise for him when he entered the dining tent, but he was not amused. They had wanted to blindfold him, but he had refused, and they were thoroughly entertained by his squirming. Suddenly the music stopped, and everyone got silent as it changed to a more rhythmic beat, many of the men giving Demetrius a sly grin. Then he saw her. He could tell she was Greek, but she was dressed as a Persian whore. Most of her body was exposed through sheer material as she gazed at him seductively. He felt his mouth go dry as he realized what his *surprise* was. She was beautiful, but this was not a surprise he wanted. This was not the woman he wanted. She swayed and danced her way to him. She was only a few feet away when he started to rise, but he felt two hands on his shoulders push him back down. He saw the girl's eyes widen as she looked at the person behind him. The music and talking stopped, the men all looking shocked by the new guest. He looked at the small feminine hands on his shoulder and felt his stomach jump, knowing exactly who was behind him.

"Oh, don't stop on my behalf. I was profoundly enjoying the show." Cassiopeia leaned down and he felt her breath on his ear. "So seductive, don't you think, Colonel Demetrius?"

Her soft, melodic voice made him break out in chills, as his groin jumped. Demetrius didn't answer. As he closed his eyes and took a deep breath, the edges of his lips twitched as he held back a smirk. Cassiopeia was toying with him. She wasn't mad because she knew how uncomfortable he was. Now, this was a game for her, and she liked to play games. Her voice got quieter, so only he could hear her.

"Did you really think I would be content with just a letter?" She pressed her hands down firmly on his shoulders and spoke louder. "Stay."

He felt her hands slide off his shoulders and across his back as she walked around his chair. She looked heavenly. She was in a simple, short, light blue and white peplos, her hair falling down over her shoulders in light curls. There was a glint in her eyes as she looked him over, ensuring he would stay. He could see the smirk she was also trying to hide.

Cassiopeia then turned to the dancer, and as she approached her, a golden drachma appeared between her fingers, which she held aloft. The woman was awestruck by the coin, for to her that was a large payment. Cassiopeia pushed it against her own lips as she looked at the woman then to Demetrius. She bit her lip and stood next to the woman and held the drachma out a few inches in front of her, putting her lips to the dancer's cheek. She looked back to Demetrius and his stomach dropped as he heard her next words roll off her lips.

"Make. Me. Jealous."

She winked at Demetrius before she tucked the coin into the woman's cleavage and manifested a goblet of wine and a small throne to sit in and watch. The music started again, and the dancer continued where she had been before the interruption, more determined than before. Demetrius could see the men whispering and snickering. He tried to rise but he felt an unknown force holding him down. When he looked at Cassiopeia, he could see the smirk that she was no longer trying to hide.

As the dancer reached him, he tensed. She swayed against him, rubbing her body against his. He knew one way he could get back at Cassiopeia right now, as she was watching closely, enjoying his squirming. He reluctantly relaxed and put his hands on the dancer's hips, never breaking eye contact with Cassiopeia. He saw her amusement turn into a small smile. He ran his hands from the dancer's hips and down to her buttocks and then her thighs. He then ran his hands back up.

The men were whooping and cheering, but they were a distant noise in her head as she watched him. He was playing a dangerous game, but he knew it. Since she was going to make him squirm, he was going to get back at her by making her do the same. Little did he know, it was turning her on even more. She bit her lip. The dancer turned around in Demetrius' lap and he ran his hands up to her breasts, kneading and teasing them, all while continuing to keep eye contact with Cassiopeia. They were dancing on the line of who would break first, when the dancer leaned back against him and turned her head to capture his lips, Demetrius watched Cassiopeia look away. He felt her powers release him from the chair. The game was over. He had won. Demetrius gently pushed the dancer away, her expression upset and confused, and he stalked over to Cassiopeia's chair. He leaned over her, bracing his hands on the armrests and placed his lips on her ear.

"My tent, *now*," he growled quietly, the baritone in his voice rumbling through her body, setting her on fire.

The music had stopped, and the men grew completely silent. Demetrius walked out of the dining tent. Cassiopeia looked over her shoulder and could see the tension in each step he took. She smirked. She liked it when he was stirred up. It made him more demanding, more heated. When she looked around, remembering she wasn't alone, the men were staring at her, not knowing what to do.

"Music?" she said.

The band regained their senses and began to play again. The dancer still looked confused, not knowing if she had earned her pay, but Cassiopeia waved for her to go.

Cassiopeia toyed with a piece of her hair; she was waiting. She wanted him to steam for a moment before she followed. Glancing over at her wine, she saw it was half full. She knew the men were still watching her closely, but they had begun to return to the conversations amongst themselves. Cassiopeia lifted her goblet to her lips and drained the rest of her wine. She set the goblet down and stood. The music continued, but no one said a word as she stalked out of the tent after her prey.

When Cassiopeia entered his tent, she didn't see him there. She looked around for a moment, then heard movement behind her, and someone grabbed her arms, twisting her around quickly. She looked up into his aggressive light blue eyes. They seemed to glow in the dim lighting. Demetrius pulled her to him, kissing her roughly, growling at the feel and taste of her lips. Cassiopeia reciprocated, her tongue dancing against his. She tried to put her hand on his cheek but he held her arms to her sides. He stepped closer to her, pushing her backward toward the bed.

He pulled his lips away from hers. "Move."

"I don't know if I'm in the mood for sex, especially after seeing you kiss another. Maybe you should ask her."

He looked at her slyly. "She would be scared of the things I want to do to you. Now, don't make me have to carry you over to the bed."

Cassiopeia felt herself becoming more heated at his words. He pushed her lightly, and this time she obliged. When they reached the bed, he turned her around and pinned her body against his with one arm while he trailed kissed up and down her neck and ear, the smell of her perfume filling his head. He reached up and unfastened the ties of her peplos. Sliding his hand down her body, he slipped the cloth down, then removed her undergarments. Demetrius turned her back around and looked at her and the body that he had become so familiar with. She was completely naked, while he was still completely dressed. He smiled at his luck. Of all the people she could love, she chose him. And she didn't want him change, she loved him for himself. He became serious again.

"You come here and try to embarrass me in front of my men," he chided. "What happened to having discretion?"

"No regrets," she said with a tone of defiance and a glint in her eyes.

Demetrius turned her back around, and when she couldn't see his face he smirked lightly. He pushed her onto the bed with her feet still on the floor. She groaned lightly as she hit the soft bed. He unclasped his belt and lifted his chiton. He was already hard for her. Placing his hand on her back, he pinned her down and pressed the tip of himself against her core, feeling her wetness.

Cassiopeia moaned in anticipation as he rubbed against her. He let go of his manhood and smacked her buttocks, just hard enough to startle her. She yelped in surprise. He rubbed the spot that was now pinkening. He smacked her again, but this time her whimper was quieter. When he lined himself up with her body, he spanked her once more as he plunged into her at the same time. Her gasp turned into a cry of pleasure, and he continued to thrust against her. Demetrius could see his handprints lightly forming on her cheeks before his eyes rolled back into his head and the feel of her body around him consumed his mind. He leaned down and kissed her shoulders and neck. Cassiopeia moaned at his touch. He squeezed her sore bottom and he heard her hiss, watching her bite her lip.

"See what happens when you don't listen?" He watched as her eyes rolled back.

"Yes, Demetrius."

He loved the sound of his name on her lips. He pulled away from her as she groaned in protest.

"Roll over."

She quickly obeyed. He grabbed her hips and slid her down to the edge of the bed. She looked up at him with dusky, lust-filled eyes. Demetrius lined himself up with her and plunged in roughly, her body tensing around him. He kneaded and toyed with her breasts as their bodies joined in the throes of passion. He could feel her tightening around him as she was getting closer to climax. Smiling, he took one hand and moved it down to her core, just above where they were joined. She buckled as he found what he was looking for and rubbed against her with his thumb. Cassiopeia gasped as fire built inside her. Suddenly her body exploded in pleasure as she cried out and quivered around him, pushing him over the edge to his own climax only a few moments later. Demetrius felt the quivers of sensitivity and heat wash over him. It was bigger and more intense than usual, as it had been a while since they had been together. He fell down on top of her, resting on his elbows shakily, quivering at the intensity of his climax. She ran her hands up and down his torso, causing him to break out in chills as he regained control of himself. He buried his face into her neck and breathed in her scent, enjoying her presence.

"I missed you. You're back early."

"I am back early for a reason."

Demetrius pulled himself off of her and laid on the bed on his back next to her. She rolled over and looked at him, excitement in her eyes.

"I have a surprise for you!" Cassiopeia kissed him quickly, then stood and an Atlantean robe appeared on her body. She turned around to face him. Demetrius looked over at her, content with staying bare to her, pulling his peplos to just above his hips as he put his hands behind his head. She smirked at his confident stance and shook her head.

"I don't mind one bit, but if your mother decides to stop by, I don't think she will be as entertained as I am with your bareness. We can always wait and see."

"What?" he groaned. "You know I hate surprises." He sat up quickly and looked at her, confused by her words. What surprise would she have that involved his mother wanting to be here?

"You didn't seem to mind your last one." Her eyebrow rose as she toyed with him over the dance he had just received.

Demetrius shook his head and groaned, rubbing his face. He was not excited about seeing his men tomorrow after their little public flirting episode. He didn't know how he was going to explain it away. Their relationship was supposed to be completely secret.

"We are supposed to be discreet. Usually I'm not the one telling you this. How am I supposed to explain this to my men?" He asked as he rose from the bed and adjusted his peplos to cover himself.

"Just tell them the truth . . . that we are engaged to be married in the summer."

He looked at her like she had lost her mind. "Because that wouldn't tip Zeus off about our secret relationship. My mother will be thrilled."

Cassiopeia got serious. "Zeus already knows."

Demetrius froze in front of the table where he was pouring a cup of water. He turned around and looked at her, fear and worry in his eyes. "How? We've been careful."

She walked over to him. "I don't know exactly how he found out, but he gave me this."

Cassiopeia held her hand out and the small jar appeared in her palm. Demetrius looked at it confused, but she watched when realization crossed his face as he put the pieces together. He looked up at her as she removed the lid. Inside was a golden liquid that looked like honey but smelled like home, like the smells of his childhood. It seemed to be swirling on its own inside of the small crystal jar.

"Why? Is that enough?"

"I don't know exactly why. He told me that he was trying to establish peace between our people and wanted to show a sign of good faith. He swore to have someone bring ambrosia for you every week on the same day at the same time. Demetrius, he swore it which means it must be done. He cannot go back on his word." She gently placed the jar into his hands and cupped hers under his, looking up at him. "We can be married. We don't have to hide anymore. Demetrius," she placed one of her hands on his chin and cheek, "we can be together, forever, without having to worry or sneak around in secret."

Demetrius looked at the woman he loved and couldn't imagine having her suffer a day without him. He closed his eyes and focused, reaching out and praying to his mother. They both felt a shift in the tent, and he opened his eyes to find Athena standing in the tent. She looked at the small jar in their hands.

"Demetrius." Her eyes were full of emotion. "It is your choice my son."

"I have already decided my choice. I just wanted you to be here for it."

She walked over and Cassiopeia took a step back from Demetrius. He began to bring the jar to his lips but hesitated and lowered it. He looked worried.

"What if we have children? Will we have to watch them die?"

Athena stepped forward and put her hand on his arm. "No, my son, with both of you being immortal your children would also have immortality. They would be gods and goddesses in their own right. With their own powers flowing through their veins."

They had never discussed having children, due to the fact that Cassiopeia couldn't watch her children die and had never had the overwhelming desire to even have them. But, now that they had all of the time in the world and the fact that their children would be immortal, it was a possibility.

Demetrius looked back to her and raised the jar to his lips, drinking the golden liquid. It flowed smoothly down his throat, and he felt a warmth wash over him. He downed it all and lowered the jar from his lips. He waited to feel a change, but nothing dramatic happened. Athena tightened her hand around his arm. He then felt his stomach beginning to burn and he groaned, falling to his knees. The warmth that washed over him was now turning into fire. It flowed through his veins and covered his entire body. His groan turned into a cry of pain. Demetrius barely even felt Cassiopeia wrap her arms around his body as she held him close. She was whispering into his ear, but he couldn't hear her over the pounding of his own heart.

Then her words broke through. "I will be here when you awaken in the morning, my love."

He then succumbed to the darkness that consumed him.

Demetrius awoke on his bed in the war tent. He went to sit up quickly but was stopped by Cassiopeia's body laying over his arm. His sudden movement woke her with a start. He wiggled out from under her and sat at the edge of the bed, his hands on his knees. He felt like he should be sore from what happened yesterday, but he felt great. His body felt fully charged, like he could run for days or defeat anyone. Cassiopeia placed her hand on his shoulder, and he felt a sexual fire on his skin at her touch. His body was on high alert and all of his senses felt heightened.

"How do you feel? It will take a few days to get used to, at least that's what Athena said. This is a first for me too."

Her voice sounded more melodic than it usually did, it was as if her words caressed his heart. He could easily hear her Atlantean accent even though he knew she was hiding it.

Demetrius turned and looked at her. She was holding the sheets to cover her body, but her skin seemed to glow in the light. Her eyes had a light behind them that he had never noticed before. Even her hair had a glow to it as it flowed like strands of gold down here back. She didn't even look real. He reached out and touched her cheek. She closed her eyes and smiled. Her skin felt softer than usual in his hand, and he felt as though he could feel the life coursing through her veins. It was as though his eyes had been truly opened for the first time.

When she turned her head and kissed his wrist, his whole body lit up in desire, her touch causing a chain reaction through him. Unable to resist, he leaned over and kissed her. He moaned deeply as her lips felt like velvet against his and her perfume filled his head, making him dizzy. Demetrius couldn't believe the things he was feeling from a simple kiss. Usually her lips took his breath away, but this was different, more intense. Cassiopeia laughed against his lips as he deepened their embrace, leaning over and climbing on top of her. He trailed his lips from hers down her neck and throat. It was as if he could taste the powers that ran through her veins on her skin.

"All of your senses are overly heightened. It will take a couple days before they settle down."

He barely heard her words as his head swirled, filled with her. Her scent, her touch, her taste, the sound of her breathing and heartbeat, she was filling every one of his senses one at a time. He tried to move the sheet, but it got caught on his leg. He groaned, wishing it wasn't there and suddenly it vanished.

She laughed. "It seems you are discovering your new powers rather quickly."

"I have powers?" His own voice sounded weird in his head. It was as if the deep baritone of his voice reverberated through his own chest.

"Some simple powers that all immortals have. You can manifest things, you can flash places, you have heightened senses, and you can reach out and feel the power of others and determine who they are. Push your mind out toward me."

Demetrius relaxed his thoughts and pushed his mind out. As he did, he felt her power. He never realized how powerful she was until he could feel it. It ebbed and flowed like a tidal wave inside of her, crashing at the walls, begging to be freed. He felt a slight, instinctive fear wash over him. Somehow, in his gut he knew she was from a pantheon different than his and that she was Atlantean.

He opened his eyes and refocused on her face. She was smiling at him, and it lit up his world. He kissed her again, this time filled with love and passion instead of lust. She moaned against his lips and he felt the sound vibrate through his body, her pleasure fueling his own. His peplos suddenly vanished off of his body, curtesy of her, and now he could feel her bare body completely against his. His whole body sang at the feeling of her softness pressed against him. He felt her separate her legs, giving him access to her core but he didn't want to just take her, he wanted to be swimming in her. Before she could object or react, he slid down her body and captured her in his mouth. Cassiopeia gasped and squirmed in surprise. He moved his tongue against her, paying attention to her body and the most sensitive areas. He felt her hand on his head, her fingers entangled in his curly blonde hair. She gasped and moaned as he brought her closer and closer to climax with just his tongue. Suddenly, she cried out loudly and he felt her wetness surge out into his mouth and he lapped up her juices. His head was swirling with her, he couldn't think or feel anything other than her. He started to lick her again, but she begged him to stop. Laughing, he kissed his way up her over-sensitive body. He captured her lips as he easily slid inside of her. Cassiopeia pulled him against her, her nails gently raking his back. His eyes rolled back into his head as he felt waves of pleasure roll over him. As he moved against her, she felt like heaven. She was better than the elysian fields. She gasped into his ear and he felt her beginning to tighten around him as she was reaching another climax. Demetrius quickened his strokes, hoping to get at least two more orgasms out of her but, as he felt her power surge against him when she came, it was too much. His whole body erupted in a firework of pleasure and overstimulation. He had never in his life felt so engulfed by one person. Cassiopeia was the only person in the world besides himself in this moment. Their powers crashed and mixed together, increasing everything they felt physically and emotionally. As his mind came back down to his body, he could barely breathe. He was gasping deeply for air. He felt her rake her fingers down his back and even that was too much for him, as he quivered and rolled off of her. He pulled her with him so that she was lying across him. As he came back to the world a little at a time, he could feel her breathing heavily against him. He wanted to hold her tighter, but he was still trying to regain his own senses and he could tell she was doing the same. After a few moments, he wrapped his arms around her, caressing her body. Demetrius heard someone outside of the tent. He reached out and felt that it was two of his head men. They began to enter without knocking and Demetrius swore under his breath. Cassiopeia laughed and manifested blankets over them, no panic or concern in her demeanor.

"Colonel Demetrius, we were sent to ensure all is well. There was a powerful disturbance somewhere near here and we wanted to verify that it wasn't an attack…" When he spotted her his voice trailed off and went silent. They bowed. "Goddess, we did not mean to disturb. We shall leave you and the colonel to your peace."

"It is fine." She snickered lightly. "We were the reason for your disturbance. We will be more careful in the future, so it doesn't happen again."

"Of course, goddess. Our apologies for the interruption." They nodded to Demetrius. "Colonel."

They quickly turned and left the tent. Cassiopeia began to giggle uncontrollably as she fell back against Demetrius' chest. He looked down at her, a little less amused, but her contagious giggles flowed over him and he couldn't help but laugh with her. He nuzzled his forehead against hers.

"We should really get out of bed sometime today. We could go spar, so that you can be used to your new powers before the battle tomorrow," she offered.

"What of the men who have seen us together? What does this mean for us moving forward?"

Cassiopeia looked up at him. She leaned away and turned around to face him. She looked nervous, which confused him because she always had an air of confidence around her. "If this is too much let me know and we can wait a little longer."

She held her hand out and manifested a small box onto her palm. When she opened it a simple golden ring was inside. As he lifted it out of the box, he saw engravings along its border. They were Atlantean in style on one edge and Greek in style on the other. The two designs intertwined in the center of the ring. Two cultures and two pantheons intertwining as one. Demetrius smiled as he put it on, and it fit perfectly.

"It's beautiful." He leaned forward and kissed her. When he pulled away, she was smiling.

"I didn't think you would want something elaborate, so I kept it simple. It's not just gold. It's Atlantean steel coated in Atlantean gold, no weapon can damage it except for the fire from an Atlantean forge. I had one made for me too, but mine is a little more elaborate and made of Greek steel and gold." Another box appeared in her hand and when she opened it, he saw that the band had the same design but hers had three stones on the top. The center stone was a black diamond and the two on the sides were red rubies.

"Beautiful, just like the woman who will wear it." He took the ring out of the box and, grabbing her hand, he slid the ring smoothly onto her finger. "I don't want to wait another day hiding what I feel," he said.

"Good, because I don't want to hide my love anymore either."

Chapter 9

A Pantheon is Born
2037 BCE

Let us sacrifice our today so that our children can have a better tomorrow.
—A. P. J. Abdul Kalam

Cassiopeia was in her family's new villa. They had built it many years ago as a place where they could both feel at home. Demetrius wasn't a fan of living on Vēlatusa, and because of her childhood, she didn't mind. Having a home on Earth also kept them more in tune with the mortal realm, and they both appreciated that. It was a way to never forget Demetrius' roots. Demetrius was acting peculiar, and he had been since her birthday. She found it frustrating, especially because she had news to tell him and didn't want him to be distracted.

"Can you please tell me what has been bothering you? You are driving me crazy," she said.

Demetrius hadn't realized he had been so wrapped up in what he had learned a few weeks ago that he was acting different. He just couldn't get something he had seen off of his mind. He stood and walked over to her.

"How well do you know Alexander?" he asked.

Cassiopeia was surprised by his random question.

"Alexander? The leviathan?" Demetrius nodded. "I don't really know him at all," she said. "I suppose no one does. I've met him only on a few occasions outside of council meetings. I would consider us distant friends, more so acquaintances." She could see in Demetrius' eyes that had not answered his question to his satisfaction.

She huffed. "The first time I met him was the night of the ball before his people made the prediction about my family. Then I met him when I lost control of my powers, I saw him when my brother was resurrected, and I helped save his life against demons years ago—thousands of years ago. I've only seen him for short moments on very few occasions since then outside of council meetings. So why the question?"

"No reason. Just curious."

"Did you talk to him? Did he say something?"

"No, I'm just . . . it's nothing."

He stepped toward her and kissed her forehead before pulling her into a hug. She accepted his embrace, still confused by the unusual question.

Demetrius let go of her and looked into her eyes. "You know I love you, right?"

"Of course. And I love you. I'm just still confused about why you are acting so strange."

"It's nothing you can change my dear, I'm just distracted."

She reluctantly nodded in acceptance, but knew it was something more than just a distraction. She would figure it out and she knew exactly who to talk to. Her news would have to wait a day.

Demetrius left to go to battle. After hundreds of years of peace, Zeus had started yet another war with the Persians that they had to sacrifice themselves for. Cassiopeia stayed behind and took that chance to go figure out what had been said to bother him. A few days later, she flashed to Vēlatusa, and when she arrived, she followed the sound of clashing swords to the arena. She stopped at the entryway, still mostly out of sight of the two men fighting. Caelum and Alexander were going at each other viciously. She could see Caelum was struggling to keep up while Alexander was moving like a skilled warrior against his opponent. She knew Alexander had sensed her arrival because he looked in her direction, meeting her eyes. Caelum tried to use his distraction to overpower him, but Alexander didn't even hesitate, and in two movements Caelum was at sword point.

He was upset. "Damn it!"

"You didn't feel anything change while fighting?"

"No, I was focused."

Caelum turned, looking to where Cassiopeia had been standing, but she had flashed herself to directly behind him.

"What—"

Before he could finish, she grabbed his shoulder, dead-legged him, and shoved him to the ground. He landed flat on his back, making a grunt as he hit.

Alexander began to laugh. "You didn't sense that?"

"Obviously not," he said bitterly as he rose from the ground, wiping off the dirt.

She laughed lightly. "You should really work on your awareness to your surroundings. It will help you fight better."

"Why do I feel like everyone says doing everything better will help me with my fighting?"

"Because it does!" Both Alexander and Cassiopeia said it at the same time and laughed.

"Screw you guys. I'm going to get water." He began to walk away, then he stopped and turned to her. "Did you need me?"

"Actually no. I came to talk to Alexander."

Alexander's stomach dropped as he heard her say that. Her wanting to talk with him in private never boded well for him. Caelum nodded, not caring, and left to get water. Alexander pulled his sword out of the sand. Cassiopeia was twirling her hair nervously. It was a habit that he had noticed she resorted to when she was uncomfortable.

She turned and looked at him. "Did you talk to Demetrius?"

"No."

"Look at me."

Alexander turned and looked into her blue eyes. They pierced his soul.

"I know you're lying."

He looked away. "Fine, maybe. Depends on what he said."

"He asked me about you and how well I know you, and he's been off for the past couple weeks."

Alexander didn't know how to answer.

"Did you tell him about…"

"No!"

Cassiopeia looked out toward the stands. She suddenly felt stupid for confronting him. Even if Alexander had told him about their moment in the woods, it was centuries ago and nothing had come of it. It was just a simple moment.

She stopped twirling her hair and rubbed her temples. "I'm sorry. I shouldn't have come here. I've just felt off lately and now I feel like my husband doesn't trust me and . . . you really don't care."

She turned to leave, feeling foolish, but he reached out and touched her arm.

"I do care. It's just . . ." he looked at her, not knowing exactly how to say what he knew she needed to hear. "He loves you so much, and he found out something that he shouldn't have, and it's making him worry about things he shouldn't."

Alexander knew it wasn't the best way to put it, but he didn't know what else to say to ease her mind. He looked down, realizing he was still touching her arm, and pulled his hand away. She just stood there silent for a few moments.

"Is he going to be okay?"

"He can't tell you what he saw. I swore him to it. He just cares."

"Why would you make him swear to keep a secret from me?" she said angrily.

He closed his eyes and shook his head before looking back at her, exasperated. "I can't tell you. Just know that it's my secret to carry. I am sorry that he discovered it."

Cassiopeia didn't know what to do. She looked at the ground, trying to find words to ease her stressed mind. She just felt so lost in her own life. Everything was changing, and she didn't know how to handle it all.

She took a step back and then stopped. "I'm pregnant."

Alexander was surprised by her sudden declaration.

"Does Demetrius know?"

"No." She began to toy with her hair again. "Only me and Set's wife, Nephthys. And now you. I'm sorry! I didn't mean to pull you into my problems. I really should have told my husband first."

She twisted her wedding ring around on her finger.

Alexander spoke. "I won't tell if you don't." She looked at him, and he winked. She gave him a small smirk. "I think that he would want to know that first."

"I know. I've just been waiting for him to stop being so distracted, but it hasn't passed. I was going to tell him a few days ago, but then he asked me about you, and it got me worried and—"

"And now you should go tell him. I think a baby will be a good distraction from his distraction. Can I make a prediction?"

She looked at him, confused. He looked at her tummy and narrowed his eyes. She looked perplexed, but also amused.

"I think it's a boy."

Her eyes widened. She laughed lightly. "Well, keep in mind you are betting against Nephthys. She said a girl."

He smirked at her. "Does she want to bet money?"

Cassiopeia laughed. He loved to see her smile. It made him smile too.

"You should go home and tell him."

She stopped smiling and nodded. She heard Caelum enter the arena with a flask of water.

"Thank you. You made me feel better and put my mind at ease."

Demetrius had been summoned to the front lines by his mother and Zeus once again. The Greeks had been struggling to hold back the Persian forces in the East. They had started a war that they were still trying to finish. He had stayed away from the battles for many years but, as a member of the Greek pantheon, he was being summoned.

When he arrived, many gods and immortals were already there. Normally Cassiopeia would have arrived with him, but she had decided to stay back to solidify the peace between her and the Egyptians. They didn't want the Persians turning toward their borders and she was an ally to them. Demetrius could tell, based on the number of gods in the tent that he just entered, that the intensities on each side had risen. He quickly spotted Athena and walked over to her side. Ares was in charge of the battle strategies, and he made quick work of delegating where everyone would be going. The meeting took a few hours, only because the gods wouldn't stop arguing over unimportant things. When it was finally finished, most of the gods dispersed back to Olympus and planned to come back at sunrise the next day.

Demetrius was brought to his tent and sent a beacon out to Cassiopeia so she could find him. He heard a noise outside of the tent entrance and then the flap moved, showing his mother standing there. Athena had changed into a long flowing peplos. One would never know that they were mother and son by looking at them, as Demetrius looked a few years older than his mother's current, and true form.

"Where is Cassiopeia? Is she not going to be fighting in this battle?" she asked.

"She wants to stay out of the battle because of her allegiance with the Egyptians. She's hoping to be here by nightfall for the festivities that I am sure Ares already has in the works."

Athena laughed and walked over next to him. "Yes, I am sure. Will you be attending?"

"Yes, I was going to wait until Cassiopeia arrives and we will go together."

"Or . . . since she's not here yet . . . you could accompany your lonely old mother." She winked at him and he laughed lightly.

"Of course. I would love to, Mother."

He held his elbow out to her and his outfit changed to a long black chiton with a blue himation that matched his eyes. Both had gold detailing around the edges. They left the tent and headed over to the party together.

When Demetrius returned to his tent, he could feel the alcohol in his system. He more than a little tipsy. He was surprised that Cassiopeia hadn't made it to the festivities, but he wasn't concerned. He walked into his tent and went to remove his himation but stopped when he saw a woman in his bed. He groaned quietly. Someone, probably Ares, had sent a woman for him, but he didn't want this as a gift. Many hundreds of years ago he would have happily accepted, but now he only ever wanted his wife.

He could see the woman had fallen asleep, her dark blonde hair strewn over the pillows. His brow furrowed as he got closer and realized she looked a lot like Cassiopeia. He walked up to the bed and gently rolled her over. His heart jumped as he realized it was her. Cassiopeia was still sleeping, and looked so peaceful. He loved just watching her, never getting tired of seeing her face. He leaned down and kissed her lips. Her eyes opened suddenly, then she relaxed when she realized it was him. He pulled away.

"Hello, beautiful. What a wonderful surprise."

She gave a sleepy smile. "I returned tired and decided not to go to the party. I tried to stay up, but I couldn't. You smell like wine." He chuckled lightly at her observation. "Come to bed," she said, patting the empty bed next to her.

"You don't have to ask twice, my dear."

He undressed and climbed into bed. She spooned into him, her back pressed against his chest. Her head was resting on his arm and she turned her head toward his.

"If you wake up before me in the morning, wake me. I have something important to tell you."

"Why not just tell me now?"

"Because I'm too sleepy to celebrate. And I want you to be completely sober."

He gave her a confused look, but she just gave a small smile.

"Trust me, it will be worth the wait," she said.

Cassiopeia woke to Demetrius kissing her neck and shoulder. She smiled, her eyes still closed.

"You have made me wait all night only to sleep the day away. I cannot wait any longer my dear. What do you have to tell me?"

She opened her eyes. She could tell from the dim sunlight around them that it was still near dawn. The sun had just come over the horizon.

"You're so dramatic," she groaned and shut her eyes again, nuzzling her head into his chest. She feigned as if she was going back to sleep, but she was too excited about the news to really doze off.

He groaned. "If you're going back to sleep, then I am getting up to roam around and suffer until you tell me. You know I hate surprises."

Cassiopeia pulled away from him, rising up on her elbow.

"This is definitely a big surprise, so I don't know if you're going to be happy."

He glowered at her, slightly tired of dancing around it. Demetrius just wanted to know. He could see her gazing at him, her eyes filled with love, but he didn't know why she was acting so mysterious.

"Cassiopeia . . ."

"I'm pregnant."

He went silent and his face became blank. She looked nervous, but excited, as she waited for him to respond.

"You're sure?" His eyes searched hers.

"Nephthys confirmed it. I am about four months along."

Cassiopeia watched his face change as his eyes lit up and a smile spread across it. He reached over, placing his hand on the nape of her neck, pulling her into a deep kiss. She kissed him back, leaning into him. He pulled away and leaned his forehead against hers.

"You, my dear, have made me the happiest man on the planet!" He pulled his head back, looking into her eyes. "I'm going to be a father."

Cassiopeia laughed at his excitement. She was excited too. They had both been wanting this for a very long time. He had wanted children since he was mortal, but she had been hesitant, not wanting to watch her children die of old age while she stayed the same. Then, when he became immortal, they had decided to just enjoy each other for a while, but they had never been cautious about not getting pregnant, it had just never happened. They had started intentionally trying a few decades ago, still to no avail. Until now. She was going to be a mother. Her heart jumped at the idea, but she also felt worry in her stomach. Demetrius saw the anxiety in her eyes.

"What's wrong? What could be bothering you about this?" he asked.

She looked down at her hands, almost embarrassed by what she was feeling. "What if I'm not a good mother. I've never really been around children and my mother was . . ."

Demetrius pulled her to him.

"I know you. You are kind and caring to those you love. You are going to be amazing and our children are going to love you completely. You will be nothing like your mother. You could never be that cruel."

He felt her nod against his chest. Demetrius felt worries too, the foreboding of a ticking clock, but he didn't want to concern her any more than she already was.

Cassiopeia was in Egypt. She had come to speak with Nephthys about the birth of the baby. She had appeared in the main hall and was waiting for either Set or Nephthys to answer her summons. Her long hair was pinned back, and she was dressed in a short peplos for the summer.

Cassiopeia hated being pregnant. She had enjoyed the first few months, but after month eight she just wanted to be able to move again. She felt mortal. She was clumsy and awkward. Demetrius found it entertaining, but she was not amused. She was beginning to get aggravated waiting for her little one to come out. Her emotions were heightened, and she was crying about everything and destroying anything that angered her. Set was slowly climbing up that list. She couldn't be mad at Nephthys because that was who was going to deliver her baby into the world.

This was her final checkup before the baby was scheduled to arrive. Nephthys was planning on moving to Vēlatusa for a week or two for the birth and delivery, then staying to help her with the newborn. They were hoping for a boy—a son for Demetrius.

Cassiopeia was pacing back and forth down the length of the main hall. She felt the Egyptian god she was waiting for manifest nearby.

"Finally! I have waited forever."

"It's been maybe ten minutes, so don't go giving me attitude little lady. I am sacrificing my wife for a few weeks, so the least you can do is wait ten minutes while I say goodbye."

"Well, that explains a lot if it only takes you ten minutes. No wonder Nephthys wants to get away, maybe it will give you some stamina."

Set just looked at her wide eyed. "Wow. I see being pregnant has made you saucy. Maybe I should make Nephthys stay, since your attitude could deliver the baby."

"Is that a threat?"

Out of her control, her eyes flashed red and her hands glowed lightly. Set took a step back.

"No, it wasn't a threat, my dear. Set is just being himself when he should be treading more carefully. I am all packed and ready." Nephthys had walked into the room and, luckily, her words quickly defused the situation as Cassiopeia's eyes returned to normal and her hands stopped glowing.

She began to feel guilty for attacking Set. "Ugh! I hate these heightened emotions! Now I just want to cry."

Set stepped toward her, still wary. "It's okay. The babe will be here soon, and then you won't have to deal with silly emotions anymore."

Tears fell down her cheeks. Set looked like a lost puppy and Nephthys was enjoying Set's discomfort a little too much as she just shook her head at him, telling him to be quiet.

"I don't know how Demetrius does it. That man must be a saint because I would have sent you to a mental asylum by now," he said quietly.

Cassiopeia lunged forward to smack at him playfully, but her large belly threw off her balance and she stumbled forward toward the floor. Set caught her and pulled her to his chest. She looked up at him, her eyes wide in shock.

"That's why you should never try to hit me."

She looked down, wide eyed, at the trail of wetness that ran down her leg to the floor. Set looked at it confused.

Cassiopeia turned to Nephthys. "I think my water just broke."

Demetrius was just finishing up the last of the things he needed to before going to Vēlatusa for the next few weeks. He was taking his time because, as excited as he was to see his new baby, Cassiopeia was starting to drive him crazy. She was not the type of woman who enjoyed any part of her pregnancy. She made him go get her honey cakes in the middle of the night because she couldn't stop thinking about them and said the manifested ones didn't taste right. When he had returned with them, she was crying because she didn't want them anymore. He was ready for her emotions and moods to go back to normal. Demetrius was telling their housekeepers the last few details before he left when he felt a shift behind him and turned around to see a wide-eyed Set.

"You're supposed to be in Egypt. What's wrong?" Concern and worry filled Demetrius.

"The baby is coming. Like right now. Her water broke. In my arms. I broke her."

"What?" Demetrius understood the first part, but the last was confusing and filled him with worry. "Where is my wife?"

Cassiopeia was laying on the bed, full of anxiety. Suddenly the doors to her room opened and she saw Demetrius turn the corner. She filled with relief and much of her worry was alleviated just by the sight of him. He walked over to the bed quickly and kissed her.

"Are you okay?" She nodded. "Set said he broke you. What did you do to him? I'm pretty sure *you* broke *him*."

Nephthys began laughing. "She went to punch him, and her water broke while he was holding her. Now he feels like he broke her. It's really quite funny."

Cassiopeia would have laughed too, but she felt another contraction wash over her and groaned at the pain while Demetrius held her hand and kissed her forehead.

"Demetrius, you should leave." Nephthys said. "The baby will be here soon, and I need space to work without worrying about you passing out."

"I have fought in battles, Nephthys!"

"Yes, but you have never seen your wife in extreme amounts of pain. With blood."

Nephthys held her hand up from where it was behind the sheet between Cassiopeia's legs, her fingers and palm was covered in blood and other fluids. She watched as Demetrius' face paled.

"Maybe I should go sit outside. I love you. Take care of her Nephthys, she is my everything."

Cassiopeia gazed up at him, her contraction having subsided.

"I love you too."

"I will take great care of her. She will be fine, don't you worry."

Demetrius was pacing up and down the long hall outside of Cassiopeia's room in Set's temple. He had never felt so powerless in his life. Occasionally he could hear her cries and screams but he was told to stay out. So here he paced, back and forth, like a tiger in a cage.

"Boy, if you don't sit down, I will make you."

Demetrius looked over at Set, who sat on a nearby bench and could see that the primordial god was deadly serious. Demetrius sat against the wall. He ran his hands roughly through his hair.

"Is it almost done?"

"How the fuck would I know? I'm sitting out here with your ass. Do I look like the goddess of childbirth?"

They heard Cassiopeia cry out again and both men looked anxiously at the door. Then they heard it, the noise they had been waiting for. A cry, from two small but powerful new little lungs. They both felt a wave of relief wash over them at the precious sound. Demetrius stood, staring anxiously at the door.

The moments turned into minutes as they waited nervously. They could hear the women talking inside, but the door remained shut. Just as they were about to sit back down, the door opened, and Nephthys was standing there. Both men looked at her, waiting for the news. She laughed at their eager faces.

"Both mother and baby are fine." She looked at Demetrius. "It's a healthy baby boy."

Demetrius' heart soared at the news. Nephthys moved out of the way and let them in. Demetrius looked over and saw Cassiopeia sitting propped up on pillows on the bed with a small bundle in her arms. Athena was sitting next to her.

"He's beautiful. He has a set of lungs just like his father did," Athena said.

Demetrius slowly walked over, as if scared to startle the newborn. He looked down at the little bundle in his wife's arms and he was overcome with emotions. He gazed at the perfect little baby. His perfect little baby. His son.

"Do you want to hold him?"

He looked at Cassiopeia. She looked tired, but he could see the pride and joy on her face.

"I don't think that's a good idea. I don't know what to do."

Athena scoffed. "It's just a baby Demetrius," she shook her head.

"Your father was the same way. He was always scared to touch you until you could crawl, then he never put you down. No matter how many years pass, I will always remember the way he acted when he first held you. *His* eldest son."

"I'm not scared I just don't want to break him. He's so little."

Demetrius sat on the edge of the bed and Athena walked over. She gently lifted the newborn from Cassiopeia's arms and set him into Demetrius' nervous hands. He looked down at his son and felt overwhelming joy. He could feel tears welling up in his eyes. He watched as the tiny infant opened his little eyes and began to squirm slightly.

Demetrius began to panic. "He's moving . . ."

"Relax, hold him to your chest and he will calm."

He listened to his wife and sure enough the baby stopped squirming at the feel of his father's warmth. Athena went to take the baby back, but Demetrius pulled away. She laughed.

Nephthys walked over. "Let us leave the new parents to their little one. Athena, we have arranged a room for you if you would like to stay for a few days while they are here."

"Thank you. Your gesture is greatly appreciated."

Nephthys looked at Cassiopeia. "You should be recovered enough to go home in about a week. I will go with you and stay in Vēlatusa for a few weeks to ensure all is well."

"Thank you, Nephthys. I couldn't imagine having done it without you."

Nephthys just smiled and bowed her head. "Rest. It's very important for you to sleep when you can. I'm sure Demetrius wouldn't mind holding the little one while you sleep."

She laughed lightly as Demetrius hadn't set down the infant since he was handed to him, constantly looking down to ensure all was well in his arms. He laughed as well. Cassiopeia ran her hand up and down his back as he sat there.

"This is mine now. She had him for almost a year all to herself now I get to enjoy him," he said.

They all laughed as they left the parents to their new baby. After the door closed the infant began to fuss, pushing his head into Demetrius' chest.

"What's wrong?"

"He is hungry. May I have him back?"

Demetrius looked at Cassiopeia, she had a small grin on her face. He gave her a sheepish look and very carefully handed the baby back to her. She brought him to her chest to let him nurse. Demetrius was filled with love as he watched his wife and son. When she looked back at him, he leaned down and gently kissed her. He pulled away and laid down next to her on the bed. She rested her head onto his shoulder.

"What are we to name him?"

"I have an idea . . ."

They had been in Egypt for one week and they were ready to go to Vēlatusa for the next few months. Today was the baby's name day. The day that they would announce the name they had chosen for him to the world. They were standing in the main hall. Set, Nephthys, Athena, Caelum, Sitara, and Sierra were all there to hear the name of the newborn. Demetrius and Cassiopeia were standing in the center of the hall, Demetrius holding their baby.

"After a lot of thought we finally decided," Demetrius said.

"It was a very hard decision," Cassiopeia added.

They both paused.

Set couldn't take it anymore. He stood from his throne. "Will you two just spit it out! Waiting one week was hard enough with you to going around teasing us all!"

"Mainly just you, honey," Nephthys said laughing.

Set looked at his wife, exasperated. Demetrius and Cassiopeia had decided what they wanted to name the infant on the day he was born, and they had been teasing the others about it all week. Set was the only one who was getting aggravated by it. He didn't have much patience, and they had both found it quite entertaining. Especially because of the name they had chosen.

"Will you please ease my suffering?" Set put his hands together as if pleading and looked at them. Cassiopeia and Demetrius looked at each other. Cassiopeia looked back to Set and spoke.

"Seth. His name is to be Seth. After his godfather, if his godfather wishes to accept that title."

Demetrius spoke. "Set, will you be his godfather?"

Set stood there, dumbfounded. He was at a loss for words. He fell back down onto his throne. Tears started to well in his eyes and everyone stayed quiet waiting for his response.

Finally, Athena spoke. "Will you say something!"

Set stayed quiet for a few more moments then said, "Is this a joke? You two think I am responsible enough to steer a whole person in the right direction?"

"You did for me. In my eyes you are a big brother. You are family."

He looked at Cassiopeia. She knew inside that she owed Set more than he would ever know. Sometimes he had been the only thing she ever held onto in the darkness. Set got up and walked over to her, pulling Cassiopeia tightly into his arms.

He whispered into her ear. "And you are like my little sister."

She felt a burning as he hugged her, and she gasped as she felt his powers surge into her and then ebb back. He released her and stepped away. She looked where his hand had been on her arm and saw his symbol marked onto her left arm. She looked at him wide-eyed.

"Why?"

"So I can always be there to protect you. I want you to feel safe and one day you will need it to show *me* the way."

Set's mark would remain forever. It was a rare thing to mark someone, especially someone from outside of your own pantheon. With this mark she would always have access to Set's powers no matter where he or she was in the world. It would also alert him to when she pulled from his powers letting him know she needed help. It was a rare thing to bestow upon someone because with it she could drain his powers completely and, if not stopped, could lead to his death and even weaken his pantheon. It meant that Set trusted her completely, even with his life.

Set looked at Demetrius. "Thank you for the honor of naming your son after me. Know that I will always be there for him, no matter the cost."

"You are welcome, Set."

In that moment the bond between the Atlantean and Egyptian pantheon was sealed forever in an immortal bond that would last millennia.

Cassiopeia smiled as she watched Demetrius, Athena, and Set argue over how to teach battle strategy. She was sitting in the noble's booth watching them with Nephthys beside her. Poor little Seth just stood there getting more and more confused as they taught him conflicting tactics. Tired of watching his distress, she flashed down to the arena. Seth looked relieved to see her.

"Mitéra!"

He ran over and hugged her waist. Seth was still young to learn how to fight, not quite to his eighth birthday. But he had wanted to learn, so they decided it was time. They just hadn't expected it to turn into a whole family debate. The others looked at her and all started to tell her their points of view at once.

"Stop!" she said. They all fell silent. "Why don't you let Seth decide who he wants to teach him? I am sure that once he knows the basics, he will want to spar with all of you to learn more specific techniques. He will find a style that he likes eventually and stick to it and nothing you teach him now will change that." She paused and knelt down next to Seth. "My little chosen one, who do you want to teach you first?"

Seth suddenly looked very shy. She could tell that he didn't want to upset anyone or have anyone angry at him for not choosing them.

"I don't know, Mitéra."

"Let the boy spar with his father. Fathers should be the first ones to teach their children how to hold a sword, to carry on their lineage."

They all turned to see Alexander walking over. He stopped a few feet away and crossed his arms over his chest. Cassiopeia looked down at Seth.

"Do you want to spar with Patéras?"

Seth looked up at her and she could see in his eyes his answer was yes. He gave a small nod.

"Then it is settled." She stood. "Demetrius will teach him the basics and you two can help round him out later. Alexander, welcome. Can we help you with something?"

He looked at her for a moment before he spoke. "I am actually here for Set. It can't wait."

Cassiopeia had a suspicious glint in her eyes but said nothing. Set just looked peeved and followed after Alexander, who had begun to walk away. Demetrius started to show Seth some different maneuvers and stances. Cassiopeia watched in awe at her family that she had built from nothing. She loved watching Demetrius be a father. He was amazing with Seth, even from the day he was born. Her heart swelled as she watched her husband and son.

She kept Alexander and Set in her sights out of the corner of her eye. They were having a pretty intense conversation. She watched Alexander step aggressively toward Set and she flashed over to them. Both men immediately stopped talking.

"I don't care what you two have to discuss or how important it is, if you are going to start a fight then you will leave my home. I will not have you two get into a pissing contest and endanger my family. Do you both understand."

They both looked surprised and took a step back from each other.

"We will behave. My apologies, Cassiopeia." Alexander said.

His words calmed her, but she didn't know why. She always felt relaxed around the leviathan. She looked at his tattoo and it looked different, familiar. She could have sworn she saw her name on it. Without even thinking she reached out and grabbed his arm, twisting his arm to face his palm up. She looked at his forearm, but it looked different. There was a word written on his arm, but it was in a language she couldn't read. She felt as though she was going crazy.

"What does that say?" She ran her fingers over the word.

"Why?" Alexander asked, his voice emotionless.

"Because a few moments ago I swore I could read it . . ."

"What did it say?"

Cassiopeia looked up at the leviathan. She heard worry in his voice. What was he hiding?

Set spoke. "Is everything okay, Cassiopeia?"

"Yes, I just . . ." She shook her head, looked down at his arm one last time, and released him from her grip. "I'm sorry. I thought I saw something."

Cassiopeia turned around to see Demetrius looking at them intently. She saw jealousy in his eyes and stepped away from the two men in front of her.

"Just behave," she said. She turned and walked away.

Cassiopeia had been getting a weird feeling about things lately. As if everyone around her was keeping secrets. She walked back to the booth and sat next to Nephthys.

"Is everything alright?"

"Honestly, I don't know. Nephthys, do you ever feel like you don't have the whole picture of what is going on around you? As if others know more than you do?"

The goddess nodded.

"Sometimes. Set he tends to be secretive, but not usually. Tell me what is bothering you. Why did you grab Alexander's arm?"

Cassiopeia looked out and watched Demetrius and Seth spar for a few moments as silence engulfed the two women.

"It's going to sound ridiculous. Just thinking it sounds crazy, but I thought, for a moment, that I saw my name on his forearm. But when I looked at it, the writing was in Lumerian. I can't read Lumerian. And why would Alexander have my name on his arm. Ugh." Cassiopeia dropped her head into her hands.

"How have you been sleeping?"

"Not well. I've been having weird dreams. Some make sense and others are just unusual." Cassiopeia felt Nephthys put her hand on her back as she rubbed it gently. "I just don't know what's wrong with me Nephthys."

"Well, I think I do. Pregnancy can change how your body takes care of itself. It throws off everything in your mind."

"Seth is already almost eight. Everything from my pregnancy should be worn off by now and this just started recently."

"Cassiopeia," Nephthys paused and waited for her to turn and look at her. "You're pregnant, again."

The Atlantean goddess just stared at her.

"No, you must be mistaken. We have been being careful because we want to give Seth his childhood before we talk about having another." She paused. "It took so long last time. This makes no sense."

"Now that your body knows what to do, it's easier for you to get pregnant. If you want to wait longer, I can arrange that for you."

"No!" The sheer thought made her stomach twist. "I could never imagine doing that. I'm just surprised . . . but excited. That explains some things, but not others."

"What have your dreams been about?"

Cassiopeia looked out at her family. "Death. Blood. They remind me of the dreams I had before the Atlantean pantheon fell. If they are premonitions, then as the time gets closer, they will get worse. A week before Caelum was killed my powers almost destroyed Vēlatusa when they flared up during a dream. I haven't had any power spikes, so I don't know if they are just dreams, or more."

"I don't know, my dear. I wouldn't worry about them too much. Just enjoy the moment. If you live your life constantly worrying about the *what if's,* you will never be able to enjoy it. Life will happen as it is supposed to. For example, a baby. Another Atlantean god or goddess. You, my dear, have now doubled the size of your pantheon. When are you going to tell Demetrius?"

"I will let him enjoy his son for one more day. I don't mean to seem unexcited about this baby, because I'm ecstatic. I just feel very . . . logical right now. I have for the past few weeks."

"Sometimes, if the baby is powerful enough or has a very external power, the baby can endow you with their powers while you are pregnant."

"So, I'm pregnant with an emotionless prophet?"

Nephthys laughed. "I would be curious to see what other powers manifest during this pregnancy."

Cassiopeia just shook her head. She watched as Seth handed his sword back to his father, then ran inside. Demetrius looked over to her and she watched his face go from joy to concern.

"Maybe I should tell him now. Lift his mood."

Nephthys nodded and Cassiopeia flashed over to her husband. He sensed her but didn't stop what he was doing, stowing all of the weapons and cleaning up. She waited until he was done. He looked at her and she saw his eyes light up with love, but she could see sadness hidden behind it. He wrapped his arms around her waist and gave her a quick kiss.

"You seem distracted, my love. What was that about with Alexander and Set?" He rested his forehead against her temple as he held her.

"They were getting too heated. I thought I saw something on his arm. It's really stupid, but its Lumerian, so there is no way I could have read it. I haven't been sleeping well, but I think I know why."

"Why?"

Cassiopeia placed her hands on Demetrius' cheeks as she looked into his light blue eyes.

"I know we wanted to wait a little longer but," his eyes widened slightly and he looked down at her stomach before looking back up at her. "I'm pregnant."

She watched fear and worry cross his face for a moment before it was replaced with excitement and joy.

"Another baby already! That's amazing news my love!"

He pulled her into a tight hug and just held her. She felt like he was holding onto her as if it was their last embrace.

"Why don't you and I go away, just the two of us, for a week. Get away from all the hustle and bustle of our life. Just enjoy each other." He released her and gazed down into her eyes. "What do you think? I am sure Caelum would be willing to let us stay at one of the temples alone on Vēlatusa."

"That sounds absolutely wonderful. What of Seth?"

"I guarantee that my mother would love to have her grandson all to herself for a week."

"That sounds heavenly. I can't remember the last time we had a day with just the two of us."

He smiled and pressed his forehead against hers. "I'll make the arrangements, my love."

Cassiopeia was happily progressing through her pregnancy. This time was much better than when she was pregnant with Seth. She and the baby shared their powers and she already knew that this little one was going to be a god or goddess of wisdom and learning. Cassiopeia could remember everything, word for word, and could read any language. It made her more curious about the tattoo that she had seen on Alexander's arm, but she had pushed those strange thoughts out of her mind. It made no sense.

She had just appeared on Olympus. Seth had stayed with Athena for a few days while they were getting ready for the baby and making the arrangements to move back to Vēlatusa. She had tried to convince Demetrius to move there permanently but he didn't want to. Staying there, in another pantheon's capital made him feel weakened. He enjoyed Earth.

Cassiopeia was escorted down the main path of Olympus, up toward Athena's temple. One of Zeus' rules for her visiting was that she had to be escorted everywhere and she could only arrive at the bottom of the mountain. It sounded like a long walk , but the magical cloudiness of the mountain that made it look enormous also made it so it was a short walk.

When they arrived at the temple the escort walked her into the main hall. The main hall looked very similar in layout to Set's temple, except smaller. On one end was the entrance and on the other was a massive statue of Athena. She was dressed in a floor length peplos with an armor chest plate. She had an owl on her shoulder, and her eyes seemed to follow visitors as they walked around the room. Her sword, still in its sheath, was on her hip. In one hand she had a book, and in the other hand she held a shield with her symbol on it, two crossed spears behind an olive tree with an owl in the center. The armor and weapons were gold, and they sparkled in the sunlight that poured in through the skylights in the ceiling. Her dress and the rest of the statue was a bright white marble.

A few moments later Seth ran out from one of the side halls.

"Mitéra!"

Cassiopeia laughed as she bent down and wrapped her arms around her son. She wished she could pull him closer, but her extended stomach wouldn't allow for it. She let go of him and looked down into his eyes, Demetrius' eyes.

"Where is Athena?"

"I am not one to run as fast a growing boy." Athena entered the room with a grin on her face.

"Were you good for your grandmother?"

"Yes, Mitéra. We had a lot of fun!"

"Why don't we tell you of our adventures over lunch? I am sure you could spare some time and I think sitting and relaxing for a moment would be good for you. If Demetrius has a problem with it, just tell him to take it up with me."

Cassiopeia laughed. "I suppose I could spare the time for food."

"Good! We can eat outside. Zeus is in an unusually good mood because it's a beautiful day."

They walked back into the courtyard. Olive trees were planted around the edges, making the area feel bigger. One side was a balcony that protruded off of the edge of the mountain. One could look out and see most of Olympus. Cassiopeia walked over and looked down. She could see Artemis' hunting grounds and Ares' fighting arena.

"As much as I don't like coming here, it is a beautiful place. Vēlatusa gets so quiet with there being so few of us."

"Yes, but sometimes Olympus gets too loud with so many of us. I'm happy you were able to stay for lunch. I'm going to miss you while you are on Vēlatusa. Zeus says I can go to visit, but then he gets so upset about it when I get back. It's not worth the headache."

"You will be there for the birth though, right?"

"Of course. I just won't stay for days. I know it's not ideal, but that's the only way to appease both sides of my family."

They talked about Seth's time up on Olympus and he happily chattered on about his adventures there. When they were done eating Cassiopeia stayed a little longer to enjoy the company before going back to the hectic process of preparing for the baby. It was still a month off from when the baby was due, but Seth had been a few weeks early, so they were getting ready just in case. They grabbed Seth's things and said their goodbyes. Cassiopeia took Seth's hand and went to flash away but nothing happened. She looked at Athena confused.

"Am I not allowed to leave?"

Athena looked back with the same amount of confusion. She flashed from where she was standing to next to Cassiopeia.

"You should be able to leave. There is no lockdown on Olympus. I can flash."

Cassiopeia tried again and nothing. She held her arm out and reached out with her powers and tried to move a vase that was across the room.

Nothing happened.

She looked at Athena, alarm filling her. The thought dawned on them at the same time.

"No, no, no!" Cassiopeia cried.

Athena placed her hand on Cassiopeia's distended tummy and waited a moment. Then she felt the contraction. It was small, but it was there. Cassiopeia had gone into labor. When a goddess goes into labor, her powers diminished so that she can't accidentally hurt herself or the baby while in the middle of labor. The powers from other gods and goddesses would also not work against them. Only the powers that they were born with. It was something that protected mother and baby, but in this situation, it trapped Cassiopeia on Olympus until the baby was born.

"Artemis!" Athena shouted.

The goddess of childbirth, amongst other things, appeared in front of them. She was in a short beige peplos, her light brown hair pulled up into a messy ponytail and her light brown eyes sharp with feistiness. Cassiopeia could tell that she was about to snap at Athena for the sudden summoning, but she didn't when she saw the pregnant Atlantean. Artemis looked her up and down once and already knew what Athena needed.

"You're in labor. Here. On Olympus."

"It appears that way. I know that Zeus won't let Nephthys come here, so you are my only option."

"You are not of my pantheon. I do not have to help you."

"Artemis!" Athena said harshly.

"It's fine, Athena. You are correct, I may not be of your pantheon but this child in my stomach is. I am not demanding your assistance. I am asking you as a mother to a maiden."

Artemis narrowed her eyes at her. She stepped forward and placed her hand on Cassiopeia's stomach. Artemis looked back at Athena. She still seemed aggravated at the situation, but Cassiopeia could see that the goddess couldn't resist doing what she loved, what she was created for.

"Have her set up in one of your rooms, I will return with supplies and handmaidens. You know what to do before I return?"

"Yes. This is my second child."

"Good. I will be back." Artemis began to walk away and then stopped. "I don't know how Nephthys ran her labor room, but for me no men are allowed in the room until after I am done. Mother and child come first."

"Can I speak with Demetrius before the birth begins?"

"You must hurry and get him. I don't like men around me."

Artemis vanished and Athena summoned a handmaiden. "Get them set up into a spare room in preparation for labor. Cassiopeia, I need permission to enter Vēlatusa to inform Demetrius."

"Take Seth, he has permission." She looked down at her son whose expression was worried. "Can you flash Athena to Vēlatusa to get Patéras?"

"I don't want to leave you Mitéra." Seth took a step closer to his mother and grabbed her hand. "What if you need me?"

Cassiopeia smiled down at him, his worry for her touching her heart, and then she felt another contraction, this one stronger than the others. She didn't want to be alone either. Cassiopeia reached out and grabbed Athena's wrist. She pushed two of her fingers against the tender skin of her wrist and when she removed them there was the symbol for the ancient Atlantean home world tattooed onto her wrist.

"Seth can stay but please hurry. I want to see Demetrius before the birth."

Athena quickly flashed away. Cassiopeia and Seth followed the handmaiden to the room where she would have the baby. As they walked into the room another contraction washed over her. The baby was coming quickly. Cassiopeia grabbed the bed post as the wave of pain and pressure washed over her. The handmaiden scurried around, quickly preparing for Artemis' arrival. Cassiopeia felt Seth place his hand on her back, rubbing gently. Then he took her hand and held it.

"It's okay, Mitéra."

The contraction passed quickly, but she knew another was coming soon. Cassiopeia tried to hide her worry that Demetrius wasn't going to make it. She didn't want Seth to be out in the hallway alone listening to her in labor. As she sat on the bed, she patted for him to sit next to her.

"Patéras will be here soon. Don't be worried. If he doesn't make it before everything starts to happen, I need you to be strong like your father would be if he was here. Okay? I need you to be my strong warrior while he isn't here. Can you do that for me, my little chosen one?"

"Yes, Mitéra. I can be strong for you, always."

As she felt a more intense wave wash over her Athena still hadn't returned with Demetrius. Artemis appeared near them with three handmaidens in tow. They had supplies for the birth and they began scurrying around preparing the room as Artemis liked it.

"Has your water broken?"

"No."

"How are your contractions?"

"Only a few minutes apart. They are becoming more and more intense."

"Your son should leave."

"I want to stay," Seth said firmly.

"No, Seth. It's only going to get worse, and I am going to be in a lot of pain with a lot of blood. You don't want to be here."

Cassiopeia didn't want her son to be scared watching childbirth.

"I will stay."

Cassiopeia looked at Artemis, who had a strange look on her face.

"He may stay until Athena returns."

Cassiopeia was surprised by her response but didn't want her to change her mind. She didn't want to be alone in this and she knew that if it began to become too much for him, she could send him out of the room.

"Alright. Just stay quiet and keep out of the way."

He nodded and one of the handmaidens walked over and gave him small wash bowl with a cloth and told him to place it on her forehead and neck when the labor progressed. He was happy to have something to do, especially after the labor began to progress. After almost an hour Cassiopeia was beginning to worry about where Athena and Demetrius were. It shouldn't have taken her this long to get him. The baby was coming quickly. She was about to say something about it when the door opened. Athena walked in and Cassiopeia turned to look at her.

"Mitéra, Artemis said you have to breathe. In . . . and out . . . in . . . and out . . . don't stop breathing." Seth placed the damp cloth back on her forehead. He was being surprisingly calm with everything that was going on around him. Athena walked over and grabbed her hand.

"I am sorry it took so long. Demetrius wasn't on Vēlatusa and I had to find him. All is well now. He is outside waiting." Athena glanced at Artemis. "He's sorry he couldn't make it to see you before."

Artemis groaned. She reached her arm under the blanket that was over Cassiopeia's lower half.

"You're lucky I care for you, Athena. He has one minute before I come back. If she has a contraction while I am gone, Seth and the handmaidens can handle it. Seth can stay if he would like."

Artemis left. Athena looked incredibly surprised and walked quickly to the door to get Demetrius. When he walked in, his face was covered with worry. He moved quickly over to the bed, took Cassiopeia's hand and kissed it.

"I am so sorry! I came as quickly as Athena found me."

"It's fine, I am just happy Artemis let me see you. I am—" She groaned as another contraction washed over her.

Demetrius took a step back, not knowing what to do. Seth moved back to his mother's side and held her hand.

"Breathe, Mitéra, in . . . and out . . . good." He put his hand on her stomach. "Artemis needs to come back soon. My little sister is coming."

They looked at him, confused, and then Cassiopeia gasped as she felt her water break. Demetrius' face went white. She could tell he was about to pass out.

"Mother, I don't feel well . . ." Demetrius said to Athena.

Athena looked at Demetrius. She punched him in the arm, hard.

"I swear, boy, if you can handle a battlefield but childbirth makes you pass out then I did not raise you right. Even your son has better bearing on the situation. Now hurry and say goodbye for a short while."

Demetrius gathered himself, still pale, and walked over to kiss Cassiopeia. He grabbed Seth's shoulder and started to push him gently toward the door.

"I want to stay. Artemis said I could. I want to be here for Mitéra, to be strong for her."

Demetrius looked at Cassiopeia, then Athena.

"If it becomes too much or he needs to leave, I will bring him out," Athena said.

Demetrius looked back to his son, then nodded.

"Take care of her for me, Seth."

"I will, Patéras, always."

Demetrius nodded and left the room. A few moments later Artemis returned. She looked at Seth.

"You decided to stay? Good. Let's begin, this little girl is ready to be born to the world."

"How do you know it's a girl?" Cassiopeia asked.

"I am a goddess of childbirth, I just know."

After what felt like waiting alone in the hall for hours, Demetrius jumped up when Athena finally popped her head out. She grinned as she nodded for him to enter. When he walked in, Cassiopeia was sitting on the bed looking exhausted. Seth was sitting next to her, holding a little bundle. He was softly whispering and shushing the little infant in his arms. He looked up at his father with joy on his small face.

"Patéras, it's a little sister."

Demetrius smiled as he walked over to them and sat by Seth. Seth gently handed his father the baby. Demetrius gazed down at his tiny daughter, then looked back up at Cassiopeia, Seth, and Athena.

"My whole world in one little room. I could never imagine asking for more. Cassiopeia, she is beautiful."

Cassiopeia smiled at him, but she looked as though she was about to pass out. He looked concerned.

Seth put his hand on his father's arm. "Artemis said that she lost a lot of blood. But she said that she should be fine in a few days. We can go home in about a week. I got to hold her first. Artemis let me help."

"He was a strong boy. He stayed strong through it all, I am very impressed by him," Artemis said.

"He was raised to be strong." Cassiopeia's voice was weak as she spoke. Her eyes drooped but she was trying to stay awake.

Demetrius put a hand on her cheek. "Sleep, my love. You did a lot today. You need your rest. I will take care of her until she needs to feed. I love you."

"Thank you. I love you too."

She shut her eyes and they all left the room. The baby started to fuss, and Demetrius rocked her gently.

Seth reached up. "Can I hold her?"

Demetrius laughed lightly and carefully handed him the infant. Seth took her almost expertly and the second he began to rock her, she quieted right down. Athena patted Demetrius' shoulder.

"He's a natural with her. He didn't cringe or falter once during the entire thing. He had more bearings about himself than I did."

"Does that mean anything?"

"In regard to what? The fact that he's tougher than you?"

Demetrius laughed. "I am sure that if it was any woman other than my wife, I would have been fine, but watching her struggle in pain . . . I couldn't do it. So, if I am weak for not wanting to watch my wife hurting, then I accept that. I meant in regard to his god powers."

"There has never been a god of childbirth or mothers. Only goddesses. I suppose there is always room for a first, so maybe, but I have a feeling in my gut that he is more powerful than that. I think that neither of your children are destined to be a minor god or goddess. I think they are both going to be more powerful than either of us could ever imagine. More important than we could ever understand."

Her words were almost prophetic sounding, as if she knew something in her gut about their possible future. Demetrius turned to look at Seth, who was still gazing at his little sister. He walked back over to his son.

Seth looked up at his father. "Patéras, I have an idea for her name. Can I name her?"

"Why don't we talk with your mother about it when she awakens. What name did you have in mind, Seth?"

"Antiope."

"When set against the power, she will make her own voice heard above the others and set her own path. I think it would be a wonderful name for a strong little goddess," Athena said.

"I love it, Seth. We shall see what your mother thinks when she awakens, but I am sure that she will love it, too."

Chapter 10

A Moment of Silence
2007 BCE

Death leaves a heartache no one can heal;
love leaves a memory no one can steal.
—Anonymous

Cassiopeia was back on the battlefield for the first time in years. She had stayed away for a long time, trying not to get involved in the affairs of the other pantheons as she raised her children. The Persians had made a blatant and direct threat toward the Atlantean pantheon. Cassiopeia still didn't know why they had made such a bold move, knowing that there would be repercussions, but she knew that she had to act viciously and cut the head off of the snake before other pantheons decided to follow suit and attack them again. Many thought that because they were small, they were weak, but she intended to prove them all wrong. If that meant wiping the Persian pantheon out, then so be it. She wasn't going to stand for anyone threatening her family.

Because of their alliance, and the already looming threat of the Persians against their pantheon, the Egyptian pantheon was joining them for the battle. She was surprised that Zeus hadn't decided to get involved as well, but they had been in a truce with the Persians that he didn't want to upset. He did allow Demetrius to fight alongside his family.

Cassiopeia looked over the battle plan with Demetrius, Set, Isis, Anubis, and Montu. Many other gods would be arriving tomorrow from the Egyptian pantheon, as well as Caelum, Seth and Antiope. Battles between gods were very different than gods participating in the battles of mortals. Things became much more intense and there was a greater risk of danger. Just because a mythical creature couldn't kill a god, it didn't mean that they couldn't cause some physical damage. The Persian pantheon was large, with a huge army but the Egyptians and Atlanteans were almost equal in numbers with their combined army. Their army was more powerful because the battle was occurring on what little land was left of Atlantis. Creatures and gods had more power when they were on their own homelands. After going over the plan, they dispersed out to their tents to ready for the battle in the morning.

"Maybe you should sit this battle out," Cassiopeia said to her husband.

"What? I could never sit back and watch you and the kids go into battle without fighting. I know that I am not of your pantheon, but I will be on the battlefield tomorrow," Demetrius responded as they walked into their tent.

"I don't think the children should fight either. I know that they are fully capable adults now and they have been trained well, but I want them to stay safe. I want all of you to stay safe. And I know that even if we don't win, the Greek pantheon will take you all in."

"Cassiopeia, we already talked about this. They are staying in the back lines to help with any stragglers, far from the front. They will be fine, and they would never forgive us if you didn't let them fight and something happened. Why are you having a change of mind about this? Usually once the plan is set you never second-guess yourself. What's wrong?"

He walked over and placed his hands on her arms, looking into her eyes. They were full of concern and worry.

"I . . ." She took a deep breath. "I don't know. My dreams are back, and they are worse than ever. Blood, pain, death, I'm worried that it's another prophecy like the dreams I had before Atlantis fell. I just want my family to be safe."

"Oh, my love." He pulled her into a hug. "The children have plenty of people who will be on the battlefield with them to keep an eye on them. Worry and fear will just hold you back in battle and cause you to be distracted."

"I know. I just can't shake this feeling."

"Why don't you take a bath to relax. I have an errand I need to run, and I will be back before you are done."

"Okay."

Demetrius released her and looked deeply into her blue eyes.

"Just know that no matter what happens tomorrow, I love you. I always have and I always will."

"Forever."

He smiled. "Forever and ever."

Cassiopeia smiled back and walked over to go take a bath as he left the tent. As she filled the tub, she couldn't shake her concerns. She stripped down and stepped into the hot bath water, letting it relax her tensions and wash them away. She closed her eyes and settled into the metal tub.

Swords are clashing around me, gods and creatures screaming in pain and death. I can't see much through the red haze that covers everything. The coppery smell of blood fills my nostrils. I can hear the voices of those I care for yelling around me in the midst of the battle. Fighting as best I can, suddenly the pain that I knew was coming hits me. I never see the blow coming and could never fully see the wound or who caused it but, as pain courses throughout my body and chest, I looked down to see my own heart lying on the ground, shattered into pieces. The sound of my heavy breathing fills my ears and I can hear nothing else. I look up to see my family yelling at me, but I can't reach them, and they can't get to me. Panic is filling my mind. The pain is unimaginable, cutting into my soul. I looked back to my hands and they are covered in blood, dripping off of my fingertips and onto the ground, sticky and red. Lilith appears in front of me, her face stoic and her eyes full of sadness. She pushes me hard and I fall back, unable to stop her. I just keep falling and falling, with only the red flow of blood all around me and my breathing and pain filling my mind.

Cassiopeia jolted up quickly in the tub, awakening suddenly. She was gasping for air, her body in a complete panic. Before she could stop it her, emotions overtook her and tears rolled down her cheeks in a torrent. As she slowly returned to reality, she took slow deep breaths to calm herself. She couldn't let these dreams and emotions distract her from what she needed to do tomorrow. She knew who she had to talk to, and as much as she didn't want to, it must be done. Hopefully she would find guidance on what to do.

Cassiopeia walked through the swirling portal into Khaos. When the world around her came into view, she saw Lilith sitting on her throne in the main hall. She looked surprised to see her daughter.

"What an interesting surprise. And to what do I owe this unexpected visit?"

Cassiopeia suddenly felt embarrassed and a slight regret for coming here. She hadn't seen or spoken to her mother since Atlantis fell thousands of years before. Her mother had reached out a few times to try to restore their relationship, but every time Cassiopeia had shunned her.

"I need guidance and I don't wish to worry those I actually care about," Cassiopeia said.

Lilith laughed. The sound rang out like soft music over the room.

"After that insult, why should I help you?"

"Because of all the horrible things you did to me after everything happened, the least you can do is give me some words of advice. You were the one always trying to open a dialog, but now when I come to you, you push me away. I can leave, maybe I never should have come."

Cassiopeia began to turn around when Lilith spoke.

"What guidance or advice would you like, my little star. What is troubling your mind so much that you come to me?"

Cassiopeia hesitated. She wanted to tell her, but she also prepared herself for Lilith's blunt answer. Her mother was never good at beating around the bush or trying to sugarcoat her words.

"I've been having dreams."

"What kind of dreams?"

She could see that her words piqued Lilith's interest, her curiosity coming to the forefront.

"It's always the same. I told Demetrius about them, but he tells me that they are just dreams and not to worry. But they seem so real. I am on a battlefield fighting, but I can't see much over a red haze. Someone rips my heart out and it shatters into pieces. When I look up, I see my friends and family standing there but I can't reach them. When I look back down, my hands are dripping in blood. Then you appear, and you push me, and I fall endlessly through blood and pain. They are very similar to the dreams I had before Caelum came of age. Pain, blood, a red haze, all the same."

Lilith didn't speak. She sat on her throne looking down at her daughter. They stood there in silence for a few minutes. Cassiopeia began to feel uncomfortable. It was silly to think that her mother would actually help her.

"You won't like my answer. There is no way to say it without angering you," Lilith finally said.

"Then just say it."

Lilith took a deep breath and stood. She walked over to stand directly in front of Cassiopeia.

"You are a goddess of fate. Some things in this universe can fluctuate and change but other things must go according to a set chain of events. When something happens that must happen a certain way, it is fate, events that are destined to happen outside of your control. Because you are a goddess of fate you have a link to those set events. You can get a glimpse into them. Dreams for you are more of a code of events to come. But remember, no matter what you do you can't change what has to happen. Nothing you do can change what you see in your dreams. If you do something to stop it, then it will just happen anyway at a later time. I don't fully know what your dream means, but it is going to happen because it is fated."

"So, you are saying that I should just ignore my dreams and their meanings?"

"No. Take them as a warning. A sign to help prepare yourself for things to come."

"So, your advice is don't do anything about the dreams and just accept their consequences. I am so happy I traveled all this way for that sparkling piece of knowledge."

"If you try to fight it, it will just make it worse. I have tried to fight fate multiple times and here I sit, trapped in the fate that I tried to avoid. It will happen no matter what you do. The universe is stronger than you or anyone else. One day you will understand."

Cassiopeia felt her anger rise. She hated it when her mother said that. She treated her like a young child that didn't fully understand the adult world.

"I am not a child anymore. What is there left for me to understand? Have you kept more secrets from me?"

"There are many secrets that those around you keep and there is also much that you still have to learn. In the course of the universe you are just a child. They wouldn't be secrets if I told you."

"So, you admit to keeping things from me?"

"They are not important to know yet. One day."

"It is not important for me to know who my true father is?"

Cassiopeia watched Lilith's eyes widen slightly, confirming what Cassiopeia already knew. She was not Magnus' daughter; she never had been. Her mother had lied to everyone. Lilith quickly hid her surprise, but smirked at Cassiopeia.

"Well, well. Someone is more insightful that I had thought. Why wait until now to confront me? I am sure you have known for a while now. Since Atlantis fell, I would presume."

"Why did you never tell me yourself?"

"It wasn't safe. The fewer who knew the better. You needed to completely believe that Magnus was your father, otherwise he would have noticed. He was too preceptive for it to be any other way. Even after that pathetic prophecy you had to still believe without a shadow of a doubt that he was your father. It was the only way to keep you safe. Everything I do is to keep you safe."

"Stabbing me was to keep me safe? Abandoning me was to keep me safe? Giving Vēlatusa and the pantheon to Caelum was to keep me safe?"

Lilith glared at her daughter. "So naïve. I thought I raised you to be more attentive. One would think that you would have at least picked it up from Magnus." Lilith turned away and walked back over to her throne. She sat and looked at Cassiopeia for a few short moments before sighing. "Vēlatusa was Caelum's birthright from the beginning, the only true child of Magnus. Yes, technically you were raised as his eldest child, but the universe would end if it was run on technicalities. I never abandoned you. I was always there for you and still am. Not living in the same place as you and you keeping your distance never changed that fact. Lastly, I will admit that stabbing you was not one of my proudest moments, but I did it and it is done. If you wish to hate me forever because of it than so be it, I suppose."

Her words held no true regret. She spoke them in a very unsentimental manner.

"You are so frustrating. Do you not care? Do you not regret the choices that you have made?" As Cassiopeia spoke, her eyes began to glow red. Her words upset Lilith.

"For being not a child, you very much act like one. I would have hoped that at almost seven thousand years old, you would be wiser and more mature. That you would have better control over your powers and emotions, more aware of the reality around you. I see you are just as innocent and weak as when I left you."

"I have had to make sacrifices for my family that you never made. You know nothing of my life, because you chose not to be in it! I should have never come to see you. I don't need your insults and useless words. Goodbye, Lilith."

"I will see you again, my daughter. Sooner than you would like, I fear. I am sorry that you are so important to the universe."

She was confused by Lilith's cryptic words, but she didn't care anymore. She didn't care about anything the woman who birthed her had to say. Cassiopeia opened a portal and returned to the war camp.

Shortly after she arrived Demetrius walked in looking somber. His expression quickly changed when he saw her, his eyes filling with love and his expression softening.

"Did the bath help?"

"Yes, very much," she lied. There was no point in having everyone around her share in her worry.

He removed his chest plate then walked over to her and moved a piece of hair that had fallen into her face to behind her ear. Leaning down toward her, he captured her lips with his. She leaned into him, all her worry and stress melting away at his touch. His kiss quickly deepened into something more passionate and forceful, as their tongues danced against each other. His arm wrapped around her waist and his other hand went to the nape of her neck to pull her body closer to his. She moaned as she pressed against him. After a few moments of enjoying the taste and feel of each other Demetrius pulled his head away to gaze down at her.

"Cassiopeia, will you let me make love to you?"

She blushed lightly at his simple request.

She gave him a small smile. "I don't know… I'll have to think about it."

She watched as a smile grew on his face as he shook his head. He kissed her roughly and scooped her up, carrying her over to the bed. He set her down next to the bed and kissed her shoulder and neck, working his way up to her jaw line to her lips. She felt as he slid the top of her dress off of her shoulders and it slipped down to the floor. He pulled away just far enough to gaze down her body. He let out a small moan as he looked at her naked in front of him.

"All yours, my love," Cassiopeia said softly.

"Every single inch. Mine," He said, looking into her eyes.

He pulled her back against him and kissed her. She unbuckled his belt and let it fall to the floor. Then, grabbing his peplos at his hips, she pulled it up, over his head, and heard as it dropped to the floor. She ran her hands over the muscles of his chest and shoulders.

"And you are all mine. Every single inch."

He let out a small gasp as she took him in her hands while she spoke, gently stroking him. He buried his face into her neck, breathing her in and gasping lightly every now and then as she touched him. When he couldn't take being teased any longer, he grabbed her and lifted her, laying her onto the bed on her back. He moved himself on top of her and slowly sank his fullness into her. She moaned lightly at the feel of him entering her. He kissed her, from her lips down to her collarbone and back up, while thrusting slowly and sweetly into her. She was his everything and he wanted to savor every moment in her arms. Cassiopeia felt the same way as she gazed up into his eyes.

"I love you, Demetrius," she said softly.

His heart swelled at her words.

"I love you too, Cassiopeia."

Even after being together for over fifteen hundred years they still felt the same amount of love as they did in the beginning.

Cassiopeia felt her body beginning to tense as he moved against her. He increased his pace and she gasped and moaned loudly as she reached her climax. Her hands gripped at his shoulders and back as pleasure coursed through her body. Demetrius sat up so that he could see her body moving as he made love to her. He gripped her hips, allowing himself to plunge more deeply into her body. He moved one hand to her breast and the other to her core, feeling her squirm and moan at his touch. When he moved his fingers against her, he could feel her body beginning to tense for another orgasm. Knowing he couldn't hold back much longer, he laid back down against her, taking her hands in his and entwining their fingers. Feeling her body tensing again and hearing her cry out his name pushed him over the tipping point, and he joined her in blissful ecstasy. His body quivered over hers as he regained his senses. Demetrius stayed on her for a few more moments, enjoying the simplicity of the moment and the feel of her body before he pulled away. He looked down at her as she gazed up at him, satisfied.

"What did I do to deserve you in my life?"

He smirked at her as he spoke.

"I ask myself that every time I see your face looking at me or the children with love."

He smiled and she got up to go clean up. Demetrius was in bed when she returned and she crawled into bed next to him, spooning against his warm body. He ran his fingers gently through her long blonde hair as she rested her head onto his chest. She could hear his heart beating and feel her head rising and lowering with every breath he took. They were both trying to distract themselves and ignore the fact that they had a battle tomorrow, one that could change both of their lives forever. This wasn't just a battle like the others they had. This one could mean life or death for those they cared for. Gods they knew could meet their fate and die in the battle.

"Are Seth and Antiope here or are they coming in tomorrow morning?" she asked him.

"They are spending the night on Vēlatusa. I told them that it would make you feel better to know they are sleeping somewhere safe. They reluctantly agreed."

She laughed lightly. "Thank you. The less I have to worry about, the better. Let's sleep. Tomorrow is a big day. I love you."

"I love you too."

They both drifted off into dreamless sleep. Cassiopeia was grateful for the dreamlessness.

Cassiopeia awoke the next morning still wrapped in Demetrius' arms. She could tell that he was awake but didn't want to disturb her as his fingers lightly ran through her hair. When she opened her eyes to look up at him, he was watching her. She smiled at him.

"Some might think it's a little weird to watch someone sleeping," she reminded him.

He laughed lightly before kissing her forehead. "It's time to get up, my love. We need to get the troops ready. Others have already started moving around."

She nodded, then reluctantly sat up and stretched. They dressed in their battle armor and walked toward the main planning tent. Many Egyptian gods were already inside, including Set and Isis. Caelum, Antiope, and Seth were also already there.

"I spoke with Lilith and she said that she will be sending additional Vantha demons to help us increase the number of warriors on our side," Caelum said.

"Good. Very good. We are over twenty-five thousand strong, and with additional troops I have no fears that we can easily take out the Persians. Especially if we have additional troops that they don't even know about," Set responded.

They talked for a little longer and shifted around some troops to accommodate for the new ones before they dispersed to go to their places. Their army was an array of faces and creatures. Mortal man would be pointless, easily cut down and killed.

The Atlanteans had thousands of Vantha demons at their disposal and now more with the additional troops. The Vantha demons were not to be underestimated. As one of the first demons ever created, they could kill and eat almost any creature on the planet with ease while also being almost indestructible. They looked beautiful up close when relaxed, but in battle they were insanely quick and lethal, with their sharp teeth and claws on their hands and feet. They chirped excitedly, ready to kill things.

The Egyptians had an array of creatures, mainly Anubis' army—dog-headed men who stood eight feet tall, with jagged, sharp teeth, and griffins, their eagle wings and muscular lion bodies moved swiftly and lethally. There were more than fifteen gods and goddesses between the two pantheons.

The combined army was a frightening site, with the Egyptians in their gold and black armor contrasting with the Vantha demons scattered throughout and their unnatural unique-colored skin. It was a mind-blowing sight with the rainbow of colors flying over and dispersed throughout the black and gold. As the gods went to their places on the battlefield, they watched as the Persian army appeared over the nearby ridge.

They looked at the Persian army and they could see the descendants of Fulad-zereh, huge horned demons with armor for skin and sharp, jagged horns, marching toward them. For mortals they were a sight to be feared, but she knew that the Vantha demons could make quick work of them. There were also manticore scattered throughout their ranks, with the head of a man but teeth like a shark. They had the body of a lion like the griffins, but also tails like a scorpion. Cassiopeia knew that she would have to be wary of their tails, because they could shoot their barbs great distances with amazing accuracy.

Usually the leaders of the two armies would gather in the center to discuss possible surrender, but the Persians were not planning on discussing anything. As they marched forward, they stopped for a moment, leaving hundreds of yards between the two armies. It was a fierce sight, the three pantheon's armies lined up, ready for battle. You could hear the melodic chatter and hisses from the Vantha demons and the growls and snarls from the Egyptian army. The Persian army cried out and ran forward to begin the battle. Surprised, the Egyptians and Atlanteans gave the order for their armies to also advance.

Shouts and battle cries were heard through the ranks as they ran forward. The sound of swords clashing and cries of dying creatures quickly filled the air. Cassiopeia started fighting on the sidelines, using her powers to eliminate large numbers of soldiers and thin their numbers. Once the enemies began to close in, she jumped from her horse and fought with her weapons and powers combined.

She kept an eye on where the Persian gods were at all times. Cassiopeia was currently the only god on the battlefield who could kill another god without repercussion. But, only with battles like these, any gods captured in war on the losing side would be brought to the leviathans to be finished off.

As she fought, her strikes were smooth and quick. She didn't need to waste time or energy on toying with the enemy, she just wanted them dead. Cassiopeia cleared the area directly around her and looked around to check on the others. Set was on the other side of the battlefield, but his gold armor and weapons shone brightly in the sunlight. Seth and Antiope were too far back in the ranks for her to see, but the enemy hadn't reached that far yet and they hadn't pulled from her powers for help, so she wasn't worried. Demetrius was fighting only a short distance from her, his armor and weapons drenched in blood. He locked eyes with her for a moment and nodded to let her know he was fine. She did the same.

She grazed her eyes over the fields, slowly spotting most of the others. She could see Ahura, leader of the Persian pantheon, moving in her direction, constantly looking toward her to check her position. Suddenly, Cassiopeia felt a goddess flash next to her. She dodged her initial attack and lashed back just as violently. The other goddess' eyes were glowing a bright light brown. They fought viciously, but Cassiopeia could quickly tell that her skill was greater than the other goddess'. A few movements and blows later, she felt her sword sink into flesh. The goddess' eyes widened and slowly faded back to their normal dark brown. Cassiopeia watched as the life drained from her face as she removed the sword and the blood poured out. As her body fell to the ground Cassiopeia saw the black dust of the fallen goddess' powers flow out of her body and into herself. She gasped at the sudden invasive feeling and regained her senses.

Some of the enemies who had been fighting around her paused, their eyes widening at the sight of their fallen goddess. She used some of the new gained power to lash out, killing them. When she looked back to find Demetrius, she saw him fighting Ahura.

Demetrius was fighting the Persian god fiercely. They matched each other blow for blow, each of them swinging with deadly force. Blocking a blow from Ahura, Demetrius turned to attack back. As he turned, he felt the sharp pain of a blade penetrate his abdomen and go up to his chest as the Persian god twisted and sliced up his body. He gasped out in shock, but felt no pain. Demetrius looked across the field to Cassiopeia. She had seen what happened and the expression of pain on her face cut him worse than the sword that was still in his side. He looked at Ahura, who was still holding him up. The god looked just as he did on the day when Demetrius had fought against his army as a mortal. The first time he had ever fought alongside his wife.

"This is so that your wife feels the same pain that I did when she killed my brother."

Ahura let him go and Demetrius fell to his knees.

Cassiopeia watched as the Persian God plunged his sword into Demetrius' side. Her stomach dropped to the ground as she saw him twist and slice. Every piece of her heart shattered. Every wall that she had up, every cage that held back her demons, broke. She couldn't breathe as her entire world came crashing in on itself. She stopped, frozen in place by her pain, her sword slowly slipping from her hand. The entire world had gone into slow motion around her.

She flashed over to his side and fell to her knees next to him. Tears had already begun to run down her face. Cassiopeia looked at the wound and she knew he wouldn't make it. Not even a god could have recovered from a wound so severe. It still didn't stop her from instinctively holding his side to try to stop the bleeding.

"No, no, no. You're going to be fine. You can't die. You can't leave me. Please." Her voice pleaded with him as tears poured from her eyes.

He brought his hand to her cheek. "Cassiopeia, stop . . . I love you. Kiss me."

Her heart ached even more at his final request.

"Please don't leave me," she whispered.

"Shh. Just kiss me. I just want to feel you."

She cupped his cheeks and kissed him. Her lips were full of love and feelings as she pushed every ounce of herself into their kiss. She pulled away and looked into his light blue eyes.

"Please . . . Demetrius, I love you. I love you so much. I can't go on alone. I can't . . . please."

Cassiopeia knew her pleas were futile, but she had no power to do anything else. She leaned back down and kissed him again. She could feel his hand getting weaker against her cheek, she pulled her lips away and buried her head into his neck, breathing him in.

"Tell Seth and Antiope that . . . I love . . . them . . . so much."

"I will." She sobbed the words into him.

She wanted to use her powers to heal him, but she knew that his wound was too severe. She wouldn't have enough energy and power to stop the inevitable. Her heart was finally accepting what her mind already knew. He was going to die. She was never going to snuggle up to him in bed or hear his voice again. She was never going to run her fingers through his curly blond hair or gaze into his light blue eyes. So many other things that she wished they had done one last time.

Cassiopeia kissed him again, pressing his hand against her cheek. The tears wouldn't stop flowing from her eyes as she slowly felt his palm slip from her face and he slid into the darkness. Cassiopeia felt as Demetrius took his last breath and his body stilled to sleep, never to awaken again. She felt the cold weight of death as she had never felt it before. It sat on her chest and crushed her heart like a pit that would never recede. This was a pain she had never felt before. Something even her dreams could not prepare her for. As if a piece of her had died as well. She pulled her body against his and just held him close, her own body heavy with the pain. Her hands touched the ground and she could feel where his blood had stained the soil beneath his body. She hadn't even noticed that one by one the gods and creatures around her began to cough blood and fall to the ground. She could hear the Persian god, Ahura, yelling something, presumably at her, but her mind didn't hear him. Only her pain filled her. She couldn't contain it anymore. She dug her fingers into the Earth. She felt all the living things in the world. She reached out to every Persian string within miles as far as she could reach without dropping any of them. She grabbed them with her mind and screamed as she lashed her pain out at them.

The whole world froze at her heart piercing cry and every Persian, god and creature alike, fell to the ground dead around her. Cassiopeia could feel the dust from their powers pouring into her, filling her body and charging her powers, charging the demon inside. She could feel the shock of her actions over the planet. The sudden shift of power. Cassiopeia didn't care if it destroyed the world, she didn't care about anything. She created a force field around herself and Demetrius. All she felt was a cold emptiness inside. She couldn't focus on anything other than the aching in her heart. There was yelling and talking in the distance, but she didn't listen. It didn't matter to her. Nothing mattered anymore.

Time passed, she wasn't even aware of how much, and then she heard a voice she never expected to ever hear in this realm.

"Oh, my little broken star."

Lilith.

Cassiopeia pushed the force field out harder, her powers surging forward.

"That won't work, my sweet girl. I am just a shade. Caelum didn't free me; I just felt your pain. Your children felt your pain, they share in it."

"Your words mean nothing to me. You knew and you lied. I have no want or desire for you to be in my life. Shut up and go away!"

"There was nothing we could do. Please listen to me, my little star. Your children need their mother."

"Don't call me that! That's what Magnus called me! I never want to see you again! What would you know about a child needing their mother after what you did to me? I don't want to hear your voice!"

Lilith paused before responding. "Then I shall stand here in silence, but remember I am here for you when you are ready."

Cassiopeia didn't know how long she had been sitting there in her misery, but she didn't care. Here she still felt his body against her. His cheek next to hers. She could run her fingers through his hair. Just be with him even though he was gone. Suddenly she felt someone push against the barrier, but she held it strong. Then she felt it again, but differently. This time she didn't want to fight it, she couldn't fight it. Cassiopeia felt the newcomer break through and flash over to her. She could vaguely hear Lilith speak to the intruder before they walked over to her. She heard a deep voice say her name then silence. A few moments later he spoke again.

"It's Alexander. You have to get up." He waited a few moments. "Cassi—"

"Go away. Leave me to my misery."

She didn't want to speak to him or to anyone. What did he think he was going to do for her? Give her a hug? Make her a cup of tea? He didn't know her, and he couldn't bring Demetrius back, therefore he was of no use to her.

"You know I can't do that. Your children are worried. They don't need to lose two parents today."

She turned to look at him.

"Go away!" The demon inside of her yelled out. She didn't want to hear about her children. She didn't want to have to face them. Her own sadness was overwhelming to her. She couldn't imagine seeing that sadness on their faces. She looked into Alexander's lavender eyes and she could see his sympathy and the pain that he felt for her.

"I'm not leaving you." He crouched down closer to her. "I will always be here, whenever you need me."

She wanted to leave and go with him back to her family, but she couldn't leave Demetrius. She promised him forever. She turned back and looked at his face. He looked peaceful. As though he were sleeping, bound to wake any moment. A new wave of pain crashed over her. Then she felt Alexander touch her shoulder and she cringed, standing quickly and whipping around to glare at him.

"Don't touch me!"

He stood with her and grabbed her arms. The anger and rage inside of her went to lash out. Cassiopeia pushed her powers out and reached into the earth for his string but there was none. She pushed her powers against him to shove him back but again nothing happened. She glared into his eyes, that were glowing as brightly as hers but his were a deep royal purple. She realized her powers had no effect over him. He was immune. Then she saw a window into his mind. He was trying to show her something. As she pushed her own mind toward it, the image became clearer.

"How?"

"He wanted me to show you this, after it was over," Alexander said quietly.

Cassiopeia saw, in her mind Alexander's conversation with Demetrius from the day before.

"She will need you more than ever. I know that one day she will be strong again, but not on this day. I don't know when it's going to happen, but I know it's soon." Demetrius looked over at Alexander. "And, based on your expression, I'm not wrong . . . Damn." Demetrius looked away sadly out into the expansive ocean just off the shore of Isle Del Alexandrius, Alexander's private island.

"Just keep her as she is, not like her father or her mother. I want my Cassiopeia raising Antiope and Seth. I don't want them to lose both parents whenever it happens. Promise me." Alexander nodded. Demetrius continued, "I just want her to be happy. I want them all to be happy again."

"Me too. That's all both of us have ever wanted." Alexander replied.

"Take care of her. This was always her biggest fear when she married me, and we thought we beat it. I guess even immortals must die. She gave me a life I could have never imagined if I had stayed mortal and never been with her. I regret nothing. I want her to know that. Even knowing what's going to happen, I wouldn't change a thing. I would always choose to be with her. Don't let her

carry the guilt of my loss with her forever. You know what's going to happen I want her to have that future. I want her to be happy again."

"He didn't want you to be consumed by your pain and hate." Alexander said quietly as he watched more tears fall down her face. She pulled her mind away from his.

"He knew he was going to die, and he didn't tell me. Why?" she said quietly.

"It had to happen. Demetrius knew that. He knew what his future was every day he was with you. For him, being with you for the time you two had was worth the sacrifice he would have to make later."

Cassiopeia looked up at Alexander. She felt her pain taking control over the rage and anger. More tears poured from her face as she felt the waves of anguish wash over her.

"It hurts and I . . . I don't know what to do," she said desperately.

Alexander's eyes stopped glowing as he stepped closer and pulled her into a deep embrace. She could feel his emotions in his touch, how her pain spread to him. She cried into his chest and just let it wash over her. His body warmed her from being on the cold ground and she relaxed, giving in to her sorrow.

"I am so sorry you have to feel this pain," he said sadly. "Forgive me for this."

Before she had time to react to his words, she felt a pressure wash over her and then darkness consumed her mind as she shifted into unconsciousness. The last thing she felt was the demon slip back into its cage in her mind.

Cassiopeia awoke in her bed on Vēlatusa. She felt peaceful for a moment before reality crashed back down onto her. Moving slightly, she could feel someone on either side of her. She opened her eyes and sat up a little to look around. Antiope was curled into her on one side while Seth was pressed into her, lying on his back on the other. Athena had her arms around him, her hand resting on Cassiopeia's shoulder from under Seth's head. Antiope began to awaken at her mother's movement. Cassiopeia looked down at her daughter, she could tell that she had cried herself to sleep. As her eyes opened, she focused on her mother's face.

"Mitéra." Antiope said, her voice barely above a whisper.

Cassiopeia kissed her daughter's forehead and pulled her in closer. She felt the waves of pain returning to wash over her, but she knew she had to listen to Demetrius' last wishes and be strong for her children. As much as she wanted to crawl into a hole and wallow in her sadness, she knew she couldn't. She had to rise above it, at least in front of them.

"How long have I been sleeping?"

"Two days. Alexander told us not to worry. That your body had to recover from absorbing and releasing all of the power from the dead gods. It's been really hard not being able to talk to you."

Antiope snuggled closer to her mother. They had always been so close. Even when Cassiopeia was pregnant she could feel her daughter's presence in the world, and as she grew that bond only became stronger. It made her worry for Seth, who was very close with his father.

"How has Seth been?"

"He's not doing well. He says he's fine but . . . Mitéra, he hasn't cried. He's just holding it all in and I'm worried."

"Everyone grieves in their own ways my sweet little one."

Cassiopeia stopped speaking as she felt Seth awakening. He groaned lightly before opening his eyes. As he looked up at his mother, his eyes widened slightly in joy at seeing her awake.

"Mitéra, do you feel better?" He saw her eyes tear up and realized his mistake. "I meant physically. Alexander said you needed to sleep to heal and absorb the powers. I meant physically, as in the power . . ."

"Seth, my sweet chosen one, I know what you meant. Yes, I do."

She honestly didn't know, as she couldn't feel anything other than her pain and her love for her children, but she didn't want them to know that. He rolled over and hugged her and Antiope tightly.

"We're going to be okay. We are strong. Patéras made sure we would be. He would want us to be strong for his memory."

Cassiopeia felt a tear slide down her cheek. She tenderly ran her fingers through her son's hair.

"Sometimes you don't have to be strong. Sometimes you can let the pain in for a little while. You can be weak to make yourself better."

"I am fine."

She could tell that he was barely holding on. Athena was now awake. She sat up and looked over at Cassiopeia. Cassiopeia could see the rim of red around Athena's eyes and the sadness that still consumed them.

Athena spoke. "Seth, he wouldn't want you to be just fine. Demetrius . . ." Her voice cracked when she said his name. "He would want you to be able to move on and be happy again. To mourn him and then enjoy his memory. Just as Priamos wanted when he passed to the underworld."

Athena leaned over and wrapped her arms around her grandson. She gently rubbed his back.

Cassiopeia spoke, her voice cracking as the words came out. "He told me a few days ago that if anything ever happened to him, he wanted us all to be happy. To always stay together as a family and to support each other forever. Even in his absence. He knew he might not leave that battlefield. I don't know how he knew, but he did. And even facing death, his final wish to all of us was for us to be there for each other in his memory. It's okay to cry, Seth. It's okay to let the pain in. You have to feel to be able to heal."

Seth stayed quiet, but then she felt a gentle sob against her chest. His small sobs became more intense as his emotions poured out with every tear and every breath. This pain was the one she never wanted know, the pain of her children being hurt, of their hearts getting broken. Cassiopeia looked at Athena as she felt more of her own tears returning. She watched as a tear fell from the Greek goddess' eyes at the thought of her son. Cassiopeia remembered that even when Priamos and then Markus died, Athena hadn't showed this much emotion. She had felt the same security that Cassiopeia had taken for granted. The security that immortals couldn't be hurt. That they were exempt from death.

Cassiopeia would mourn a little longer and then, for Demetrius and her children, she would get up and be strong. She would hunt down the Persians who were involved and got away in the unjust murder of her husband and she would kill them all slowly. They would feel her wrath to the point where no one would ever dare come after her family again without threats of death. They would know the pain of the destruction of their pantheon and families. She would be cold and heartless to take care of what needed to be done, then she would return to her children and slowly their family would heal together.

Cassiopeia heard gasps and then silence as she entered Alexander's domain. She could feel Alexander and all the other gods looking at her, but she didn't care. She was wearing black and gold Atlantean mourning robes and her hair was pulled up in a pile of braids. She kept her face expressionless. They all knew why she was here: revenge. She could feel Alexander's surprise at her arrival. While she did still hold a seat on the council, she was staying away while she mourned. No one expected her to come unannounced.

Cassiopeia turned to look at Alexander, and she watched as the realization of why she was here hit him. She knew that Alexander was going to try to keep the peace and talk her out of what she was here to do, but she wasn't going to let him.

"He will pay. I am here to collect my debt," Cassiopeia said firmly.

Alexander stood and stepped toward her. "There is a process, I can't just let you kill him without proper evidence that what he did was malicious and unjust."

"I can get you your evidence with one touch!"

She glared over at the Persian. Ahura had escaped the day that he killed Demetrius, leaving his men behind to die at her hands.

"She will not touch me! She is biased!" Ahura shouted. But before anyone could object either way, Cassiopeia flashed to right next to him. He stood quickly and angrily, trying to move away from her, but she grabbed his shoulder, her fingers touching his bare neck. She felt her eyes shift from their bright blue to a deep vivid red. They glowed as her powers flowed forward, showing her his whole life. Every evil thing he had ever done.

"You lie. You have lied to your own people and you have lied to this council. You gave the permission for the attack on my pantheon, leading to an unjust war. You have also led the attacks on, and deaths of, numerous other creatures and gods from other pantheons, even after peace treaties were signed. As your punishment you—"

"Stop! You do not have the authority to assign punishment here!" Alexander shouted, his voice full of anger.

Cassiopeia could see on his face that he wasn't ignorant to the fact that the Persians had been more involved than they were letting on. She glared at him, infuriated that he wouldn't let her have what was rightfully hers.

Alexander spoke again. "Step away. He will receive a punishment deemed appropriate by the council."

Not wanting to fight him, Cassiopeia reluctantly obliged, taking two steps back. He could have his charade, but she knew that she wasn't going to let the Persian leave this council room alive. She also didn't want to clash with Alexander if she didn't have to, because she honestly didn't know who would win.

"May I stay?"

"No!" The Persian god shouted, full of rage. "Make her leave. She is biased. She has no right to be here. Her interjection is not valid!" he insisted.

"Yes. This involves you," Alexander said.

"Can you not control who enters your home or who rules over you anymore, leviathan?"

Alexander's head whipped around toward the Persian, who had now greatly overstepped his bounds. Cassiopeia saw his eyes beginning to glow.

"Excuse me?" Alexander spat angrily.

The arrogant god realized his mistake, but it was too late. Now he had angered the leviathan. He had challenged his authority and power. Cassiopeia could see Alexander was fed up with Ahura's games and watching him dance around the truth as if he thought Alexander were stupid. His eyes glowed more intensely, and she could feel his powers surging forward.

"Yes, I can control who enters my domain. I can also control who leaves it."

Before anyone could react, the Persian god caught fire and burned until there was nothing left but a burn spot on the chair and that section of the table. The black dust of his powers flowed across the room and into Alexander.

"And who leaves all the other domains of the living." Cassiopeia looked up from the burn mark to Alexander.

"They're will be no more council discussions on the matter of Demetrius of the Greek pantheon. The entire bloodline of Ahura's family is gone from the realms. Let this be a reminder of my power and of the laws that we have governing the pantheons. This council was set up to keep all of the pantheons in check, but I will not be treated as if I am ignorant or stupid. Justice is done. Have I made my standing on these matters clear?"

The members were in agreement.

"Meeting adjourned. Leave my domain."

All of the gods and goddesses left quickly with no arguments, all afraid to anger Alexander more.

Cassiopeia was still standing behind the Persian's chair, slightly unsure of what to do. She looked up at Alexander, who walked over to her. He had sorrow in his ancient lavender eyes. She looked back at the burned table and chair.

"I don't know what to do now. I thought his death would bring me some peace, but it doesn't. I am happy he has paid for the crimes he committed, that all of them involved have paid but..." she trailed off, looking up at him with a glint of anger in her eyes. "I had it under control. I didn't need your help."

"I know, but you are in my domain and this is my council. If I let every god or goddess come in and take out their wrath on the other council members, firstly there would be no one left on the council and secondly no one would respect my authority. I know you could have handled it, but you also don't have the authority or my permission to kill council members without a proper trial."

She glared at him. Cassiopeia wanted to argue, but she knew he was right. She knew that if he didn't know her, if he didn't care for her, he would have destroyed her the second she entered the council room late without his permission. She looked back down at the burn mark. While she knew he did certain things for her, she never understood why.

"Thank you," she said gently. "I think I would still be in that field if Antiope hadn't gotten you, or if you hadn't come." She paused, "How were you able to get through? How did I not kill you?"

"Did you want to kill me?"

She paused as she thought. "At first, I wanted to kill everything, so yes. But mainly I just wanted to be left alone, to be swallowed by my grief and rage. Somehow, you pushed through. How?"

"Maybe you didn't want to hurt me. Maybe you just needed someone who wasn't family." He paused, winking playfully at her. "I'm also pretty awesome and powerful."

She cracked a small smile as she looked up at him.

"One day I'll be better. One day I will be back to my normal, happy self."

"I know you will be."

She touched his arm softly. Then she stepped back from him and with those final words she left to go home to her children.

Chapter 11

Party Time
2019 CE

One of the happiest moments in life is when you find the courage to let go of what you cannot change.
—Anonymous

Cassiopeia was standing outside of the Immortal Fire bar in New York City. Run by Dionysis, it was the favorite of many other supernatural beings because it catered to them better than mortal bars, even though mortals were still allowed inside. New York had become the East Coast hub for supernatural business. Even Cassiopeia had an apartment in the city to keep up her more *mortal* business appearances, but she still primarily resided in Vēlatusa. With modern times came modern changes to how the gods needed to run things to stay in power, and business was one way to stay on top.

She approached the bar with her long, dark blonde hair down in loose curls. Her makeup was perfectly applied, and she was dressed to the nines in her black jeans and cropped blouse. There was a fire in her bright blue eyes. She wasn't planning on going home alone. She had been in a dry spell for too long for it to continue.

Sierra was with her and just as dressed up, except she wasn't on the prowl, she was just excited for the party. She was dressed similarly but in a more gothic style, with her hair straightened and purple streaks throughout. The Vantha demon was disguised as a human and matched heights with Cassiopeia as well as in hair and eye color. One would think they were sisters, but everyone who knew them knew they were a lethal combination of an immortal goddess and a powerful demon.

Cassiopeia looked over to her Vantha companion and guard. "You ready for a good night?"

"Yes! I am very excited for this party!" Sierra said excitedly. She loved to spend time with other demons.

"Let's go kill it!" Cassiopeia paused. "Not literally please."

Sierra looked disappointed but nodded her head. They skipped the line and walked up to the bouncer.

"Hey Henry! It's nice to see you again." Cassiopeia smiled kindly at him.

"I don't know how you always look so beautiful! It's like you never age. Your brother is the same way." He chuckled as he moved aside to let her in. "If you need anything, my youthful goddess, just ask. Have fun!" He winked and she smiled at his surprisingly accurate endearment, especially since Henry had no clue what she was.

She winked back as they strolled inside. As she surveyed the room, Sierra was already halfway to the dance floor heading toward Sitara, the birthday girl, Caelum's Vantha demon. Technically it was Caelum's birthday as well but he didn't get as much enjoyment out of celebrating as his demon did. When Sierra reached her, Cassiopeia could hear their squeals of excitement from across the loud crowded bar. She chuckled. She looked over at the bar and spotted Sara, the bartender. She walked over and found an open stool.

"Hey girlie! Welcome to the party! I just hope we have enough food!"

Sara looked genuinely worried as she spoke.

Cassiopeia laughed. "Worst case scenario, you'll have to sacrifice the humans!" she said sarcastically. They both laughed.

"What can I get you my dear?" Sara asked.

"Bourbon, on the rocks."

"Gotcha! I'll be right back."

Cassiopeia nodded at her and looked around. She could see that they had roped off almost half of the seating areas in the bar for the private party. She and Sierra had gotten here before most of the guests. Good. She needed to relax before being social with half of these buffoons. As much as she liked most of them, they took a lot of energy. Especially when she was facing them alone.

"Here you go, have fun!"

Cassiopeia smiled at Sara before she slid the drink closer. She hated bourbon, but it was the only way she could stomach the powdered lotus she was about to add to her drink; otherwise, it was way too sweet for her palette and she would want to spit it out. Gods had a natural revulsion to lotus. If they did ingest it, it worked just like it does on humans, removing inhibitions, the concept of time, and all stress, giving the user a sense of peace even in dangerous situations. She hadn't taken lotus in years. But Athena had gotten her hands on some and shared with her, knowing she needed this mental break.

Cassiopeia sprinkled half of the powder into her drink, ensuring no one saw her. She swirled her glass around in the air to stir it in. She was about to raise it to her lips when she heard a voice she hadn't heard in a very long time.

"Well, this party is so much fun you're starting the night with a bourbon. Now that's my kind of night."

She set her drink down and turned around in her seat. There he was. Less than a foot away. Alexander. She hadn't realized how she had missed seeing his face. Nothing had ever happened between them since they had parted ways all of those years ago, as he had kept a distance between them, even when he had been there for her as a friend. His wavy black hair hung down to his shoulders, and he looked down at her with his devastatingly unique lavender eyes. They stood out from his tawny skin. She could see his muscles through the black T-shirt he wore. Cassiopeia had forgotten how overpowering and intoxicating he was, as she smelled the sandalwood and jasmine on his skin.

She gave him a sly look. "Sounds like you're just jealous that I already have my drink." She turned back to drink her drink and it vanished from her hand.

"Hey! What the—"

She looked at Alexander to see the bourbon in his hand.

"Oh. What? Thanks!" he said with a sarcastic smirk, before tilting his head back and downing the whole glass in one large swig. Cassiopeia hadn't even had time to react. She just looked at him with her jaw dropped. Based on the expression that he gave her he wasn't expecting it either. It tasted weird.

"That was some shitty bourbon," he said with a scowl.

"I . . ." she started to laugh. "I am so sorry. I wouldn't have done that! That was for me."

She giggled, turning away toward the bar. She waved Sara over and asked for another. Cassiopeia looked back over at him smiling, with a guilty look on her face.

"Well, you're about to feel really good."

"What?" he asked, confused by her statement. Sara came over with the new bourbon.

"Thank you," Cassiopeia said as she took the glass. She shook the rest of the powdered lotus into the glass, swirling it around. She took a breath and slammed it back. She made a face at the bitterness of the bourbon and the nasty sweetness of the lotus.

"Please tell me you didn't just drug me," he said slowly.

"I actually don't know what will happen to a leviathan, but we're going to find out. And I didn't drug you. *You* stole my drugged drink." She looked at him slyly and said, "It's okay, it's just lotus."

She watched his face twist slightly at that news, then he looked calm.

"I should be pissed or upset, but I'm not . . . why am I not?"

She started giggling. "That's cuz you're drugged, honey!"

Laughing harder she could feel the effects start to take hold. She leaned into him, laughing, and he smiled back at her. As much as he hated seeing her drug herself, he enjoyed seeing her smile again. Seeing her face again. He had stayed away for too long. Alexander realized that if he didn't stop smiling, someone was going know that something was up. He tried to be stoic, but it wasn't working. He looked over at her and she was looking at him intently.

"You've never done drugs before have you?"

"When I was mortal. But we had nothing like this." He leaned closer to her. "Why do you smell so good?"

She laughed. "Well, it's definitely working. Now I get to enjoy watching how well you can hold your drugs." She winked at him.

He felt his groin stir.

Damn. Self-control, dude, Alexander thought.

He knew that he couldn't make an advance anyway, but for reasons she didn't need to know, yet. But she didn't know that, and he knew her feelings based on how she was eyeballing him.

He felt that tingle again.

Ugh! This is going to be a long night.

He walked away a few steps, and she followed. She grabbed his hand and pulled him gently toward the dance floor.

"No," he said firmly.

"Just one?" she said, pouting and opening her eyes wide.

Damn.

He could feel more of the lotus slipping over his mind. He just followed. She turned to him when they got to the edge of the floor and whispered into his ear.

"By the way, lotus, is an aphrodisiac."

She pulled her head back and looked up at him with lust-filled eyes. He had already started to figure that out based on the aching that was growing more and more insistent between his legs. Cassiopeia spun around and walked further into the dance floor. She turned back to face him. He knew he should have felt awkward because he had never danced in public before, but he felt no worry or anxiety.

Before he could start making a fool of himself, he heard a cheerful voice shout out. "Alex! You made it! Yay! And now you came out to dance with me!" Sitara squealed.

Cassiopeia laughed at the demon's over-exuberant excitement. Alexander chuckled too. She was one of very few creatures that could get away with calling him Alex.

"Happy birthday, Sitara!"

He pulled a small present out of his pocket.

Sitara squealed in delight. "Oh! For me!"

She grabbed the gift and flitted off through the crowd toward a table covered with presents to add it toward the growing mountain. He turned back to Cassiopeia, who was dancing by herself even though she was surrounded by people on the crowded dance floor. He enjoyed watching the way she moved. The way she swayed her hips and rocked her body back and forth.

Alexander tried to look away but couldn't. He couldn't resist as he prowled his way to her. She smiled as she saw him get closer. He knew if he didn't say it now then he would be too far gone and wouldn't say it later and bad things would happen. She reached out and ran her hands down his arms when he got within reach. He knew exactly what she wanted. He could feel the tattoo on his arm stinging slightly as she touched it.

"Dance?" she asked playfully.

He leaned in to her and whispered in her ear. "I will do *whatever* you want tonight, but you must make me a promise." She looked up at him, excited at that prospect. "We will not have sex tonight." He could sense her disapproval, but he finished his thought to save himself from sounding like a prude. He touched his lips to her ear. "If I am going to have sex with you, I don't want it to be when we are both drugged. I want to remember it. Every. Single. Second." He felt her body break out into chills.

He pulled back and looked into her eyes.

She gave him a shy little smirk and she nodded in agreement. "I promise. No intercourse. But that's all I can promise." She winked as she looked him up and down.

She glanced behind her, grabbed his shirt, pulled him with her, and took about five steps backwards. Her back was now pressed against a wall. He realized they were hidden from sight in a small side hallway. Alexander looked back down at her as she slid her hand from his shirt up to the nape of his neck and gently pulled his head toward hers. He knew he should pull away, but looking into her eyes, he couldn't resist. He placed his hand on her lower back and pulled her body closer to his and leaned down to find her lips. He placed his other hand on her cheek as he kissed her passionately, pulling her body in close to his as their kiss deepened.

She had heard of kisses as good as sex, but this was different. She had seen fireworks in a kiss before, but this just felt like it was meant to be. Like the universe itself had put them together for this one purpose. She was starting to vastly regret the promise that she had made only a minute before. When she thought that he was about to pull away, he just deepened the passion of the kiss. His tongue danced with hers and his smell filled her senses. She could have stood there in the back corner of this bar all night and the world would have gone on without them. His body was pressed into hers, as she felt every curve of his muscles against her body. When he drank the lotus, she had changed her plans to sleeping with Alexander tonight. But then he made her promise there would be no sex with that sweet statement: *I want to remember it. Every. Single. Second.* That did it. There would be no sex tonight. But tomorrow morning was fair game.

Alexander didn't know how long they were standing there kissing, but he felt her gently pull away. He lifted his head from hers and she looked up at him with lust-filled eyes. Cassiopeia looked out toward the bar with a bit of distain, then looked back up at him and grabbed him back into a quick passionate kiss. He groaned. She gave at little giggle at his pleasure. She nibbled his lip as she pulled away and looked up at him.

"I have to go. Others have arrived and we need to make a non-drugged appearance."

Alexander focused his mind toward the people who had arrived. He knew who she was talking about. Antiope and Seth. He nuzzled his forehead against hers, and with a reluctant moan he took a step away from her to let her leave. She looked up at him and followed his step, keeping her body pressed to his.

"Don't think that this means you are off the hook tonight. There are *plenty* of things we can do besides sex."

Alexander could tell, based on the look on her face, that her list was growing longer by the minute. His groin felt like it was going to explode. It physically pained him to let her go and watch her walk back toward the party.

He turned and leaned with his back against the wall. Running his fingers through his hair, he let out a ragged breath.

What did you get yourself into tonight? This was supposed to just be a stupid birthday party.

Cassiopeia walked out of the shadows and toward the bar. She was still on cloud nine from some of the lotus but mainly from that kiss. It had been a very, very long time since someone had taken her breath away.

Focus. You are drugged, but no one can know that. Focus. Make an appearance. Make it respectable, and then you can leave and go have the best no-sex night of your life with Alexander.

She never thought she would hear herself think that last part: *with Alexander.*

He always seemed to pull away from her when they started to get close. Even as friends. He basically vanished from her life shortly after everything happened with Demetrius. Since then they had only seen each other at council meetings and events like this, but that was it—polite interactions and nothing more. But tonight, he was so forward.

It must just be a really good batch of lotus. I'll have to thank Athena later. Maybe he will regret the whole thing in the morning. Maybe he will enjoy it so much you can stay forever. Wow. *Okay. That last bit was definitely the lotus talking.*

Cassiopeia walked toward the bar where she spotted her children standing with Caelum. They were all grown and looked to be in their mid-twenties, the same as her. Both were more than 4,000 years old, though, but they would always be her babies. They turned around and saw her. Cassiopeia watched Antiope's face light up.

"Mitéra!" She jumped up from her seat and bounced over happily to her, pulling Cassiopeia into a tight embrace.

Cassiopeia laughed. "It's wonderful to see you too sweetie! How's school?"

Antiope was working on her tenth college degree. This time she was majoring in nuclear technology. As a goddess of wisdom and education, she was always eager to learn, absorbing knowledge like a sponge. She never forgot anything. Standing equal in height to her mother, they could be doppelgängers. She did have some of her father's features, including his light blonde, wavy hair, but she had her mother's eyes.

"It's great! I have my own place and Seth just moved in! As you can tell, he's super excited."

Cassiopeia looked over at her son, Seth, just in time to see him roll his eyes playfully. He too had some of his mother's features, but he stood almost eight inches taller than her. At six feet, five inches, he stood taller than most. He had floppy, light blonde hair that fell just past his eyes, when it wasn't flipped back, and he had his father's light blue eyes. They were both very attractive; a perk of being children of gods.

"Yay! It's wonderful sharing an apartment with my little sister," he said sarcastically.

They all knew that he had the means to have his own place if he wanted, but he always tried to stay close to his little sister. He was her protector and had been there for her since before she could walk. Cassiopeia was so happy that they had kept their bond through all of the centuries. If only Cassiopeia and her brother, Caelum, had gotten to have the same relationship growing up. Cassiopeia held her arms open for Seth and he reluctantly hugged her.

He acted like it was so difficult, but he pulled her in a tight embrace.

"I have missed you, my strong boy," she whispered into his ear. "I hope you're happy too."

"I am Mitéra. I just wish you were around more," he said quietly, as he pulled back to look at her longingly. She had been traveling more and more lately, and it had been taking a toll on their little family. She hadn't been able to settle for long before she would start to get restless. She had been like that for many years. Maybe it was the universe's way of trying to tell her something.

"I will be. Things are changing. Hopefully after the next couple months there will be no more traveling."

She smiled up at him and looked over at the bar. Alexander was sitting there talking to Sitara. It was actually probably the other way around, with Sitara talking and Alexander just nodding in agreement. Cassiopeia couldn't get him off of her mind.

"I'm gonna go get a drink and see if Sitara wants to dance," she chuckled, looking at Caelum.

He laughed too, rolling his eyes sarcastically. "Sitara? In the mood for dancing? Never."

Cassiopeia walked toward the bar. Alexander saw her heading his way. He smirked at her and she smiled back. He felt himself stirring again.

Damn.

She had him wrapped around her finger tonight. That lotus worked wonders. All he wanted to do was get her alone and touch every single part of her body. The part that worried him more than that was the fact that he wanted to tell her everything, too. Even the things he knew he shouldn't, the things he knew he couldn't. As she got closer, he saw she was looking at Sitara.

"Hey birthday girl! You wanna dance?" Cassiopeia winked at her.

"Yes!! Oh, I'm so excited! Bye, Alex, we're going to dance the night away!"

"Okay just give me one second, I have to order my drink, then I'll be out there!" Cassiopeia said to the excited demon.

202 The Atlantean Constellation

"Ugh! Fine. Hurry!"

Sitara skipped away toward the dance floor to get started without her. Cassiopeia leaned toward the bar, brushing over Alexander's lap. He was too focused on her body to even realize what she was doing. She stood back up and he saw the drink menu in her hand.

"I have to see what I want . . ."

"Why do I have the feeling that you know that menu by heart? You have been coming to this bar for the past two hundred years. I'm pretty sure you have tried every alcoholic drink on the planet twice over." He lowered his voice. "So that begs the question of whether you really wanted the menu or you leaned over me just to turn me on?"

Those words made her tingle. She was fighting the urge to just take him to the back room and make him hers for the night. The sexual tension between them was brutal. She didn't look up from the menu, pretending to be reading it intently.

"Maybe they added something new." After a few seconds, she looked up at Sara. "Rum and coke. Oh, and two tequila shots." She leaned back over him to return the menu, but when she finished setting it down, she turned toward the floor to look at Sitara, rubbing her bottom gently against his leg as she turned. He groaned.

"You're brutal," he muttered under his breath.

He heard her chuckle quietly. A few minutes later, Sara came over with her drinks.

"Here are your drinks, honey!" Sara said cheerfully.

"Thanks!"

Cassiopeia pushed one of the tequila shots toward him. She put the salt on her hand and picked up the lime.

"Cheers!" She lifted her shot, as if tempting him to take the other shot with her. Alexander looked down at the clear shot. He picked up the salt and sprinkled it onto the lime. Looking back at her he lifted the glass, clinked it with hers and downed it. He got to enjoy watching her lick the salt seductively off of her hand as he sucked on his lime. She smiled at him slyly and grabbed her drink. She started to walk away then turned back.

"Oh yeah, I forgot to tell you, silly me, alcohol makes the effects of the lotus stronger." She winked at him. "I probably should have mentioned that earlier."

She gave her hand one last slow lick as she turned and walked away. As he watched her go to the dance floor, he shook his head, feeling the alcohol take effect. She knew exactly what she was doing. He turned in his chair to see Caelum looking at him from across the room. Hopefully he didn't notice anything unusual. Alexander nodded at him, lifting his glass slightly. Caelum did the same, then looked away. Good. Alexander felt better. He didn't want his drugged lust to get him into a fight with one of his best friends. Caelum was very protective of his big sister and nothing was going to change that.

Several hours passed without incident. Cassiopeia had already come back over and ordered her last drink and closed her tab. She looked at Alexander when she did it, as if letting him know she was planning to leave soon. Sitara had Cassiopeia and Sierra out on the dance floor for almost the entire night. Alexander had wished she was closer but at the same time was grateful for the distance to allow for him to settle down. As he sat there, his right arm tingled and shivered. Something was wrong. Where was Cassiopeia? He looked around the dance floor. He couldn't find the demons, but then he spotted her. Cassiopeia was being cornered and corralled toward the back corner of the dance floor by a group of men. Mortals. They hadn't touched her, but he could sense she'd had enough of them, and they wouldn't let her pass. She turned toward Alexander, meeting his eyes. He could see she was beginning to get upset. He started to stand when one of the men grabbed her roughly by her upper shoulder, with his fingers touching her throat. He saw her eyes change from blue to red.

Shit!

Before he knew it, he was across the floor. Even Caelum hadn't noticed and didn't have time to react to what was happening.

"Come on babe, we're just having fun," one of the men said as they pressed her toward the back hallway. Cassiopeia was unimpressed with this game they were trying to play. It may make human women scared, but she wasn't human. She went to move away, and she looked over to where Alexander sat. He already had his eyes locked on her. She felt one of them grab her shoulder, his fingers touching the bare skin of her neck. She closed her eyes as she felt them beginning to change from blue to red. Before she could even see any of his memories or judge him, she felt his hand pull away from her neck. Someone else would have had to pull him away, a mortal would not have been able to break the connection alone. She heard a grunt and yelling. She opened her eyes to find Alexander next to her and felt his hand on her shoulder. A wave of relief washed over her.

"Are you okay?" The amount of concern in his voice warmed her to her core.

"Yes. I'll be fine." She looked over behind him and saw two of the employees picking up the unconscious bodies of the guys who had just tried to assault her. "Are they dead?"

"No," Alexander said angrily. "But they should be," he mumbled, his eyes glowing slightly.

"Thank you," she said gently, looking up at him and leaning into his chest.

"What happened?" Caelum said sternly, as he and Seth reached them.

"It's all fine now. Alexander saw it and stopped anything from happening or from being seen. I am fine. They would be dead if it were up to me."

She looked at Alexander, then spoke to the demons. "I think I am ready to leave. Sierra, you can still have a sleepover at Sitara's, if you would like to."

The demons squealed excitedly at the idea.

Caelum looked at her worried. "Are you sure you're okay to go home alone?"

"I'm not afraid of humans, they just took me by surprise. Let them come try to find me. Then I *will* give them my wrath." She glared at the men being carried out. "Really, I'm fine." She smiled at her brother.

"At least let me take you home," Caelum said.

"Oh, I'm good, Alexander already offered," she said, looking at Alexander.

He knew he didn't, but he wasn't going to argue. He cleared his throat. "I got her, don't worry. I'll make sure she's safe."

"Okay," Caelum said curiously.

Cassiopeia walked over to her table and grabbed her jacket. Alexander was already waiting by the door. She said goodbye to everyone and walked out of the bar. They walked over to the alleyway right next to the bar so they could flash to their domains without being seen. As they rounded the corner, she turned around to face him.

"You were watching me," she said firmly.

"What?"

"When I was dancing. You were watching me. That's the only way you would have been able to react that quickly."

"Maybe. Or perhaps I got a feeling, like a spidey-sense."

He winked at her. Little did she know that the latter was actually the more correct reason why he knew she was in danger.

She looked up into his lavender eyes. "Kiss me," she said softly.

He obliged. Leaning down he kept his hand on her lower back and placed his other hand on the nape of her neck. She reached up toward him, placing one hand on his cheek and the other on his chest. As their kiss deepened, he pulled her closer. He turned, lifting her up, and gently pinned her to the brick alleyway wall. His hand moved from her back to her bare waist. He slid his hand between her skin and blouse to her ribs, caressing her body. She wanted him closer. This was not close enough. Not much room to move. Too many clothes. She, reluctantly, pushed him away. As he broke away from her lips, he leaned his head down to kiss her neck. She could feel his stubble from the day scratch against her. That feeling usually bothered her, but right now it was a huge turn on. She wanted to say something, but all thoughts in her mind vanished when his lips touched her neck. She moaned deeply and it encouraged him. His hand made its way up to cup her breast. She could feel him kneading at her clothes and she wanted more. He wanted more. She finally remembered what she wanted to say. Just three little words.

"Your place. Now."

Nothing else had to be said. Alexander smiled and flashed them to his domain.

Chapter 12

After-Party
2019 CE

We were together. I forget the rest.
—Walt Whitman

Cassiopeia smelled the crisp ocean air of Isle del Alexandrius. She could feel a light breeze stir around them. He lifted her up, never breaking their kiss. She wrapped her legs around his waist, causing him to have to look up at her. She ran her fingers through his hair. He moaned at the feel of her touch. Right now, he didn't care about anything else but having her. He just wanted to lay her down and touch every part of her until she begged him to stop. He turned around and placed her on the bed, laying on top of her and supporting his weight on his elbows. She felt his body press against hers lightly. She really regretted wearing jeans tonight. They were so restrictive. Almost as if he was reading her mind, she felt his hand slide across her jeans. He lightly groaned in protest, then she felt her pants and shirt vanish. He leaned back and looked at her, lying there in just her lingerie. She was truly perfect. Every inch of her made him harder. Alexander knew that he shouldn't be doing this, but he was tired of fighting against what he wanted, and all he wanted was her. He leaned back down to kiss her. She felt his hand run down and then back up her bare leg.

Well, two can play this game, Cassiopeia thought playfully, as she made his shirt vanish.

He snickered against her lips as he felt her smirk. She trailed her fingers down his body, from his chest, over his abs, and down his hip bone until she reached the top of his pants. She unbuttoned them and wiggled her hand in past his waistband. No underwear. Commando. That made her feel even hotter for him. She continued her mission down a little further until she reached her goal. She took him in her hand. She could feel the soft velvety skin that was also as hard as a rock. He hissed with pleasure. It had been too long. He bit back the urge to finish right there. She began to move her hand up and down the length of him while grinding against his body. He could barely hold himself up as he felt waves of pleasure overcome him. He felt his body cover in chills. He pulled his lips away from hers and buried his face into her neck, groaning in pleasure. He didn't want to seem like he had no stamina but, with how long it had been and with it being her, he couldn't hold back any longer. It sent him over the edge. She felt him quiver in release. She smiled at her success and kissed the top of his head. He looked down at her. His eyes filled with love and longing. She leaned up and kissed him as she manifested a towel and wiped her hand.

He knew it was now her turn and he was going to make up for his lack of control. He lowered his head back to her neck and began kissing his way from her neck down to her collarbone, then down to her breast. Pushing her bra aside he took her nipple into his mouth. She felt fire course through her veins. His tongue flicked feverishly against her nipple. She felt his mouth pull away from her, as he slowly slid down her kissing every couple of inches. Cassiopeia looked down at Alexander as he raised his eyes to hers. He moved her underwear aside without breaking eye contact. She had already begun to ache in anticipation. Still looking at her, she felt him take her in his mouth, his tongue flicking expertly. Her moans filled the air as she burned with pleasure. Fire filled her veins. She gasped as he plunged his fingers inside of her, amplifying her pleasure. After a few moments she went over the tipping point. Her whole body erupted into waves of pure bliss. She grasped at the sheets and put one hand on his head, entangling her fingers in his long black hair. Her toes curled as he continued to lap at her tender folds. When she didn't think she could take much more, her body erupted again. She cried out his name as she arched in pleasure, tugging at his hair as he licked up her juices.

Alexander felt himself growing hard again. He couldn't wait. All his inhibitions where gone. He looked up her body as he made all of their remaining clothes vanish. Now he could see her completely bare to him. He growled as he slid back up her body quickly. He felt her pressed against him and that made his hunger even worse. He held her hands in his and pinned them above her head. She looked at him in surprise at his sudden ferocity. Cassiopeia felt the tip of him press against her core. She wanted it too. Badly. She could feel that she was ready, and he was too. Just one hip motion and all would be done.

No! You promised him, she thought.

Cassiopeia knew she couldn't break her word. She wasn't that kind of person. She looked into his hazy lavender eyes. She wanted him to truly want her, not just respond to drug-induced lust. Even though he felt *so* good, she knew she had to stop. He started to lean into her, and she was gone. Alexander looked down in surprise at his now empty bed. He looked around the dark room, confused. Then he saw her, standing out on the veranda breathing heavily, her hands leaning on the railing.

Cassiopeia couldn't believe that she had actually pulled away. She didn't know where her strength had come from. Part of her was furious at herself, and another part was happy that she kept her honor. She felt him flash to behind her.

"Are you alright?"

"Yes. I just . . . I made you a promise earlier tonight, and I want to keep it."

He chuckled lightly. She could sense that he had sobered slightly, due to her sudden exit. She breathed in the warm, crisp ocean air trying to clear her head. She could feel a light breeze stir around them. Then she felt him drape a soft blanket over her shoulders, and she reached up to hold it around her.

"Thank you. This view is . . . breathtaking," she said in awe, trying to distract herself from him.

"Yes, it is," he said softly. She looked back to see him staring at her.

She rolled her eyes. "Nice one, Mr. Cheesy Pick-up-line." They laughed together.

Alexander walked over to her and wrapped his arms around her. She looked out at the expanse of ocean and stars as he held her, her back to his chest. He closed his eyes, feeling at peace in this moment. This was all he had ever wanted. The two of them in the home that he had built for them. He could feel his emotions swelling.

Not yet. Hopefully soon this will truly be reality. Just savor this night.

She shivered a little and leaned deeper into his chest.

"Let's go back inside," he said quietly.

She turned around in his arms and looked up at him. Her eyes were full of emotion, but he couldn't figure out which one. She leaned up and kissed him softly. He lifted her into his arms and carried her back over to the bed. He lowered her onto the bed, their kiss deepening.

She pulled back, looking up at him and whispered, "Why now? How have we known each other for thousands of years but only now we realize all of these emotions?"

"Maybe it just hadn't been meant to be yet. Maybe our patience will pay off."

He nuzzled his head into her hair, lying next to her and breathing her in as he closed his eyes.

"Maybe," she said quietly, as he pressed into her back, pulling her tightly into his arms. She felt herself easily drift to sleep in his warm, safe embrace.

Maybe the universe does have a plan for us . . .

Alexander sat up quickly, awakened by the sound of the shower running.

Someone broke into my domain to take a shower? What the hell happened last night?

He groaned as his head pounded. Falling back into his pillows, he smelled her perfume on his sheets. He turned into the pillow and breathed in deeply. It was her. Cassiopeia. What the hell happened last night?

No, no, no, no . . .

He lifted the comforter and looked down at his nakedness. This was not good. Not good at all. He heard the water turn off as he looked toward the bathroom.

Cassiopeia walked around the corner, her hair wrapped up in a towel and another wrapped around her body. Water was still dripping down her legs.

"Oh, you're awake!" she said cheerfully. "There's aspirin, coffee, and water on the side table. I recommend all three if you want to feel better before the end of the day."

She smiled and turned to walk back into the bathroom.

"Wait," he said. She stopped and turned back around. "What the hell happened last night?"

She just looked at him, then she started giggling. Her giggles turned to laughter. His frustration was growing quickly.

"You really don't remember? It's okay, it happens sometimes." She paused and walked over to the bed, sitting next to him. "What's the last thing you do remember?"

He tried to think, but the fact that she was sitting on his bed with just a towel between them was making thinking difficult.

"Do you remember stealing my bourbon?" she asked him.

"Yes. That I remember."

"Do you remember what I told you after you downed it in one gulp?" She looked at him slyly. He thought for a moment.

"Something about . . . lotus. Fucking lotus!" He laid back, rubbing his temples. She drugged him. Not intentionally, but it still happened. This was horrible. He felt hungover. He honestly could not remember the last time he felt this sick. Maybe when he was mortal. Definitely when he was mortal.

"I remember . . ."

He looked at her. She was at his place taking a shower and the last thing he remembered was pinning her to a wall in the alley next to the bar. Now he was panicking.

"Did we..."

He waited for her to finish his sentence. She just looked at him slyly, her lips curved into a small smirk. She was enjoying this way too much.

"Did we have sex?" she asked him. He nodded and concern filled his eyes. She rolled her eyes at him. "I don't know why you are so concerned with us *not* having sex." She looked up as if to think "I mean, technically, most of the things we did last night would count as sex for most people." She winked at him, turned toward him and, leaning over his chest, looked down at him with her face only inches away from his. He felt himself stirring. If only she knew the power she had over him. She could rule the world.

"But no. Technically we didn't have intercourse." She leaned back slightly. "But if you want to go over the list of things that we did that are not included in that category, I can." She slipped her leg across his lap so she was straddling his body. "I can demonstrate for you, if you'd like."

He could almost see her peeping out at the bottom of the towel. He felt himself growing harder. She felt it too, as she wiggled around to tease him. He cleared his throat and started to sit up. If he didn't move her soon, some more things were going to happen. She pushed him back down and held him there.

He hated being pinned. He couldn't stop his reflexes. Before she could comprehend what was happening, he had her pinned on the bed with his hand on her throat. His eyes were glowing. She suddenly knew what she had done. A trigger. Someone had once pinned him down and caused him pain. She grasped on his hand on her throat.

"Alexander," she sputtered. "Alexander, stop. It's just me."

She saw his eyes flicker as the realization of what he was doing hit him.

He gasped and pulled his arm away.

"I'm sorry. I don't know what happened. I . . . I'm . . ."

He went to flash away, but she grabbed his arm and placed her hand on his cheek. He hadn't hurt her.

"Hey. It's okay. I'm fine. It happens. I understand," she said, rubbing her throat, "I shouldn't have pinned you. You've been through . . . stuff. I get that."

She ran her hand up his arm comfortingly. He looked away. Trying to lighten the situation, she leaned up toward him.

"But you on me like this, minus the intense choking, is kind of hot."

She thrust her hips up to have her towel brush his bare groin. He had forgotten that he was naked. He jumped back grabbing the blanket that was on the bed in his departure. She looked him up and down, giggling softly at his reaction to remembering he was naked.

"Are you sure you're alright?" she asked.

"Yes, I'm fine."

The concern in his voice made her heart swell. Clearing his throat, and still coming to terms with how many times he has already embarrassed himself in the last twenty minutes, he ran his hands thru his hair. He needed a moment. He walked into the bathroom. Cassiopeia watched him walk away.

Damn. That is one fine man.

His muscles rippled as he moved. When he put his hands up to brush his fingers through his hair, she could see his hip bones and every fiber of his muscles as his torso stretched. She was getting turned on just watching him move. If only he knew the power that he had over her. He could have her wrapped around his finger in a heartbeat.

She was getting up to check on him, when he walked out of the bathroom, still in the blanket. He looked stressed. She walked over to him and was about to lay her hand on his chest when he stopped her.

"Can you please tell me what happened last night. After I was drugged. Please."

He needed to insure he didn't do or say anything that would change things.

"Tell me what you remember, and I will fill in the blanks."

After about ten minutes of her telling him about what happened the night before at the club, he was all caught up on what he had forgotten. They had moved from the bedroom to the veranda and were sitting on the lounge chairs. They had upgraded from towels and blankets to robes. But they still hadn't talked about what happened after they got back here.

"I am kind of worried to know what crazy things I did," he said.

She looked into his eyes and spoke softly. "No worries, it was . . . amazing."

He felt his stomach flutter at her words. She turned to look out at the ocean. After a night like that and with how lovingly he treated her, she just couldn't understand why he was so reluctant or how he was single. She looked back at him and found him staring at her longingly. His lavender eyes were filled with undertones of sadness.

"What?"

"You're amazing," he said softly and looked back out toward the ocean.

He was so ancient and mysterious. Maybe that's why she was drawn to him. She looked out, seeing his surfboard sticking out of the sand on the beach. Trying to change the subject, she started a normal conversation.

"Who taught you how to surf?"

He chuckled lightly.

"A close friend. Someone who was very important to me. Do you wanna go surf? I'll never say no to surfing." He winked at her and she laughed at his enthusiasm.

"I would but—and don't hate me—I don't know how. I've just never learned. I've had no one to teach me."

He looked at her, his mouth hanging open. He was speechless.

"Wow, I didn't expect you to be that shocked. It's just surfing!" she said, surprised by his reaction.

He shut his mouth. "Come on! I'm going to open your eyes and blow your mind," he said as he grabbed her hands in his.

"You already blew my mind yesterday," she said slyly. "I can't wait for round two." She winked.

He rolled his eyes with a smirk and flashed her to the beach to begin Alexander's Surf School 101.

Cassiopeia flashed herself to her room on Vēlatusa. She felt an emptiness when she left Alexander. She looked around the large room, happy to still be able to call this palace her home. It took her and Caelum a long time to befriend each other, their friendship mainly stunted by her. For so long she pushed everything away. She wanted to be independent and free from her burdens and the past that always seemed to overshadow her. People she leaned on had hurt her, and so she learned how to live by herself. When she finally let Caelum in, their bond grew, and it continued to grow even with the small family she had made with Demetrius. Caelum fit right in. She felt a sadness wash over her as she thought of Demetrius. It had been almost 4,000 years since he was murdered, but she still felt her heart ache with joy and sadness when she thought of him. She missed him, but she had longed for the past for too long. Now she just needed a shower.

She and Alexander had been out surfing almost the entire day. He insisted on teaching her all the details. He didn't leave out anything. Normally she didn't have the patience to be taught something new, but she found that she had actually enjoyed surfing, and enjoyed him. She felt herself already longing to go see him again. She hadn't felt this way in a long time, a very long time. She walked into her large bathroom and started the shower. As she slipped under the hot water, she felt the seawater and sand rinse down her body. The heat felt good on her muscles after the workout she had gotten in the ocean. Once she was done, she turned off the water and got out. She walked back into her bedroom and got dressed for a cozy evening in.

She walked out into the main hall in her leggings and T-shirt. The house was quiet.

Caelum and the demons must be out.

She walked toward the kitchen in search of food. When she opened the refrigerator, it was empty. She looked in the pantry and found a can of soup and some crackers. One of the downsides of living with demons is that they ate everything. She opened the can, put the soup in a bowl, and set it in the microwave. She was about to start the machine when she heard a noise behind her. She hadn't felt anyone flash into the realm and the whole house had been empty when she had gotten out of the shower. She turned around and was greeted with nothing but silence. Shrugging, she turned and started the microwave. Suddenly, she heard it again, but this time she saw movement out of the corner of her eye. Before she could comprehend what was happening, someone grabbed her roughly and covered her head with a cloth. She screamed and struggled, but her powers weren't working against her attacker. The beast inside was pounding violently at her, begging to be released. Just as she was going to let it out, she felt herself being pushed through a time vortex. Her mind started to spin as she felt herself beginning to lose consciousness. She continued to try to fight her attacker, but her strength was diminishing as her body went limp. She thought back through her life as her final thoughts slipped into the darkness.

Epilogue
A New Beginning

Alexander had just gotten dressed from his shower when he felt Cassiopeia's panic, her fear. It coursed through his body for a few moments, causing the mark that ran down his right arm to glow, before the emotions abruptly stopped. He watched as the glow on his arm faded away leaving only the black tattoo that ran from his neck and shoulder all the way down to the back of his hand. His heart and stomach dropped as he knew what happened, where she went. He had known it was coming, and that it was going to happen soon. As much as he had wanted to stop it, he also didn't want to. She needed to go down this path to become the person she needed to be. The creature they all needed her to become.

Alexander stood on his balcony looking down at the great expanse of the ocean, listening to the waves crashing on the shore. He felt someone flash onto the beach. Caelum. The god looked up at Alexander on the balcony and disappeared, reappearing behind the leviathan.

"It is done. She is gone," he said.

"I know, I felt it."

Caelum walked over to stand next to him on the balcony. "It has to happen this way. It's the only way, we both know that. We always have."

"That doesn't make it any easier. It's just one less thing that is in my control in this universe."

Caelum stood silent for a few minutes. He was one of the few people who Alexander could stand to be around in silence. There was never any tension or awkward energy in the air, just quiet.

Caelum spoke. "You cut it close last night. I was very worried you were going to ruin everything."

Alexander laughed. "I almost did, fucking lotus. She drugged me. She fucking drugged me! Under normal circumstances I honestly wouldn't have cared!"

"From what I saw, you stole her drink . . . but sure. She drugged you." Caelum smirked at his friend.

Alexander rolled his eyes. "Whatever. Nothing was ruined. Everything is aligned exactly as it should be."

"Just like the constellations in the night sky."

They looked up. Alexander could see the Cassiopeia constellation glowing lightly above them. He felt his worry return to him. The pieces were in place, now they just had to wait. While she was being pulled through time, he would be here waiting for her return—for the prophecy to be fulfilled.

"She will return soon, and she will be stronger than ever," Alexander said with determination in his voice.

"Do you think all of this will be enough? Do you think she will be strong enough to stop it?"

Alexander stood there silent. Honestly, he didn't know. She was the most powerful being he had ever met, but would it be enough? Enough to save the world, gods and man alike?

"For all of our sakes it better be. It has to be."